"I don't want to play anymore"

Holt walked across the loft and placed his hands on the mantelpiece on either side of Emily, his long arms barring her escape. "Neither do I," Holt said, and reaching out, drew Emily full against him.

He brushed his lips quickly across hers, a barely restrained tension gripping him. "Open your mouth," he said shortly.

Instinctively, she complied, and when she did, Holt kissed her without mercy, again and again, to ease the torment he felt when he couldn't touch her.

Other Regency Romances by
Barbara Reeves

GEORGINA'S CAMPAIGN

Other Regency Romances
from Avon Books

BELLE OF THE BALL *by Joan Overfield*
CLARISSA *by Cathleen Clare*
LORD FORTUNE'S PRIZE *by Nancy Richards-Akers*
THE MISCHIEVOUS MAID *by Rebecca Robbins*
MISS GABRIEL'S GAMBIT *by Rita Boucher*

Coming Soon

FAIR SCHEMER *by Sally Martin*

Avon Books are available at special quantity discounts for bulk purchases for sales promotions, premiums, fund raising or educational use. Special books, or book excerpts, can also be created to fit specific needs.

For details write or telephone the office of the Director of Special Markets, Avon Books, Dept. FP, 1350 Avenue of the Americas, New York, New York 10019, 1-800-238-0658.

The Much Maligned Lord

BARBARA REEVES

AVON BOOKS · NEW YORK

If you purchased this book without a cover, you should be aware that this book is stolen property. It was reported as "unsold and destroyed" to the publisher, and neither the author nor the publisher has received any payment for this "stripped book."

THE MUCH MALIGNED LORD is an original publication of Avon Books. This work has never before appeared in book form. This work is a novel. Any similarity to actual persons or events is purely coincidental.

AVON BOOKS
A division of
The Hearst Corporation
1350 Avenue of the Americas
New York, New York 10019

Copyright © 1993 by Barbara Reeves Kolaski
Published by arrangement with the author
Library of Congress Catalog Card Number: 93-90229
ISBN: 0-380-77332-5

All rights reserved, which includes the right to reproduce this book or portions thereof in any form whatsoever except as provided by the U.S. Copyright Law. For information address Perkins Literary Agency, P. O. Box 48, Childs, Maryland 21916.

First Avon Books Printing: September 1993

AVON TRADEMARK REG. U.S. PAT. OFF. AND IN OTHER COUNTRIES, MARCA REGISTRADA, HECHO EN U.S.A.

Printed in the U.S.A.

RA 10 9 8 7 6 5 4 3 2 1

For Bob Allgeier, my favorite chessman. Bob knows all the moves.

Also for Adelaide Ferguson, connoisseur of wine and life, whose brilliance never fails to exhilarate, and who always leaves that glowing aftertaste, her own elegant, unmistakable farewell.

The Much Maligned Lord

One

The frantic blowing of the horn was the first intimation Emily Wilton had of the impending wreck. She barely had time to clasp the window strap and brace herself before their carriage was struck by another vehicle and sent violently tumbling onto its side in the shallow ditch.

The noise was terrific. Emily could hear the splintering of wood, screams of horses, cries of the drivers.

All this, added to the shrill hysterics of her Aunt Nicole Quimby, Lady Hume, made Emily's head ache even more than the sharp rap her forehead received when Cousin Demetria was launched into her lap, and they were flung headlong together against the lacquered ceiling.

Stunned, Emily lay perfectly still, tangled in a heap with her cousin and aunt.

An encompassing silence prevailed; even Lady Hume was blessedly quiet for the moment.

Struggling to disengage herself, Emily wished her aunt might stay in her faint long enough for them to sort themselves out and assess the damage. Alas, Lady Hume revived and set in to wail.

Emily blinked as a stranger loomed over them, peering down into the open carriage window, which was now slanted above her.

Could this be the man who had rammed them? His stylish

shallow-crowned beaver was pulled low over his forehead, casting his strong dark features in shadow. Black eyes, cold and opaque, gauged their condition. His lips, full-cut and well defined, were compressed.

"Are you all right?" he demanded sharply. Without waiting for an answer, he leaned in and roughly hauled the dazed Demetria upright, lifting her without ceremony straight up and out of the overturned coach.

Handing her cousin to someone out of Emily's line of vision, the man now turned to her. Reaching out his lean brown hand again, he said, "Come! No need for hysterics! Grab my hand and we'll have you out immediately. Ingram's my name, and I don't believe you're hurt at all. Only a small scratch on your forehead."

Such an uncomplimentary tone, coupled with a total lack of sympathy, would have made Emily excessively angry had she not agreed with him.

"No, Mr. Ingram," she said clearly. "You may rest assured that it's not I giving vent to these wretched sounds, but my aunt. Excuse me one moment."

Holt Ingram, Baron Ingram of Ravencroft, eased his bad leg and watched while the young lady shifted herself to stand over her aunt.

He almost grinned at the unexpected lash of her words. Here was one who didn't know or care who he was. From what he could see, she was a handsome girl, small and extremely slender, with a wealth of heavy brown hair escaping her dangling bonnet. She looked to be somewhere in her early twenties and her left hand was free of anything resembling a wedding band.

"Aunt Hume," Emily said calmly. She squatted gracefully and shook her ladyship's shoulder.

Nicole Quimby, a wispy woman of undetermined years, was given, as Emily could have told anyone, to burnt feathers and smelling salts.

Lady Hume suddenly opened her eyes, took in the topsy-turvy aspect of their situation, and set in to scream in short, high bursts. Her traveling hat tilted rakishly over one rolling eye and her ermine cape bunched about her neck.

Briskly, Emily shook her aunt again. This availed nothing. Methodically, she retied Lady Hume's bonnet strings and smoothed her frizzled bangs. When these ministrations failed to calm her ladyship, Emily sighed and straightened resolutely.

"Sorry, Aunt," she murmured, and deliberately slapped Lady Hume across one cheek.

The shock cut short the woman's lamentations. Holding her injured jaw, her ladyship stared blankly about and then at her niece-by-marriage.

"We had a wreck!" she cried, as if this were Emily's fault. Then, yielding to her nature, she shrieked, "Where is Demetria? She's killed! Oh, I know my daughter is killed!"

"No, Aunt," Emily said, her voice echoing strongly in the well of the carriage. "Demetria is perfectly all right. This kind gentleman above has rescued her and shall do the same for us if only we'll help him. Don't begin screaming again," she warned sternly, "or I shan't hesitate to repeat my slap!"

Looking up, Emily saw that something was distressing Mr. Ingram. He was white about the lips, as if experiencing pain.

Doctor's daughter that she was, Emily knew suffering when she saw it. "Are you hurt, sir? Were you injured in the wreck? Can you ask one of our coachmen to get us out?"

"No, not injured—I wasn't involved in the wreck," Ingram said on a wincing breath. "I've merely wrenched an old war wound."

He turned his head and spoke to someone else. "Very well, Cecil. I'll resign my place, but you'll need help. Call the guard. I'll see what I can do for Lindsay."

So saying, the black curly head and powerful shoulders were withdrawn from view.

There now appeared over the window a pleasant-faced younger man, dressed much like the other, except that his coat of superfine was brown rather than blue.

From what Emily could see of him, he carried considerably less muscular bulk than his companion and was shorter. Before she knew his name, Emily came to regard this second stranger as the small brown one.

He stood balancing upright on the carriage door frame.

Looking down, he smiled reassuringly. "Don't worry, Miss—er—"

Emily obligingly supplied her last name. "Miss Wilton," she said, and added, "Thank you."

"Miss Wilton. I'm Cecil Jennings and while I'm not nearly as large as Lord Ingram, I can engage to have you and the other lady out in a trice."

Turning his head, Mr. Jennings said, "That's right, my man. You're the guard, eh? Up here. You stand on that side, and I'll remain here, and Miss Wilton shall give us each a hand. After that we can bring out—"

" 'At other one's 'er ladyship, sor," the guard interrupted. "Lady Hume, 'er as is the old earl's niece-by-marriage, is wot 'er name is. And I'm John Wardlow, raised in Mursey Castle and born there."

Mr. Jennings was accustomed to garrulous servants. "Fine, John. Only hurry. Lord Ingram may need us. Miss Wilton? Your hands, please."

But Emily placed no confidence in Lady Hume's being calm enough to obey orders. "It would be quicker to let my aunt go first, sir. Once she's out, I'll come up."

But, although Nicole Quimby was thin and knew herself for a featherweight, trusting herself to the hands of the sturdy guard and a complete stranger was obviously something she deplored. "You'll drop me," she protested over and over, until she was deposited safely on the ground.

When Emily was lifted from the carriage, her eyes encountered a scene of carnage.

The light racing curricle that had hit them lay twisted and broken some seventy-five yards down the road, the fine animal in the shafts threshing and screaming in agony. A young man, obviously the driver, lay crumpled on the ground. Lord Ingram had just reached him.

Emily thanked Mr. Jennings and asked him to take her aunt and cousin in hand. "I shall go to the injured man," she said. "I must help him."

"Yes, certainly," Mr. Jennings said, but Emily was already crossing the road, lifting her skirts, running.

Wondering, Mr. Jennings gave the reins of his and Lord

Ingram's mounts to the guard and took Lady Hume and her daughter Demetria by the arm. He then moved with them to where the servants were attempting to right the carriage, blocking their view of the disaster.

Emily, arriving breathless beside the lanky victim, found him even younger than she'd thought. She judged him to be about her own age. He was probably still at Oxford. A tiger dressed in livery was weeping and supporting his master's head.

"I'm Emily Wilton, Lord Ingram," she murmured hurriedly. "Do you know this person?" She indicated the young man lying on the ground.

Holt Ingram straightened. "Yes, a neighbor of mine, Valerian Lindsay, Viscount Renton."

Lord Renton's condition, Emily grasped, was serious. Obviously in great pain, he had one leg twisted at an impossible angle and his right arm was bleeding, soaking his pale buckskin riding breeches. But he was trying his best to raise a large pistol in order to put his horse out of its misery.

"Shall I, Renton?" his lordship asked, stepping forward.

"Ingram! Yes, if you would be so kind. Can't seem to shoot with my left."

Lord Renton relinquished the firearm and watched intently as his lordship took it and fired directly into the suffering beast's temple. Then he seemed to pass out.

Valerian Lindsay didn't know a young lady had knelt beside him, ignoring the dust in the road.

"I must have access to Lindsay's wound so I can get at the bleeding. Will you cut away his jacket?" ordered Emily.

After one startled glance at the girl's calm face, Holt Ingram snapped open his pocketknife and hacked at the sleeve of what he was sure was a Weston jacket. The white cambric shirtsleeve suffered the same fate. He was about to cast these away when the girl—had she said her name was Wilton?—stopped him.

"No," directed Miss Wilton. "Save that cloth, if you please. I require a tourniquet. His radial artery seems to have been severed, or at least nicked, and this leg is certainly broken. I must have a strong short twig. And get me some blankets from our coach, or have them brought. We must keep this man warm or he'll go into shock."

When Ingram stared blankly, she jerked her head about and blazed, "Well? If you can't or won't help me, send someone who will! Where is Mr. Jennings? Surely he won't blanch at the sight of a little blood!"

His lordship's face broke into an appreciative grin. A dancing light appeared in his coal-black eyes and the stiff mask he usually presented to the world dissolved, leaving him quite handsome.

"You're wrong, Miss Wilton. Not only would Mr. Jennings blanch, ten to one he'd go off in a dead faint. You must forgive my surprise. I can't imagine—"

"I'm a doctor's daughter, sir," Emily explained impatiently. "Just now I need your assistance. No, my aunt and cousin are completely useless," she said, when he glanced to where Mr. Jennings was engaging the pair in conversation.

Holt Ingram threw up his head and his jaw clenched. He knew about women, especially the more delicate ones. His own mother claimed she was too sensitive to look at the wound on his thigh, and his sister Isobel's eyes sometimes filled with tears when he limped into her presence.

He'd found little to admire in the fair sex until he met Miss Wilton. Locating a smooth stick for the tourniquet, Holt gave it to her and watched as she expertly wrapped the torn shirtsleeve about young Lord Renton's arm and started the pressure.

After a moment, he crossed to the carriage and returned, favoring his limp, carrying two blankets. He knelt in the road beside Emily and spread one over the viscount. "What else can I do?" he asked.

Just at that moment, the girl's long hair came undone, flaring around her shoulders, obscuring her vision.

Impatiently she said, "If you'd be so kind, my lord, cut a piece of that blanket and tie my hair out of my way."

Standing behind her, taking her abundant hair in his hands, Holt complied, hoping his trembling fingers wouldn't give him away. Apparently they did not, for Miss Wilton nodded her thanks and continued counting the seconds over the tourniquet.

Emily flashed him a side glance and then a brief smile of thanks. "If you really want to help, you might rip that blanket into long narrow strips. And find me some flat boards. Lord Renton's leg must be immobilized until we get him to the nearest doctor. We shall bind the whole with those strips you're making."

To the tiger she said, "You may ease your master's shoulders to the ground now. I prefer that he lie flat." Emily nodded when this was accomplished.

"What's your name?" she asked the servant. "Arnold? Well, Arnold, you must stop crying, for there's no need. Lord Renton should recover nicely once we get this bleeding stopped and his leg set."

Releasing the tourniquet, she counted and then tightened again. Her wide gray eyes swept up from her task a moment, surveying the thin youth who was valiantly struggling to stop his tears.

"Excellent, Arnold! Now, perhaps you would help Lord Ingram find some straight boards about two feet long and three inches wide.

"Yes!" she said, when the boy's eyes darted to the wreckage of the viscount's curricle. "You should be able to salvage some useful splints there." She gave him an encouraging smile.

Emily's father had a large medical practice near Hereford. Many of his patients were sturdy country folk. She'd been taught that clearly explaining what she and her father were doing almost always calmed unwarranted fears and brought satisfactory, intelligent responses from their patients. Her father's teachings had always stood her in good stead, she thought.

Sometime during that half hour while Emily efficiently went about the business of controlling Val Lindsay's bleeding arm, Holt Ingram stood up to relieve his aching leg. Absently, he rubbed his thigh, and Emily, without ceasing her medical aid, said matter-of-factly, "You said you'd sustained a war wound, Lord Ingram. Your thigh, is it? I see you have a pronounced limp. Did it happen very recently?"

There was no pity in her voice and her eyes held his steadily, with none of the spurious sympathy Holt had come to expect from females who never could decide where to look when they were confronted with the fact of his wound.

"The night of January eighth, last year, some fourteen months ago," he replied. "I was with Colborne when he attacked the Renaud redoubt, just before we besieged Ciudad Rodrigo."

"I see," Emily murmured as she tightened the tourniquet. "And did the surgeons get to you immediately?"

"Within an hour. The attack on the redoubt lasted only ten minutes, you know. I was operated on almost immediately."

"And your prognosis?"

Holt suppressed a grin. Such an entrancing frown on that bruised little brow. "The wound was laid open to the bone. My doctor is urging an operation, but I confess that until now, I've been loath even to think about it."

"I understand," Emily said. "It's possible— Never mind, my lord."

"Please," urged his lordship.

Emily's lashes swept her eyes, hiding them from Holt's view. "My father would say that you probably have a pocket of infection along the bone. Are you having low-grade fevers?"

Suddenly she gave a little start and shook her head. "Forgive me, my lord. Only your own doctor should give you medical advice. Besides, if my aunt heard me discussing such a subject, she'd be—well, shocked isn't the word. She would probably swoon dead away."

"I appreciate your comments," Holt said softly.

Emily held his eyes a moment, then looked away. She fell silent, becoming very businesslike in her attendance upon her patient. It wasn't long before she was able to cease the on-again, off-again procedure with the tourniquet. The viscount had produced an excellent clotting action.

Her hands and arms bloody, her skirt streaked, she murmured, "Good, good! You're a fine patient, my lord."

THE MUCH MALIGNED LORD 9

Emily rubbed her finger over the puncture wound on the arm, clearing it. No foreign matter, no debris left in the small gaping wound. Three stitches would secure it, and she had every reason to hope the local doctor was up to such a simple task. The artery wasn't severed, but she must make sure the arm was kept elevated for the next few hours; otherwise, the bleeding could break loose and start again.

She bound the viscount's forearm with the tail of his shirt, and in a very few minutes, with Ingram's help, was setting his leg and holding it rigid in the makeshift splint.

Her patient fainted when Emily straightened his leg, but she merely nodded. "Good. He won't feel it now. Hurry, my lord. From what I can tell, it's a simple broken tibia. We must reduce the fracture and finish before he regains consciousness. Arnold, brace his shoulders in case he comes to, please."

When their task was finished, Holt Ingram watched as the remarkable girl sat back on her heels in the dirt and wiped at one cheek, leaving a faint streak of Lindsay's blood. She caught him looking at her and grinned.

Holt found his own face relaxing and told himself he'd never seen a more beautiful girl. Woman, he reminded himself. She was small of stature, but clearly a woman.

Holt extended his hand to help her from the roadbed.

She laughed and said, "I'm very bloody, my lord."

He smiled lazily, his eyes taking in the interesting cheekbones and smooth, perfect brow. "Haven't I proven myself, my dear? I haven't fainted once," he reminded her.

Refusing to acknowledge the endearment—she was certain it was mere courtesy—Emily laughed again and let him pull her up. "An excellent surgeon's helper, sir. You could walk the ward at Guy's Hospital with the best of them. After paying your fifty pounds, of course."

"You may explain that remark when I get you home," Holt told her. It occurred to him that he liked the idea of taking her home with him—to Ravencroft.

"I've had your carriage lifted from the ditch," he said. "Your coachman got a knock on his head and has a sprained ankle. However, he insists he's able to drive. And your horses seem uninjured. We shall load Val Lindsay inside and—"

"Have my Aunt Hume faint all over him," Emily broke in. She stood nibbling her lip a moment. "How far is it, your lordship?"

"Ravencroft? The gates are less than half a mile around the bend. And up the mountain some seven hundred feet. The road is even all the way."

"Could you put Lord Renton on the roof? Someone—John Wardlow—could hold him. While they're getting him secured, may I have some water? There's a padded jug in the boot of the carriage. I'll dampen this last piece of blanket and clean up a bit. Otherwise, we'll have my aunt fainting all over *me!*" A conspiratorial smile and a twinkle from her expressive gray eyes accompanied this statement.

"Who are you?" blurted the baron.

Emily raised her brows. "But I told you, my lord. I'm Emily Wilton. My father is Dr. Amos Wilton. We live at Beacon Hill in Herefordshire, where he has an extensive practice."

"But Lady Hume . . . ?"

"Ah!" Emily replied, busily scrubbing her hands and arms with the dampened cloth after Arnold had brought the water jug. "She's an aunt-by-marriage. She married my mother's brother, the late Viscount Hume, you see."

"And your grandfather?"

Emily nodded. "Was the late Reginald Quimby, Ninth Earl of Mursey. My great-uncle Leland is the present earl."

So! Holt thought. She was Mursey's granddaughter. And if he remembered his peerage, kin to half the Midland families back to the Conqueror. Better and better.

Holt had always known he must marry again. But he'd thought to put it off as long as possible.

His youthful marriage, arranged by his father and grandfather, had been so miserable—and then poor Muriel and the baby had died—he'd sworn off taking another wife until he was at least forty.

He grunted. He wasn't forty yet, but he was getting there. Shortly after they transported him home from Spain last year, he'd had his thirty-sixth birthday. Time to try again, he thought, remembering how Emily (charming name) had smiled at him so unself-consciously.

He hoped she was at least twenty-two. Twenty-three or -four would be better. Twelve years wasn't too great a difference, Holt assured himself, taking Emily's arm and helping her into her aunt's carriage for the ride to his home.

Two

Ravencroft was a tall, narrow fortress of great antiquity, a hilltop castle perched on a steep cliff overlooking the Vale of Gloucester. Its dark brick tower—the new tower built ninety years ago, as Holt later explained to Emily—was octagonal in shape and reared a hundred feet above the rough black walls of the stronghold.

They put young Valerian Lindsay in one of the back parlors, fearing to jolt him by carrying him up several flights of stairs.

The viscount groaned and opened his eyes as they lifted him to the bed Lord Ingram's servants had hurriedly set up. Val glanced about, knew immediately where he was, and pressed his lips between his teeth to keep from crying out against the pain. He swallowed back a moan as they arranged him on the mattress, his eyes clearing when they lit on the young woman he'd seen shortly after Holt Ingram shot his horse. He couldn't understand what she was doing here—Ingram never had females about.

Val Lindsay had visited Ravencroft often enough to understand Holt Ingram's impatience with women. Ingram's sister Isobel, only two years younger than he, was very nice; she never had much to say. But his mother, smiling, probing, and with a tongue as sharp as a knife, was enough to put a man off the weaker sex for life. It was only last year that the Dowager Baroness Ingram had reluctantly taken up residence at Abbingdon, an Elizabethan manor five miles away, the dower house of the Ingrams for generations. Poor Isobel, bowing to custom, had perforce moved out of Ravencroft and gone to Abbingdon Manor with her mother.

Val was grateful Lady Ingram wasn't present now. He tried to grin at Holt, his voice faltering as he thanked him for putting an end to his horse's misery and apologizing for any inconvenience he had caused.

"No, Val," Holt said. "Don't thank me, but rather Miss Wilton here. She saved your life, stopped your arm bleeding, and set your leg. Thank her, not me."

"But the doctor—?" Val tried to ask.

"Dr. Steele hasn't seen you yet, although he has been sent for," Holt assured him. "He should be here soon. Now I want you to take this potion Miss Wilton has prepared. That's a good man; yes, it's vile. Miss Wilton learned how to mix medicine from her father. Lucky for you, she was able to patch you up. And you must say you're sorry for ramming her carriage, you know. How did it happen? You're usually not so reckless."

The opium was speeding through Val's veins. He barely had time to mutter, "Runaway. Young horse in harness ... fox dashed across the road ..."

Viscount Renton went to sleep before he could finish his explanation or offer his apologies to Emily Wilton.

"Miss Wilton is twenty-three," Cecil Jennings told Holt. They were standing in the library.

A day had passed, during which Holt Ingram's life had taken a complete turnaround. Instead of the solitary recluse he had become since leaving the army ten months ago, Holt found his thoughts, his very being, dominated by a gray-eyed girl he hadn't known existed two days ago.

He raised his brows at his friend's statement. "And how, my dear Cecil, did you come by that piece of information? Surely Miss Wilton didn't voluntarily disclose her age to you?"

"No, she didn't. Miss Demetria Quimby and I had a conversation. That's where I came by the facts. And don't tell me you aren't dying to know everything about Miss Emily Wilton."

Limping to the sideboard, Holt poured himself some wine. After offering a glass to Cecil, he asked, "What else did you learn? Out with it; I can see you're bursting with details. Don't bother telling me her father is a country doctor and her mother was the Earl of Mursey's daughter. Why have I never seen her in town?"

"Ho! And when have you taken to mingling so freely with the *ton,* Holt? It's been years since you were at Almack's. It's all a man can do to get you to London. The hostesses have quite given up on you, you know."

Unlike Holt Ingram, Mr. Jennings looked forward to the Season each spring. Sociable and urbane, he lived quietly at his country place in Kent the rest of the year, engaged in the pursuit of agriculture and blood sports. Just last week he had traveled into Gloucestershire for the purpose of coaxing his friend to town.

"But you must come, Holt," he had urged in his most persuasive manner, sodden from a thundershower and tired after his two-day trip from London. "All your special friends plan to be there. Everyone who is anyone will be in London this time of year." Cecil wondered if Holt eschewed society and avoided the *ton* because of his limp.

Well aware his habit of immuring himself at Ravencroft was unhealthy, Holt shrugged at his friend's importunings and said, "My sister wants to go, and my mother, too. I've told them they are welcome to open my town house. As for me, I hadn't planned on being in London for the Season. I always avoid that if I can. Perhaps I shall change my mind."

Cecil hadn't failed to notice Miss Wilton's effect on the baron; quite unusual. Holt Ingram had previously seemed oblivious to the charms of women of their own class. And what dealings he might have with the demimonde were well hidden. Miss Wilton couldn't have come into their lives at a better time.

Despite the six-year difference in their ages, Cecil liked Holt Ingram. He would have liked him even if they weren't

THE MUCH MALIGNED LORD 15

both fascinated by chess. They had met eight years ago at the Chess Club in London and kept the habit of games going year-round through correspondence, even after Holt joined the army.

Holt was much the better player; Cecil freely admitted he wasn't a master at the game, as was his friend. There weren't many who could play blindfolded. Holt was one who could. When he was in London, he frequently challenged Scanlon, a pupil of the late, great Philidor.

Cecil watched as Holt walked to the chessboard and stared at it absently. It held his and Scanlon's long-distance game, in-progress.

"So you've changed your mind about going to town, then?" Cecil asked.

"Yes, I believe—I think I'll go this year. I do need to see my doctor about this leg," the baron said slowly, as if thinking of something else. He lightly tapped the white queen with the tip of one finger.

But he was frowning, and Cecil couldn't understand why.

When Emily and Demetria visited Val Lindsay shortly before breakfast, the young viscount tried to apologize for wrecking their traveling coach.

Emily laughed and said, "It's my aunt's carriage, not mine. And I understand they have tightened the wheels and are replacing some of the leathers, putting it in perfect trim for our journey to London. Although when we will leave, I can't tell. My Aunt Hume seems to have taken an aversion to travel. She claims she is so shaken and pulled about that she must rest for several days. Fortunately, Lord Ingram has invited us to remain as long as we need. I, for one, am glad. This gives me the opportunity to follow your progress. How do you feel?"

"Hungry," Val declared, looking past Emily at the lovely face of her cousin, Miss Demetria Quimby, and producing a smile of great charm.

That smile was good-natured, Emily thought, but a trifle calculated. Well, the young man had met his match in Demetria, she decided.

Demetria smiled at the viscount in turn. She wasn't at all loath to carry on a light flirtation with this lordling Emily had saved; it would pass the time in this medieval castle. Flirting was what Deme Quimby did best, as she herself freely admitted.

Used to being the center of attention in the countryside around Mursey Castle, Deme cast down her eyes in mock shyness. "Good morning," she murmured, as Val Lindsay offered her a warm greeting. "What would you like to eat, my lord?" She pinned him with a lethal sweep of her eyes. "Emily says you may have anything short of a roast oxen."

"But that's exactly what I want, a whole roast oxen," Val teased, taking her hand and kissing it.

Emily, deducing that Valerian Lindsay, at the age of twenty-one, was every bit as practiced in the art of flirtation as her cousin Demetria, shook her head and left them alone, except for Mr. Dodson, Lindsay's valet, a chambermaid, and the cook, who had called in the sickroom, ready to proffer a variety of broths and other invalid dishes.

Hoping she wouldn't encounter her aunt or their hostess, the Dowager Lady Ingram, Emily made her way to the stone terrace.

Her ladyship had arrived breathlessly yesterday, in the late afternoon, some three hours after Lord Ingram escorted their carriage into the dark passage, a sort of enclosed porte cochere, situated alongside the craggy wall of the fortress.

Ravencroft rose two hundred feet above the jagged boulders that comprised the retaining wall, which in turn dropped away another five hundred feet to the valley floor.

The tunnel-like entrance, guarded by a portcullis, was directly under the terrace where Emily now stood. The baron's ancestors, Emily thought, had built for defense as well as siege.

She wanted to view the early morning scene alone; surely the baron's mother and sister weren't early risers. Her Aunt Hume could be depended on to sleep until noon; she hoped Holt Ingram's mother would do the same.

Emily had found Lady Ingram obdurate in her opinions, and given to an embattled style of conversation. She seemed determined to rule all who came within her orbit, as evidenced by her first words upon her arrival at the castle.

After explaining to Nicole Quimby that she had come to act as her son's hostess, and announcing that she would go to the kitchens to make sure there was something fit to be served to guests, Annora Ingram had immediately changed the time her son had set for the dinner hour. "No," she stated, "eight is too late. I have no good opinion of such fashionable *modern* notions. Six o'clock, that's the proper time to eat, and if anyone wants to call them country hours, let them."

Holt Ingram deflected this Parthian shot by bowing rigidly. "Yes, madam, anything you please."

This might have been a conciliatory remark, but Emily didn't think so, for she had observed the hard glance emanating from those extraordinary black eyes of his. His lordship had raked his mother with a cynical look that should have frozen her where she stood, then he had turned from her, frowning.

Emily had looked away, not wishing to believe the baron so devoid of feeling that he could hold his own mother in disdain. And why had he addressed her as madam?

Later, after enduring an endless two hours at the dinner table and an evening of card games played under the woman's hubristic eye, Emily felt she had the dowager's measure. After a lifetime of such unyielding arrogance, Holt Ingram had just cause, she admitted. And his sister Isobel, subjugated and mutely enduring her mother's pitiless strictures: no wonder Miss Ingram tended to fade into the background, seeming to dwell in her own thoughts.

Now, putting the unpleasant Lady Ingram and her unfortunate daughter from her mind, Emily concentrated on the breathtaking view.

Behind her, to the west, the land lay wrapped in shadow. But in the east, long brilliant streaks broke over the disappearing fog that shrouded the terrain.

Emily could see farther than she'd ever thought possible. She seemed to be facing an ocean of light. What manner of men devised a refuge like this? she wondered. To constantly behold the hills emerging from the shadows each morning must surely shape their characters, their very destinies, bonding them to the vast panorama. And the view from the pinnacle of the tower must be fantastic.

There was majesty in such height; no wonder Holt Ingram was so relentlessly sure of himself. He seemed solitary, as if he needed no one. He was part of this, part of Ravencroft, blood and bone.

As if the thought of Lord Ingram made him materialize, he spoke from behind her. "You should see it from the tower," he said.

Emily turned as he came round her, facing her with his back to the sun. She raised her eyes and was blinded by the brilliance behind him; he seemed immensely dark, his face nearly hidden, all his features in deepest shadow but outlined by a golden nimbus of radiant light.

Holt Ingram was shining, Emily thought fancifully, as if he were the source of the effulgent rays surrounding them. She shook her head, trying to dispel the idea that had taken hold of her imagination.

"Will you come with me?" Holt asked, reaching for her hand and holding it strongly in his. When she did not protest, he took Emily to a steel-latticed door inside the long hall.

Emily didn't have breath to protest. His touch had stunned her. The heat generated by his hard palm pressed against hers—it was the most intimate contact she had ever experienced. And she'd been kissed twice—three times, if one counted Jeremy Norville, when she and Jeremy were quite young. How could such a thing as the palm of Holt's hand, the lacing of their fingers, make her feel as if he possessed her completely?

She allowed him to pull her up the sheer stone steps of the tower. They circled upward, ever upward, and finally arrived at the round, sun-filled room, where that fatal physical contact between them was broken at last.

Holt's eyes held hers, his mouth a straight savage slash in the dark planes of his lean face. Emily felt mesmerized. Reluctantly, she turned and gazed at the faraway horizon. "We're at the very top of the world," she murmured, taking in one view, then another.

The windows were numerous, tall and set in the stone. So much light and empty space affected her strongly; Emily felt at one with the rising sun. She went to another window and trailed her fingertips across the glass.

Momentarily, she closed her eyes, aware that Holt Ingram was watching her instead of the spectacular scene unfolding before them.

Holt crossed his arms over his chest. Emily Wilton. Such a small, vibrant girl, wrapped now in sunlight. Her reaction was all he'd hoped for.

He had shared this view—so much a part of him—with no other woman. Certainly not with Muriel. His wife had been scared senseless of heights. Even below, in the castle proper, she never went near the windows, declaring over and over that she hated the place. As she came to hate him, Holt thought.

Thrusting those memories aside, Holt saw Emily stir. Beyond her, the Severn River was a flat silver ribbon widening down to the Bristol Channel.

"Are those the Malverns?" she asked at last, pointing to a clearly discernable blue ridge way in the distance. The sun was fully up now.

Holt came to stand beside her. "Yes, you can see the entire Herefordshire range from here, some forty miles away. You'd be able to see your home if we had a glass strong enough." He pointed. "And look there: across the river, the Forest of the Dean."

Emily shook her head. "I'd never leave this place," she said. "Not if it were mine."

She glanced up at him and then away, wondering what he made of her words. To think she'd lived so near this man all her life and never dreamed he was here. And Ravencroft. She'd heard of it, but never thought to see the place. It was true. If she held this great feudal stronghold, she would stay here always.

"I feel the same way. Always have," he said, and she couldn't tell from his flat tone what he was thinking.

Emily gazed past him, became entranced with the prospect again, and forgot her embarrassment. "What I mean is, how could anyone prefer a city to this? Oh!" she cried, as if a sudden thought had struck her. "What is it like up here in a storm? It must be truly magnificent."

"Yes," he said, one corner of his mouth twisting in a parody of a smile.

His eyes—totally black, she thought, where all light disappeared—idly roved her face.

"You're not afraid of storms?" he asked.

Emily shook her head. "No. I realize how foolish that sounds, but—" She paused, searching for the right words. "There's something so—so stirring about the fury of a storm, don't you think? When I was a child, I ran out in one. I was eight at the time."

"Oh?" he murmured lazily. "What happened?"

Emily laughed. "I got wet; Papa spanked me. But it was worth it; totally glorious. I've never forgotten. Being part of all that unleashed power was . . ." She closed her eyes and shivered in an ecstasy of remembrance. "It was sublime."

Three

"THE GIRL is a heartless flirt," Mr. Jennings said, clucking at his horse. The day was far advanced, and he and the baron had ridden out to inspect one of the Ravencroft sheep folds.

Holt, whose mind was filled with Emily Wilton, said sharply, "Oh?"

"Yes," said Cecil. "She has had a chessboard brought to Renton's room, and is entertaining him while Miss Wilton sits by, calmly doing her needlepoint and correcting their play."

"You are referring to Miss Wilton's cousin, Demetria? She is the one who is playing chess with Valerian Lindsay?"

At Cecil Jennings's affirmation, a reluctant grin—directed at himself—spread across the baron's stiff features. This was ridiculous. He'd barely met Emily Wilton, yet his heart had thumped when he thought Cecil said she was flirting with young Lindsay. Jealous, by God. He who had never been jealous in his life. Already the girl had breached his defenses. This wouldn't do. He must watch himself.

"Yes, of course it's Miss Quimby. No doubt she has cut a wide swath amongst the yokels in Herefordshire. I make no doubt she will continue in just such a way in London. She is very beautiful," Cecil said darkly.

Holt Ingram looked at his friend in surprise. Here was

something new. Cecil Jennings had never been in the petticoat line. He seemed content enough to remain in the background at those brilliant soirees he professed himself enamored of. He made friends with all the Incomparables, danced with them, joined the ranks of their cicisbei, but, insofar as Holt knew, never seemed in danger of succumbing to their various charms. Had Cecil fallen to Cupid's arrow?

"Have you developed a *tendresse* for the admirable Miss Demetria Quimby?" he quizzed.

"What? Certainly not! The girl is barely eighteen, a mere child."

"And you an old man of thirty. Go carefully, my friend. The girl is a stunner."

The subject of this conversation was brushing her cousin Emily's long dark hair in their bedchamber in Ravencroft Castle.

"Emily," Demetria said, "what do you think of Mr. Jennings?"

Thankful Demetria hadn't asked her opinion of Holt Ingram, Emily frowned and met Demetria's eyes in the mirror. "Mr. Jennings? Rather good-looking, quiet, polite, pleasant. Obviously a great dandy, if not a complete Pink. Why?"

"I've decided to make him fall in love with me." Demetria's grin was mischievous.

When Emily exclaimed and shook her head at Demetria, the younger girl said, "No, it will do him a world of good. He is entirely too sure of himself. He treats me like a fourteen-year-old."

"I thought you were busy setting up a flirt with Valerian Lindsay," Emily said.

"Oh, no. Well, yes. But Val is too young, barely out of Oxford. He doesn't interest me. Besides, he has just gone on the town. Val Lindsay and I are two of a kind; we understand each other. He isn't about to be serious yet, and I've made up my mind to have several men desperately in love with me by the time the Season ends."

"You don't think you might lose your own heart in the process?" Emily asked.

Demetria laughed and threw herself across the counterpane of the large bed they shared. "I mean to have at least two Seasons before I fall in love and decide to be a wife, Emily. I want a score of beaux, and then, in my third Season, I shall allow myself to be snatched up by the tallest, most handsome lord of the realm. Very eligible, of course, and he must adore me."

Emily asked, "And who shall this paragon be?" Her mind wasn't on her question. She suspected Demetria of joking, but her words had struck home. Emily had insisted—ever since Uncle Mursey conceived of sending her and Demetria to town—that she wasn't interested in marriage. But she couldn't help noticing that in depicting this husband she planned to snare, her cousin could have been describing Holt Ingram to the inch.

Demetria flopped onto her back and stretched. "I have no idea whom I shall fall in love with. Love can wait until later. By the by, what do you make of the baron? Such a dark visage; and those black eyes of his! Emily, I must say, I suspect he is secretly taken with you. When Mr. Jennings and I came to the top of the tower this morning, he fairly glowered at us. Did we interrupt a tête-à-tête?"

Emily bit her lip. Demetria's sense of intrigue was uncomfortably accurate. "No!" she protested. "How can you think such a thing? Lord Ingram was simply showing me the view."

After giving her opinion that Ingram could be dangerous where women were concerned, Demetria went away to see her mother.

Emily was unable to decide if her cousin had believed her story. More to the point, did she?

The whole episode seemed unreal. Ingram had been playing the good host, and so she'd told herself all day. What she couldn't forget was the way he'd taken her hand, his touch an act of intimacy.

Emily spread her fingers and examined her palm. How could such a thing, simple in itself, affect her so acutely? Closing her eyes, she laid her fingers across her mouth, imagining she could feel his touch. Holt Ingram was so vital, so forceful—no wonder she'd been overwhelmed when he held her hand. And his eyes had gazed into hers in a way Emily was sure she hadn't imagined.

She jumped to her feet and ran to catch up with her cousin before she reached Lady Nicole's room. She and Demetria were almost certain that there was nothing wrong with her ladyship, for yesterday Nicole had claimed bruises and injuries that she said were sustained in their wreck, and all day she had lounged in her bed, arrayed in her most fetching gown.

Catching Demetria's arm, Emily spoke in a low murmur. "Do you think there's anything really wrong with your mother, Deme? She refused to see Dr. Steele when I made the suggestion."

They paused outside her ladyship's door as Demetria said softly, "No. I think these *injuries* of hers are pure inventions, Em. Watch and see if she doesn't find herself able to come down to dinner. Nothing bores Mama more than having nothing to do, and one can read in bed only so long."

Lady Nicole was reviving herself with a cup of tea and two macaroons. She cried, "Oh, my dears, have you come to see the invalid on her bed of pain?"

Shooting Demetria a warning glance, Emily moved to her aunt's bedside. Demetria went to the other side.

"And how much pain are you actually having, Aunt Nicole?" Emily asked, amused to see a fleeting look of exasperation cross her ladyship's face.

Nicole Quimby had been a famous beauty when she was young. Emily always thought her portrait by Gainsborough, done twenty-five years ago, the most fascinating picture in the long gallery at Mursey Castle. In spite of her now-petulant expression, her aunt was still very pretty.

"Emily," she cried, "if you have a fault in the world, it's a tendency to pin one down—you've been like that since you were a little girl. Now I really don't wish to discuss it. I refuse to be one of those women who delight in recounting every ache and pain. However, when you're my age, being pulled about isn't pleasant. Suffice it to say that I'm not able to travel."

When Emily raised one skeptical brow, Nicole rattled her cup in her saucer. "Very well, Emily. If you must know, I feel perfectly fine. But only think what an opportunity this presents—Demetria in the same house with three eminently eligible men. My daughter must be given her chance, and before we get to town, where there will be dozens of girls thrown on the Marriage Mart. My adorable Deme will shine like a diamond in this broody fortress Lord Ingram calls home."

Demetria's eyes twinkled at her cousin. "But Mama," she said, "what about Emily?"

Emily bit her lip to keep from smiling. It was obvious that Nicole could not conceive that anyone could possibly prefer her to Demetria.

"Oh!" Nicole said, stricken, when she realized what she'd said. "Emily, dear, surely you understand? After all, you are no longer in your salad days, and Demetria is a glowing eighteen." Nicole turned to gaze dotingly at her daughter. "That's the perfect age to snap up a husband."

"Then you are planning to come down for dinner?" asked Emily, conscious that Demetria was stifling her laughter.

"Oh, certainly," Nicole assured them, jumping nimbly from bed. "I was just calling the maid to help me dress. I shall wear my green gown. I've never liked it, you know. It gives me a positive pallor, the very thing when one wants to look sick as a cat. Never," she said earnestly, catching the girls with an arm around each of their waists, "fail to include an unbecoming dress in your wardrobe. One never knows when it may be necessary to look wan. Very useful," she said, shooing them out her door and warning them to look their prettiest this evening.

Holt leaned back in his chair and allowed the butler to place decanters of brandy and fine humidors filled with Spanish cigars on the dining table. Dinner over, the women had retired to the Blue Saloon, leaving the men to their drinks and the pleasures of blowing a cloud.

Valerian Lindsay, ensconced in a wheelchair the servants had located in one of the lumber rooms, raised his glass and said, "To the beautiful damsels dropped in our laps by a kind fate. And to that damnable fox that ran in front of me."

Holt drank, but said, "Yes, that fox almost got you killed. If Miss Wilton hadn't been there, you certainly would have bled to death. Isn't that right, Dr. Steele?"

The doctor, a man well into his sixties, nodded his grizzled head. "Most assuredly. Without a doubt, Miss Wilton saved your life, young man. And did as good a job reducing that fracture in your leg as I've ever seen. She even helped me put the plaster of Paris cast on it, when I arrived later in the afternoon. Remarkable girl," he said, and then chuckled.

"Fired up when I mentioned bleeding you. Not that I was going to, mind, but lots of doctors would. No, I didn't need her to tell me you'd lost more than enough blood. I agreed with her entirely. Ingram's right. Girl saved your life."

"What I want to know," Val said, after they'd drunk another toast to Miss Emily Wilton, "is when can I walk? Or dance? Dammit, this is my first real Season, and I was looking forward to squiring all the pretty young things about London, even to Almack's. I suppose that is out of the question now. So, how long, Dr. Steele?"

"Can't have the cast off for at least six weeks. You can bear a little weight on it by then, but should take it easy. You can ride, of course. But you can easily lame yourself for life if you don't take care of a leg fracture."

"Damn! Just what Emily said." Val frowned and sipped at his brandy.

"Well, take heart," the doctor said. "That broken leg will have the young ladies fluttering around you like a pretty flock of doves, all cooing and murmuring soothing words in your ears, ready to fetch and carry and wipe your noble brow. Only contrive to have yourself and your chair transported to all the great dos, and you'll be the center of attention."

Yes, thought Holt, listening to the conversation. Some women were quick to offer sympathy; others were horrified by lameness, especially if it seemed permanent.

What he'd first liked about Miss Wilton—Emily—was her composure when confronted by the broken and bleeding Val Lindsay. And she'd made light of the bump on her forehead. It was, as she said, the merest scratch. But this morning in the tower, she'd had a bluish bruise over her left eye, and Holt thought he'd detected a slight swelling, though he hadn't said anything.

He'd gotten away as soon as he could after they descended the tower stairs, because he had the most overwhelming desire to take Emily Wilton in his arms and kiss away her hurt. He shook his head. He'd been too long in the country.

"Shall we join the ladies?" he asked.

"Good idea," Val said, swiveling his wheelchair and rolling away. "And Holt, if you should decide to invite Emily Wilton to a game of chess, don't be surprised when she beats you."

"It *would* surprise me," Holt admitted, then added, "Might be interesting. I've never played chess with a woman before."

The Blue Saloon, where the ladies had retired after dinner, was also known as the Lace Room. It was a large apartment, with a handsomely carved ceiling and a fireplace at each end.

Emily had not previously toured this part of the castle, and was intrigued by the displays of ancient lace, all framed and kept under glass.

She asked about the collection, and Lady Ingram said, "Several of my predecessors gathered them up. I can't tell you, but I'm sure my daughter can. Ravencroft is full of history, and Isobel knows it all."

Annora Ingram was tall for a woman, and very thin, her arms and legs bony, her body lost in the Empire style that was so modish at the moment. Emily had seen her portrait in the gallery, and she had been handsome when it was painted, though with a cold, disdainful air. Now she looked brittle, as if she might break if one so much as took her arm. Her hair was snow-white, full and abundant, and she wore heavy braids wound round the crown of her head like a diadem, creating a regal effect. Emily wondered how the woman could have produced two offspring as warm and vital as Holt and Isobel.

When applied to, Isobel led the cousins about the room, explaining about the lace, pointing out several examples that were quite ancient and yellow with age. At the dinner table, or when she was serving tea, Isobel had seemed unnaturally subdued, especially in her mother's presence. Now that she found the cousins' interest in the laces genuine, Isobel grew animated, her eyes vivid, her expression lively.

Emily had learned that Isobel was thirty-four, which seemed impossible, but Demetria had wormed the information out of Mr. Jennings, so it must be true.

"Now here," Isobel was saying, "is a set of doilies given to an ancestor of ours by Elizabeth. She was one of the queen's ladies-in-waiting at the time."

Emily decided Isobel looked amazingly like her brother, especially when she smiled. She wasn't as dark as Holt, and her eyes were more expressive, but Emily had seen Holt smile, and he and his sister were much alike.

Isobel was dressed in a rose-colored gown that showed her slender figure to its best advantage. Her features were strong. Under sweeping black brows, her eyes were compelling, and the healthy glow that suffused her rather olive complexion made her very attractive. She moved gracefully and was almost as tall as her brother.

Some twenty minutes were consumed by their leisurely examination of the laces, and when their tour was completed, the three younger women returned to sit with the other ladies.

Emily was amused at the enthusiasm with which Nicole Quimby greeted them. Her ladyship had indeed worn the green dress, but Emily couldn't see that it made her look pale, and certainly not sick.

"I should have come with you to view the lace," Lady Nicole declared, which only showed how bored she was with Lady Ingram. Emily knew her aunt had no interest in antiquities. Their hostess had been droning on, idly trying to engage Nicole in a long discussion concerning a dreary set of people in the *ton,* all special friends of hers.

Emily was very fond of her aunt, and couldn't resist subtly teasing her. "If you are positive it wouldn't hurt you to move from your chair, Aunt, I shall endeavor to escort you about. Come."

"No, no," protested Nicole. "Not now, Emily dear. I believe I hear the gentlemen coming."

* * *

"Deme," called Val, wheeling himself into the room. "Come push me to the pianoforte. I want to play you a waltz I heard in town the other day."

Demetria leaped from the banquette where she was sitting and grasped the handles of his chair, pushing him down the long room. "Do you have any music sheets?" she asked.

"I play by ear," Val said. "Never studied music. But I'll try to play a little for you. This is a pretty song. I heard old Lady Maitland—do you know her? She's Evan Ryder's grandmother—heard her ladyship sing it at the Countess Felbridge's musicale during the Small Season last November. It was the first time I'd heard it, though Holt told me it was composed over two years ago by one of the musicians in the 10th Dragoons. It's called 'Espana', and Holt says it was a great favorite of Wellington's. I can do it much better on my guitar," he complained, as Cecil Jennings removed the long piano bench so Val could get his chair to the tall Broadman.

Soon the viscount was running his hands over the keys.

"I didn't know you played, Val," Demetria said. "Emily and I love to sing, and she plays—badly, *she* claims—and I don't play at all."

"Well, neither can I, and I don't try, except when I'm a little disguised." Val grinned, looking boyish and rakish at the same time, as he essayed a jangling arpeggio. He grimaced when he hit several bad notes. "Bear with me," he said.

Holt and Cecil Jennings had gathered near the piano, as had Emily and Demetria, and they stood by as Val said, "Oh, well," and proceeded to thump out a lively waltz tune, grinning as Demetria grabbed the flustered Mr. Jennings and made him waltz her round and round the room.

When Val finished the song, amidst applause, Deme said, "That was wonderful, Val."

And she laughed at Cecil Jennings. "And you, sir, are an accomplished waltzer. Do you realize you're the first man I've ever waltzed with in my life? I've only practiced with Emily, and she's so little, I had to lead. No, they don't allow the waltz in our country assemblies. I thank you. Promise you'll dance with me in town."

Mr. Jennings swallowed and turned an amazing shade of

red. Then he recovered and said, "My pleasure, Miss Quimby, I assure you. May I have your first waltz at Almack's?"

Holt Ingram, now leaning against the fireplace, could not forbear looking at Emily, who stood nearby. Her eyes met his, and they were smiling.

Holt went to her side. Bending his head, he murmured, "Poor Cecil. I see he has fallen into your cousin's silken snare. Ought I to warn him off?"

Emily gulped, swallowing a gurgle of laughter. "I can't imagine that he would appreciate such advice. Tell me, your lordship, is Mr. Jennings in the habit of falling head over ears with every pretty girl he meets, or is this a new thing with him?"

"Entirely new," said Holt. "Cecil Jennings, to my certain knowledge, has never been in love in his life. Won't you call me Holt?" he asked, and was surprised at his impulsive question.

Emily gave him a measuring look. "Do you think I should?" For two days, she'd been calling him by his Christian name inside her head.

"Yes."

"Very well. Then you must call me Emily."

Before Holt could answer, Demetria called, "Lord Ingram, does 'Espana' have words? Val says he doesn't know any."

Taking Emily's elbow, Holt guided her past his mother and Nicole Quimby, who were conversing with Dr. Steele. His sister sat slightly apart, having lapsed into one of her quiet moods. Isobel gazed at nothing, seemingly absorbed in her own thoughts.

" 'Espana' does have words. I don't know if I can remember them."

Demetria clapped her hands. "Oh, do try, please."

"Belle, come here." Holt held out his hand. When his sister came to him, he casually placed his arm around her shoulder and smiled down at her. "Help me, please. You're better at remembering lyrics than I. I've heard you sing this. I'll go first, then you can add some harmony. Ready, Val?"

THE MUCH MALIGNED LORD 31

Val nodded and played a small introduction, after which Holt sang in a strong baritone:

> "Come, love, hold me
> Under a Spanish moon,
> Say you want me
> Never leave me soon,
> Kiss me, thrill me
> Tell me you'll always be true.
> Wait for me, stay for me
> Promise you'll pray for me,
> Under a Spanish moon."

Holt grinned down at Isobel, nodded encouragingly, and signaled for her to sing with him. He sang again, his sister adding a surprisingly strong alto voice, blending in perfect harmony.

They all crowded about the piano, and Val played the song several times, while everyone joined in, learning the words.

To Emily's surprise, Isobel Ingram had a very good voice, and proceeded—at her brother's urging—to sing "Mama Bids Me Bind Up My Hair," with Mr. Jennings lending a soft tenor on the chorus.

Under her brother's obviously loving eye, and with warm compliments ringing in her ears, splashes of becoming color filled Isobel's cheeks. Emily had thought her attractive before. Now she realized that Belle Ingram was a beautiful woman.

Demetria begged Emily to join her in their favorite duet, "Hark! Hark! The Lark," and the singing ended with Holt and Cecil—who was possessed of a really fine tenor—rendering "Drink to Me Only with Thine Eyes."

All that marred the evening was Annora Ingram's scathing comment to her son as the tea tray was rolled in. "How can you encourage your sister in making such a show of herself?" Annora asked, not, it seemed to Emily, caring who heard her.

Glancing at the flush on her daughter's cheeks, Annora continued. "You see how agitated she becomes. Isobel hates to be in the limelight. And after all, she doesn't sing well."

"Oh, but Lady Ingram," Demetria cried, "I think she has a lovely voice, so deep and husky. Isobel, I enjoyed your singing very much."

Annora dismissed this comment with a frigid smile. "How nice of you to try and make Isobel feel better, my dear Demetria. However, I am her mother and should be the best judge of the situation. At her age, Isobel must be made to realize it's no longer becoming to force herself in with a group of young people."

Emily glanced at Isobel, who had dropped into a chair and sat with a bent head. She seemed intent on studying her hands. Two spots burned in her cheeks and her mouth was set in a mutinous line.

Four

All the next day, Isobel Ingram remained secluded in her room.

The cousins discussed sending her a note. "Emily, think of something," begged Demetria.

"I've been trying," Emily said, "but everything I hit upon smacks of interference. Perhaps we should leave well enough alone."

That afternoon, at tea, Nicole Quimby had noted Isobel's absence. "Is your daughter unwell?" she had asked Annora.

"Not that I can tell," said Annora, reaching for the jam pot. "It's just as I predicted. So much attention has overset the delicate balance of her nerves."

When Lady Nicole had properly exclaimed, Annora said, "I'm afraid poor dear Isobel has never been strong. She is unable to sustain herself amidst the rigors of society. Her Season was a disaster. As much as I enjoy it, I dread going to town each spring.

"Isobel," Annora continued, "has no sense of discrimination. Well, all the time we're there, she consorts with a dowdy set of writers and artists, even *actors,* in outlandish places like Bloomsbury and Chelsea and *Hampstead.* She even fancies herself a writer. You must know she is forever scribbling something, has since she was a child. When that encroaching Mr. Locke actually wanted to publish some trashy novel she had written, I finally put my foot down. I burned the manuscript and forbade her ever to set pen to paper again. That was only last year, and I trust I got her over that hurdle.

"But she is constantly going to readings and showings and *literary evenings* when we are in town, getting into the most shocking company. And these are nobodies, you understand, existing on the fringes of society. They, like my daughter, are consumed with their so-called *muse,* and beyond Lady Caroline Lamb and that Byron person (such a horrid creature, crippled and always hobbling about), one never hears of these people. Oh, some are notorious! That Charles Lamb, a clerk at India House, has a crazy sister. She stabbed their mother, you know. And Hunt. I'm glad they sent him to prison. I believe they all eat opium—well, I know that wretched De Quincey does, but he's gone off somewhere. This is the society my daughter has fallen into. You can see, my dear Lady Hume, why the girl drives me to distraction."

Now, resting in their room before dinner, Demetria said, "I wonder if there aren't two versions of Isobel's story?"

Emily laid her copy of Jane Austen aside. "I'm sure of it. I was so shocked when Lady Ingram boasted of burning Isobel's manuscript."

Demetria idly picked up her nail buffer. "You know, Emily, I have a terrible feeling when I see those two together—Isobel and her mother. I know Mama is sometimes silly, but she does want the best for me. Well, she has admitted that she is keeping us here simply to give me an opportunity to further my acquaintance with Lord Ingram, and, possibly, Mr. Jennings, since he is so rich. She has no idea that Ingram isn't the least bit interested in *me*, and that I'm merely using Cecil Jennings to practice my flirting. No, but when I decide to marry, Mama will be delighted. She would never deny me a life of my own simply to keep me by her side."

Isobel did come down for dinner. But when the women retired to the library afterward, she excused herself, saying she was tired and needed an early night. Annora smiled and seemed pleased to have her daughter gone.

"Do you see, Lady Hume?" she asked Nicole Quimby.

THE MUCH MALIGNED LORD 35

"My daughter is still feeling the effects of that unfortunate episode when her brother coaxed her to sing. Her nerves simply will not sustain such exhilaration. It was cruel of Holt to insist, but then he is the most selfish creature alive."

Emily and Demetria exchanged glances, moving by mutual consent to view the chess game set up on a tall, narrow table near the fireplace.

Seeing the game in progress, Emily studied the board and thought it a variation of one of François Philidor's classic gambits.

Val Lindsay had told her and Demetria of Lord Ingram's correspondence games with Scanlon; this was obviously one of them. Mr. Finley Scanlon had been a protégé of Philidor's. Her father had met Philidor some twenty years ago, shortly before the Frenchman's death, and he knew Scanlon. According to Amos Wilton, no one had risen to take the late French chess master's place, although her Uncle Leland, the present earl, swore no one could hold a candle to the Italian master, Ponziani.

Emily walked slowly around the board, assessing the game, wondering if Lord Ingram was white or black.

Emily liked to read better than she liked to play games. She looked forward to visiting the lending library while she was in London; she had a list for Mr. Hatchard that she suspected would make him happy indeed. She looked forward to seeing the infamous Elgin Marbles, now in that shed at Burlington House. She also wanted to see the Egyptian exhibit at the British Museum.

She'd always wanted to visit the metropolis. The principal reason she'd given in to her father's wishes and acceded to her uncle's scheme to accompany Demetria to London was to see things she'd read of all her life. London, from Herefordshire, had seemed quite remote to Emily.

Such a country mouse as she knew herself to be would be well entertained. She was determined to see all the sights, take in the theaters, view the orangery at Kew. Her father had a small conservatory in the back gardens of their home, Beacon Hill. He had urged her to visit Kew. Emily wanted to walk where Samuel Pepys had so slyly picked an orange and tasted it.

There were many things she planned to do in London. Once she got her presentation out of the way, she could enjoy herself.

She'd wear her mama's court gown, of course. It had been preserved at Mursey Castle these many years, a stunning creation from Paris, fashioned of lustrous *peau d'ange* silk, with Flemish lace and satin knots.

Emily was excited about wearing the dress, although being presented at one of the queen's drawing rooms was a far cry from those grand affairs of her mama's day.

Her Uncle Mursey had insisted on dispatching the dress, along with several old-fashioned fur-lined cloaks, to Madame Fanchon, the famous Bond Street couturiere, sending the clothing to town in one of his carriages in the charge of Mrs. Gilruth, an upper servant who was Mama's first dresser while she still lived in Mursey Castle. Grace Garvey, her aunt's personal maid, had accompanied Mrs. Gilruth. In London, Madame Fanchon would refurbish the court gown, replacing all the limp ribbons and sagging knots. And she would design new cloaks, utilizing the chinchilla and sable furs in trimmings, linings, and muffs.

"I understand you're a chess player." Lord Ingram spoke suddenly from behind Emily.

She started; she hadn't realized he'd come into the room. The men had arrived to join the ladies in the library. A bad habit of hers, she knew, was concentrating so closely she lost herself in what she was thinking or reading.

"No," Emily said, shaking her head. "Chess doesn't interest me, I'm afraid." She smiled and lifted her face to gaze directly into Holt's eyes.

Mutely, he examined her expression. How many women had he known who could or would look at him openly and without the slightest sign of self-consciousness? Emily Wilton didn't realize her candid looks were one of the things that intrigued him most, Holt thought.

He leaned against the library table to ease his leg. "But I

THE MUCH MALIGNED LORD 37

understood from something Renton told me you were used to playing with your father and uncle."

Emily shook her head. By a strange quirk of memory, she could recall any number of chess games in their entirety, as well as beginnings, middles, and endings, so she was able to move adequately. She played often with her father, and, when she was staying at Mursey Castle, with her uncle, affording them, so they claimed, excellent games. She didn't know how that was, but most of the time, she was able to find a stalemate.

"Uncle Mursey and my father like to play," Emily said. "I'd rather do almost anything else, unless my father or uncle can obtain no other opponent."

Lord Ingram nodded.

Emily held his eyes a moment longer, then turned toward the chessboard. "I see you're playing a correspondence game. Are you black or white?"

"Black," Holt murmured. He liked the way she had her hair dressed. The dark, heavy strands were plaited loosely down the back of her head. Secured at the nape of her neck, the ends hung halfway down her back. She was so perfect, he thought, so tiny.

"Ah, yes. The black," said Emily, in a noncommittal way. She walked around the board to study the game from black's perspective.

Interesting, she thought. But wait. Surely . . . yes! She definitely recognized the play now. She stepped around to study white's position again. "Lord Ingram, who is your opponent? Could it be Finley Scanlon?"

Ingram threw back his head, his face dark and enigmatic. She didn't see the sharp gleam of appreciation in his eyes.

"How did you guess?" he asked. Inside, he was shaken with laughter. She might not like to *play,* but she certainly knew her game, by God!

"Actually, I didn't have to guess. I've seen this game, or a close version of it, before. Mr. Scanlon and my father played it two years ago." She nodded, her eyes on the board. "Scanlon has used the Ruy Lopez Opening."

"And you remember it after all this time?"

"I thought I recognized it before you came in. I wasn't sure, of course, because your middle game isn't yet begun."

"How did your father's game end? Was he playing the black?"

Emily nodded, trying to think. "Yes, the black, and I believe—" She bit her lip and screwed up her face in an effort to concentrate.

Holt studied the entrancing little frown on Emily's forehead. Not only was she beautiful, she was intelligent too.

He was fascinated—he'd never before met a woman who could even begin to play chess. And for all her denials, he was almost certain Emily could give him—or anyone—an excellent game. Not interested, indeed! Holt thought, and had to stop himself from smiling. He'd lay odds she could remember enough of the classic games to make her an outstanding player. Did the girl not realize that the ability to memorize games—and so many of them—made her a master? Perhaps she couldn't originate her own moves. Many players were not creative, but that did not preclude an admirable proficiency.

"I remember now," Emily said, nodding decisively. "Papa wasn't able to win, even using the Sicilian defense. No; that game ended in stalemate. Scanlon was barely able to castle. He was white, if you recall, and he ended with his king at queen's rook one, knight protecting."

She looked inquiringly at Holt. "You can see the play in your mind, can you not? As you may imagine on a nearly clear board, it was then black rook to king eight with black king near."

Emily turned her attention back to the game before her, which was not nearly as advanced as the game that had been played by her father and Scanlon. "Look here, my lord. Scanlon could have your majority, but you wrest it away with pawn to . . . Wait! Yes, to queen three . . ."

Emily had closed her eyes to visualize how the play might go, effectively blindfolding herself. She didn't know Cecil Jennings stood behind her and was observing her amazing feat of memory.

Cecil exchanged a speaking glance with Holt.

Grinning slightly, Holt nodded his understanding of Cecil's

THE MUCH MALIGNED LORD 39

wonderment at the girl's prowess and signed him to be quiet while she finished.

"I know," Emily said. "When Scanlon was playing Papa, he jumped his white knight to his queen's knight one. We—Papa—could only move black king to queen's knight one and it was all over—stalemate."

Emily opened her eyes and smiled directly into Holt's.

Later, stalking his bedroom—Holt was rarely able to sleep in those dim hours after midnight—he remembered how he'd wanted to kiss her in her flush of enthusiasm.

He laughed shortly. How surprised everyone would have been—Emily most of all—if he had snatched her up and laid his mouth on hers.

Holt was certain she hadn't the slightest idea of how she made him feel, all raw inside, yearning like a green boy. And good God!—that memory of hers!

Holt stretched his long body on top of the counterpane. Had he ever felt like this about a woman before? He couldn't remember. But he had only to hear Emily's laugh and desire racked him, sending lashes of heat curling round his body like a writhing cat-o'-nine-tails.

Holt came off the bed and grabbed his jacket. His servants were accustomed to his leaving the house, riding for hours, and returning just as the sun came over the horizon.

Then he would stride up the stone stairs to the tower and stand gazing over the land.

In the stables, the grooms were trained to ignore their master's comings and goings unless he called them. He liked to curry and saddle his favorite mount himself.

Holt limped into the library on his way out, gazed long on the chessboard, and made up his mind. Tomorrow, he would challenge Miss Emily Wilton to a game. Anything, so long as he could be near her and command her undivided attention.

Smiling crookedly, Holt decided against riding. He felt relaxed and pleasantly sleepy; he needed time to plan his game with Emily. He wouldn't beat her, but he didn't want her to think he was letting her win, either.

Five

The sun streamed forth, heralding a truly beautiful morning.

A knock sounded on Isobel Ingram's door, and she hid Mr. David Locke's letter—received via her maid, Gertrude—in her pocket.

Instead of her mother (who usually chose to interrupt her writing at this time of day, wandering into her room, yawning and complaining), Isobel was surprised to see Demetria Quimby standing there.

"Demetria!" she exclaimed, then lowered her voice, remembering that most of the guests must still be sleeping. "Good morning."

"Yes, it's a lovely morning," Demetria responded in a loud whisper, throwing a conspirator's look at the dowager baroness's closed door. "Shh! Come down the hall. Emily and I are having a cup of tea. We want to talk to you. My mother hasn't stirred, but Emily and I have been up for hours. Are you an early bird? I am."

Isobel grabbed her shawl. "Yes, that's when I do my best writing. I love the awakening of the day."

"Me, too," Demetria said. "My cousin and I want to hear all about your books, of course, but there's something else ... Emily didn't think we should interfere, or even comment on your problem with your mama, but, as I reminded her, she doesn't know what some of us go through. *Her* mother has been dead for years."

Isobel broke into a low, melodious laugh. She immediately clapped her hand over her mouth to stifle the sound. Her fine brown eyes danced with mirth.

"Not," said Demetria, as they passed beyond her own mother's door, "that I think Emily is lucky to have no mother. I knew Aunt Wilton well, and she was a delightful person, a good mother. And definitely romantic. She defied them all in marrying her doctor and proved them wrong because her marriage turned out so well. Just about the time Emily was supposed to be presented, she became very ill, you know. So Emily missed her Season. Yes, it's altogether too bad that Aunt Wilton died. And I certainly don't wish anything to happen to Mama, either, but she is a sore trial to me sometimes. When she is being particularly outrageous, I've often told Emily how fortunate she is. As for Mama—well, I'm her one chicken, you see, and she is possessive beyond imagining."

Isobel grimaced. There was nothing she didn't understand about an overly possessive mother. "Demetria," she said, "you can't possibly know."

Demetria shook her head wisely. "Well, Emily and I have decided to help you. At least, I have. But I can talk my cousin into any scheme; you'll see. Oh, Isobel—the three of us are going to be such good friends, just wait. And you must call me Deme," she said, grabbing the taller woman's arm, and ushering her into the low-pitched chamber she and Emily shared. "All my friends call me Deme. Look, Em," she cried, presenting Isobel like a prize. "Here she is, just as I promised."

Isobel was touched by Demetria Quimby's offer of friendship. She had only one real friend in the *ton*, and that was Allegra Lindsay Haddon, a sister of Val Lindsay's. She and Allegra had played together from childhood, they had gone to the same school in Bath, and she'd been one of Allegra's bridesmaids in her grand wedding in London. Sooner or later, Annora made Isobel's other, less understanding friends uncomfortable, and they dropped away. But not Allegra. She wasn't afraid of Annora, and Isobel suspected these Mursey cousins from Hereford wouldn't be intimidated by her either.

Isobel constantly strove to overcome her reserve. In the face of Demetria's sunny declarations of friendship and Emily's warm concern, she found herself relaxing, eagerly responding to Emily's questions about her writing. Soon, she was describing her London friends, those rather Bohemian writers and painters she knew.

"Have you met Miss Austen?" Emily asked, fascinated.

"No," Isobel said. "She lives in Hampshire. But I have corresponded with her. She wrote several letters very kindly answering my questions when I started writing seriously two years ago. Do you like her books?"

Emily's eyes sparkled. "I'm reading *Sense and Sensibility* again for the third time. I must make a confession. I do admire these modern novels, and Miss Austen's in particular. In fact, I'm addicted to the Minerva Press. But then, I appreciate books of all kinds; I'd rather read than anything. I'd love to read one of your manuscripts if you have a copy."

Emily, seeing Isobel flush, was sorry she'd introduced what was obviously a painful subject—Annora's destruction of her work in progress. That was cruel in the extreme, Emily thought. She bit her lip. How could she have been so maladroit as to have mentioned it? But it seemed her cousin did not share her reticence.

"Yes, Isobel," trilled Demetria. "I told Emily I thought it the shabbiest thing that your mama burnt your book, and I've bet her my new paisley shawl there was another copy lying about somewhere. Was there?"

Isobel smiled now. "I'm afraid, Emily, that you've lost the bet. There was indeed another copy. Mr. Locke had it and still does."

"Yes, this mysterious Mr. Locke!" cried Demetria. "When I said there was something between you, Emily claimed my romantic nature was getting the better of me. Confess, dear Belle—may we call you Belle?—confess Mr. Locke is deep in love with you. Oh, it's a romance, I know it! We shall help you, Emily and I—won't we, Em? I can't wait until we're in town. How soon can we meet Mr. Locke? Are you able to correspond?"

Emily was astounded at the look that crossed Isobel Ingram's face—a fleeting expression of yearning hope, suppressed rapture, and hidden joy. An attractive mask of dusky rose suddenly veiled Isobel's face, highlighting her wide cheekbones, giving her an exotic look, a mysterious air which revealed her as a woman in love.

Isobel had a habit, which Emily had noted before, of catching her full lower lip between her straight white teeth and widening her eyes, her dark golden gaze unfaltering, her sweeping brows lifting until her face was lit with animation. Why was this lovely young woman unmarried? Emily asked herself. She still possessed the bloom of youth. It seemed utterly impossible that Isobel Ingram could be thirty-four years old. How had she escaped the notice of those Corinthians and Nonpareils who were said to roam the glittering saloons of the beau monde searching for eligible heiresses?

"Have you never thought of marrying?" Emily blurted, and blushed at her tactless question. "I'm sorry. What I mean is, you *must* have been asked. I don't want to embarrass you, but you are very beautiful."

"No, no," Isobel disclaimed. "You're very kind to say so. However, to answer your question, I—"

"Perhaps you'd rather not," Emily said hurriedly, reluctant to pry.

"I don't mind," Isobel dropped her eyes to her fingers, which were entwined in her lap. "Actually," she said slowly, "I've been engaged twice. But I cried off both times. And—and now I'm very glad I did."

Isobel caught her lip in her teeth again. The urge to tell Demetria and Emily of her long-delayed decision to push for marriage with David Locke was overwhelming. She'd come to that decision only last night, when her mother had so cruelly humiliated her before their guests. It was the final straw. Isobel's last qualm, along with whatever loyalty she'd felt for Annora, had been swept away. She and her mother could never be reconciled. She owed Annora nothing, less than nothing, and she meant to strive for her own happiness and the happiness of the man she loved.

"Tell us," demanded Demetria. "Everything!"

"Deme," Emily cautioned, but Demetria would not be denied.

"You *are* in love with Mr. Locke, aren't you?" Demetria asked breathlessly.

Isobel nodded, smiling tremulously, and Demetria exclaimed, "I knew it! You are going to furnish us with details, aren't you? Is he handsome? Does he have a family? Not that you should let that stop you, if you're really in love. How did you meet him?"

"I walked into his office in Fleet Street and asked if he'd like to publish my book."

"Was it love at first sight?" Demetria's eyes were round. She'd learned to flirt by the time she was five, to manipulate every sprig of the quality she encountered. One day she'd find a man who gave as good as he got; Demetria was tired of easy conquests.

Isobel felt herself blush. "We—we weren't indifferent to each other," she said.

No, she thought. Not indifferent at all. She had looked into David Locke's eyes and broken her engagement that same night.

The cousins were waiting, and Isobel tried to explain. "Well, I was engaged at the time—that was my second engagement, of course. However, the greatest complication was—*is*—that David doesn't have a family as our world terms it. No dukes or earls hidden in his family tree. But in the world of commerce, he has no peers. Over a hundred and fifty years ago, his great-grandfather began a small company that published books in Leadenhall Street. Locke Publishing has grown until it's one of the premier houses in Europe. David inherited it all and was trained from his infancy to run a publishing empire. He owns several newspapers and is a brilliant journalist. He serves on the Board of Trade and innumerable commissions. All of which count for nothing to those in the *haut ton*. I, needless to say, no longer accept that attitude. David is a man to admire in every sense of the word."

"Is he handsome?" Demetria's eyes were avid. "Is he tall and dashing? Please tell us he is a 'parfait gentle knight.'"

Emily watched Isobel's expression turn dreamlike.

"Demetria," Isobel said in an awed voice, "you must see for yourself." She smiled and shook her head. "David is extraordinary-looking. Tall, yes, and powerfully built. As big as Holt and just as lean and strong. But where my brother is dark, David has the most amazing blond looks. I told him once that one of his forbears must have been a Viking."

Demetria sighed and Emily spoke. "You mentioned that you were engaged when you met him."

"Yes," Isobel agreed. "My engagement wasn't a love match. I freely admit that I had accepted Lord Jermyn in order to get away from Mama. I thought I could find contentment in a marriage with him, and he was sympathetic to my writing. He was an older man with a literary turn himself. He was very understanding when I cried off. I felt at a disadvantage, because I'd cried off from my first engagement, too. In spite of what Mama told you, my Season was a success. I had three proposals that year, 1793. Captain Conrad Gray was a dashing young officer, a second son, with a respectable fortune. Connie Gray and I fell wildly in love, or so we thought, and got engaged just before he went off to fight in the Flanders campaign with Stapleton Cotton. It was quite romantic, and I was content to wait and write furiously all the time he was gone. The captain and I broke our engagement by mutual consent when he returned to England some three years later. We'd grown apart—grown up, really—and were relieved to become simply friends. My heart was never touched, not until I met David. And now? Who knows what will happen?"

The silence grew, and Emily asked, "Are you hesitating because Mr. Locke has no family?"

Isobel shook her head. "No. *I'm* not the one. It's David. If I marry him, I shall become part of the world of trade and no longer a persona grata in the beau monde. He thinks I'll come to regret giving up my position in society. Oh, but don't you see? That is no longer my world. My friends are those writers and artists we talked about, the diplomats and all the fascinating people in that wonderful commercial world of the City. The *ton* seems so narrow to me now. Society will reject me if I marry David; I know that. Mama will be furious, but I don't care what she says. As for Holt, I know he wants me to be happy. He says he will support me in any way he can, should I persuade David to marry me. Holt, by the way, applauds David for his scruples."

"Your brother doesn't know you've made a definite decision?" inquired Emily.

"No. I'm going to tell him today. We've never kept secrets from each other and we've always found it necessary to conspire with one another against Mama. But it was only last night that I finally made up my mind to marry David in spite of his misgivings. I won't allow some antiquated notions of Society to rob us of happiness. When I get to town, I'm determined to make him propose. And if everyone cuts me dead, so be it!"

Isobel's voice shook on this defiant statement and she lifted her chin. It was true. If she could have David Locke, she'd count the world of the *ton* well lost.

"You may rely on us," stated Demetria in a steely little voice. "Isn't that right, Em?"

"Most certainly," replied Emily. "My mother defied convention to marry my father, a doctor, you know, and she never regretted it for an instant. They were meant for each other."

Isobel smiled her thanks. "What I've told you must be held in the strictest confidence, until David and I make our announcement. I'm sure the news will flash like wildfire then. I—I shall need all those who choose to stand by me." Impulsively, she held out her hand to Emily, who grasped it as hard as she could.

Demetria, however, threw her arms around Belle and hugged her. "Just tell us how we can help," she said fiercely. "That's what friends are for."

Moments later, Isobel and the cousins descended the double staircase in search of luncheon.

Spread lavishly in the large dining room, this midday meal

was served buffet-style. A bank of tall windows revealed a sweeping view to the south. The drapes had been drawn back, and the guests could see far across the countryside. The hills were pale green, fast emerging from winter's drab tones, and the sheep pastures were neatly laid in vast, darker green squares. Great flocks grazed there, scattered over the land, just as they had for centuries.

Holt Ingram and Cecil Jennings came in, declaring they were famished, laughing when Val Lindsay swore he would ride out with them tomorrow.

"Emily," Val called, obviously chafing at having remained behind while his friends went to Abbingdon on Ravencroft estate business, "I can ride, can't I, if we rig some kind of sling for my leg?"

Emily, standing close to the wall of windows, turned. Her eyes immediately locked with Holt's, and he gave her a singular smile, his white teeth flashing. He was far too handsome for her peace of mind, she thought.

She looked at Val and said, "If you are careful, I can't see why not. Have you asked Dr. Steele?"

"He's gone to Bristol for several days. Said you'd take care of me. So may I ride, doctor dearest?"

Everyone laughed except Lady Ingram, who frowned, and Nicole Quimby, who smiled absently.

Emily gave young Renton her permission, stipulating that he should allow someone to help him on and off his horse, and reminding him that under no circumstance must he bear his weight on the injured limb.

The dowager baroness shook her head and launched upon a commentary on manners.

Asserting that her father, although a simple country squire, had insisted upon the strict observance of proper form at all times, she stated, "Yes, and he, may God rest his soul, would have been shocked at hearing young ladies addressed by their given names. But more than that, he most assuredly never, ever would have approved their being applied to as *doctor dearest.*"

Lady Ingram had been directing her speech to the company

at large. Now she concentrated on Val. "Alas, my dear Renton, you are no longer at Oxford."

She smiled thinly and shook her finger at him. "We must remember that what is overlooked in a schoolboy is inexcusable in one who has lately inherited his father's honors."

The luncheon party had fallen silent. Her ladyship ruminated a moment, then continued her majestic discourse. "Yes, Renton, and I imagine you shall find yourself at many tonnish parties this Season. Only let the patronnesses of Almack's get a whiff of such ragged manners, not to mention your queer sense of humor, which I can only term frivolous, and you shall very soon discover yourself stricken off their list. If they apply to me, as your nearest neighbor, I'm very much afraid I shall find it necessary to advise them to let you cool your heels a year, in hopes of improvement. Now you must take this little hint in the spirit in which it is given; it's for your own good. But there; we know your mother has spoiled you outrageously. You were Oralia Lindsay's last child, and she is overwhelmingly sentimental; simply never got over the fact that she had given Lord Renton a boy at last. She dotes on you and your sisters, and can never perceive when she is making a cake of herself with all her cloying airs of sweetness.

" 'Spare the rod and spoil the child,' I've told her on more than one occasion, for you were very naughty, and your sisters, especially Allegra, were encouraged in every excess. I am proud to say I made no such mistake with Ingram here. Many times my husband, and Old Lord Ingram, remonstrated with me for having my footman whip him. Yes, and the child was too stubborn to cry, no matter how many lashes I had them lay on—"

The baroness closed her mouth when her son rose precipitously to his feet, almost knocking over his chair.

"Madam," Ingram said, "I feel certain our guests would enjoy other, more pleasant topics than my juvenile threshings." His voice was glacial, and his piercing eyes, bent unswervingly upon his mother, blazed with a cold fire.

Emily had never seen anger so personified. A dull flush intensified the dark cast of his features. He loomed menacingly over the table, his fists clenched by his sides. In his present barely controlled state, Emily thought Holt Ingram was more attractive, more compelling than ever.

Without waiting for his mother's rebuttal, the baron abruptly bowed, excused himself, and invited Mr. Jennings to push Lord Renton into the game room.

Annora retired to her rooms after lunch, congratulating herself on her success in goading her son into a betrayal of his anger. It wasn't often that she was able to arouse emotion in Holt. But he had been affected—oh, yes, had almost lost control of that imperturbable sangfroid he was so famous for. Annora dismissed her maid and prepared to rest upon her couch. A delicious shiver went through her body. Holt had very nearly lost his composure and made a scene. She hadn't planned it to happen; she only wished she had. But she was delighted that she had been able to shake him.

A knock made Annora exclaim under her breath, then call, "Come in,"

To her surprise, Holt himself strode into her sitting chamber. Annora was annoyed when he curtly invited her to sit, and then stood with his greatboots firmly planted on the floor, crossing his arms over his chest, and coolly telling her that she would in future refrain from embarrassing his guests.

Annora eyed her son. How like his father he was. So dark, and with that tall physique; exactly like his grandfather, too. All the Ingram men were big and forceful, and possessed of those implacable black eyes. She shuddered as he continued.

"Val Lindsay is no longer a child to be lectured on his manners," he declared. "And he had done nothing wrong. Madam, you take too much on yourself. You came here uninvited to act as my hostess when I neither needed nor wanted you. Only for Belle's sake have I allowed you to stay. Which reminds me: the humiliation you heaped upon poor Belle last night was unconscionable. I will not allow you to treat her that way, nor tell such lies about her. Make up your mind to that, or leave for Abbingdon this instant." With one last look, Holt turned on his heel and left her.

Annora lay on her couch shaking. How dare Holt say she'd embarrassed him with her commentary on manners? This all had to do with that Emily Wilton, she thought. Oh, Holt had disguised his interest well enough, never mentioning the girl's name. But Annora had seen those sly glances that passed between her son and his guest.

And, Annora thought, there had been no need for Holt to remind her she wasn't hostess here, that she came uninvited to Ravencroft. She had been obliged to hold her tongue. It made Annora ill; she almost wished she'd never had children. All the pain and bother, and then they treated you with contempt and couldn't wait to leave you.

"I was so embarrassed for Isobel," said Demetria. She and Emily were in their small sitting room, which adjoined their bedchamber, and were trying to rest.

"Yes, and Val Lindsay didn't know where to look. But more than that, what about Ingram?" Emily murmured.

She found her fists clenched in her skirt whenever she thought of Holt being whipped as a little boy, his mother keeping at it, trying to break him, determined to make him cry. No wonder he looked at the woman with such a distant air. When Annora had needlessly exposed the details of Holt's childhood pain, the force of his furious gaze was almost like an assault. Who could blame him if he hated the woman? What horrible memories he must have of his early years. "Lady Ingram is heartless," murmured Emily.

"Yes," agreed Demetria. "Val told me she called her son a cripple when he came home with his war wound. After the attack on the—what was it?—the Renaud redoubt at—at—?" Demetria screwed up her face, trying to remember. "What was that battle Lord Ingram was wounded in, Emily? You told me, but I've forgotten."

"His lordship said he was wounded at the beginning of the siege of Ciudad Rodrigo," Emily said.

"That's it!" Demetria nodded. "I can never remember that stuff, all those Spanish names. Anyway, Val swears the dowager told Ingram, in his hearing, that she thought being wounded was good enough for him. She kept reminding Ingram she'd said he shouldn't volunteer for the army.

"Val says the dowager refused to nurse Lord Ingram when he came home, or even view the great wound on his thigh. According to Val, she taunted Ingram with his lameness, contending that he must give up the idea of marrying again to gain an heir, assuring him no woman would want to be tied to a cripple. If he'd only listened to her, etcetera. Well, you know how she goes on, Emily. No wonder Ingram had her moved bag and baggage to the dower house at Abbingdon Manor. I'll say one thing, I'm going right now to tell Mama how much I appreciate her."

And so saying, Demetria took herself off to her mama's room, no doubt to startle that lady with endearments and protestations of love.

Shaking her head, Emily lay on her bed. Women, she thought, held the emotional well-being of their families in their hands. She'd never realized that so completely. Her mother had laid a warm, loving mantle over their life, creating an atmosphere of caring. Emily's parents had been extraordinarily happy together. They had expressed their need for each other by word, look, and deed. And Emily had been wrapped in that cocoon of well-being all her life. She'd always known how fortunate she was, but never more so than at this moment.

Tears started in her eyes; oh, she did miss her mother, gone these three years. Poor Holt, she thought, rising and crossing to her dresser and finding a handkerchief. He couldn't remember such love from his childhood. People who had such a legacy were lucky indeed, thought Emily. And Isobel. The woman was thirty-four and still struggling to escape her mother's grasp.

A resolution was forming in Emily's mind. She and Demetria would indeed help Isobel Ingram gain her freedom and marry Mr. Locke. And Holt—he must be the first to understand what his sister was suffering, tied to their mother.

A wave of drowsiness swept over Emily. She lost a deal of sleep while she roamed the house in what she called her night-owl hours. Now, in the middle of the afternoon, she was dead on her feet, exactly as she'd been when she was a child. An hour's deep sleep, and she would awaken refreshed. Holt Ingram stood clearly in her mind's eye as she dropped off for a nap. She wanted to hold him, to soothe the memory of his mother's dread whip.

"Miss Wilton," Holt said. "Will you honor me with a game of chess after dinner this evening?" The servants had just brought in the second course.

They had agreed to call each other by their Christian names, but since then had spent little time together. After his mother's unfortunate strictures on manners earlier, Holt felt that he must defer the pleasure of hearing his name on Emily's lips. "I should love to try your skill," he added.

Emily looked at Holt uncertainly. She had determined to refuse if he asked her to play. It had never been her ambition to put herself forward. But in her present mood, she couldn't deny him so small a thing as a game of chess.

Dropping her eyes, she nodded.

A square rout table, burled and inlaid with cherry, sat in the middle of the library, flanked by two Egyptian side chairs. A beautiful marble chessboard with ivory and ebony pieces stood ready for their play.

Emily could see that Holt's correspondence game was undisturbed on its table before the fire. Obviously then, this was a guest board. Did Mr. Jennings play, or perhaps Val Lindsay?

The baron extended his hand, and Emily laid hers lightly on his open palm. His fingers immediately curled about hers and he drew Emily to the table. After bowing her to her chair, he took his seat opposite.

Demetria pushed Val away to the Blue Saloon, leaving Emily alone with Holt and Mr. Jennings. That was just as well. None of the others was interested in chess.

The dowager baroness had seemed strangely subdued throughout dinner and opted for an early bed. Aunt Hume, who loved a novel quite as well as Emily, had gone to her room, saying she would read a while. Belle Ingram had retired to write a scene in her latest book. Emily suspected she would also write to Mr. David Locke.

THE MUCH MALIGNED LORD

Emily felt a tingle of excitement. She found herself anticipating the strategy the baron might use against her.

Cecil Jennings watched avidly as Miss Wilton tapped one of the chess pieces hidden in Holt Ingram's clenched fists, choosing, giving her the ebony piece, and allowing the baron first move as white.

Cecil nodded. White always moved first in chess, and that gave the player who had drawn it first chance at attack.

All morning, since he'd learned Holt intended to challenge Miss Wilton to a game, Cecil had tried to query his host about the opening he would choose.

Holt had laughingly declined to commit himself. "But really, Cecil, I don't know," he said. "I shall try to insist my fair opponent take the first move. I'm determined to see what the girl can do when she's forced to think. It's my belief she's never played an offensive strategy in her life."

Cecil saw Miss Wilton resist Lord Ingram's offer of the white, even after she'd drawn the black.

"No, my lord. If I'd drawn white, I should have played it. Now, if you wish to please me, you must grant me the same consideration you would a man, which is to say none. I desire no advantage. That is why I insisted we contest for first move."

Emily smiled. Was she taking the sting out of her words? Cecil wondered.

He noted Holt Ingram's acquiescent nod; that was politeness itself, and very apparent. But only someone who knew the baron intimately would have caught the hidden grimace of annoyance, revealed by that tiny downturn at the corner of his mouth. Cecil grunted to himself. Holt wasn't pleased that he'd been maneuvered into first move.

Cecil, for one, hadn't expected the girl to ask for quarter. And he wasn't surprised when Miss Wilton so adroitly refused any advantage.

So, Cecil thought, hiding a grin, the girl has already imposed her will upon Holt's. But how intriguing: such a strong resolution in that diminutive, and perfectly feminine, frame.

Mr. Jennings had a sudden premonition. It was within the realm of possibility that Ingram had just met his ultimate opponent. Perhaps not in chess, but in the larger game of life. Cecil chuckled to himself. The dear *femmes* always won. It happened to every man, sooner or later. Even Holt Ingram. Ah, they were starting to play.

Carelessly, the baron made his first move, and Emily countered.

Four moves into the game, Emily reached to touch her queen's knight, drew back, and closed her eyes in concentration. She gave Holt a look of dawning discovery.

"I believe I see what you're doing, my lord. It's Ponziani's Opening, isn't it?"

Grinning, Holt shot a glance at Cecil Jennings, who raised his brows and shook his head in amazement.

Emily was unaware of this byplay. "Yes, Papa made me learn this years ago." She studied the board a minute or two, then frowned at the entranced Ingram.

"You realize that we should stalemate in twelve moves if you continue with the usual defense."

Holt gave a delighted shout of laughter. He wanted to hug her. "No," he said. "I hadn't realized that. Do you want to finish the game? Cecil might enjoy seeing it played."

Mr. Jennings gulped a hurried plea. "Yes, please. I don't understand. What is it again?"

"Ponziani's Opening answered with Polerio's Defense," Holt told him.

Holt had unconsciously gone into a game he was familiar with. Not over two dozen players in England would have recognized it, much less had it memorized. "Shall we play it out?" he asked Emily.

Warmly aware that she had pleased him, Emily gave a small nod. They commenced to move, rapidly and without pause, until—just as she'd expected—she advanced her king one space and the game ended in stalemate.

Emily thought it the most enjoyable game she'd ever played. Or perhaps that was because Holt Ingram was an opponent *par excellence*. Playing against him was almost unbearably exciting. His physical presence, his masculine assurance—how had she dared to oppose him? Would he think her unbecomingly forward? It was considered bad strategy by all the doting mamas in the *ton* for a young lady to show herself too intelligent or too aggressive against an eligible male. But Emily wasn't hunting a husband and besides, Holt had *asked* her to play. No, she was refining too much on a simple game. It was merely that she enjoyed the interplay with the baron's mind and admired his skill—that was all there was to it. He offered her a challenge. Holt was much faster than her father. She wouldn't be surprised to learn he was able to play blindfolded.

Emily had never had occasion to do so, but felt playing blindfolded would present no problem. It might be amusing to play that way sometimes, although she would never presume to suggest such a thing.

Mr. Jennings, who knew a good chess player when he saw one, cried, "Oh, I say, Miss Wilton! Jolly good. Have you ever played blind? I can't do it myself, but it's a specialty of Ingram's. He's been doing it forever. I'd give a monkey to see you two have a go."

Holt raised one brow and murmured, "I'm agreeable to anything Miss Wilton desires."

Emily thought she must be reading too much into that statement. "I—I'd like that—" she said haltingly. "Perhaps—" She was glad when they were interrupted by her cousin and Val Lindsay.

"Emily," called Demetria, "you should see Ingram's antique billiard table. It's got bare wooden boards. The only tables I've seen have baize. Are you finished? Did you get beaten?"

"Oh, no," interposed Ingram. "Your cousin, Miss Quimby, is an accomplished player. Why didn't you warn me?"

"I didn't know." Demetria looked at Emily in surprise. "I knew she could play, but—"

Emily rose from her chair. "I'd like to see this naked billiard table, I think."

Too much attention always made her uncomfortable. She was glad Mr. Jennings and Lord Ingram were the only ones present to observe that trick memory of hers.

As they trooped down the hall behind Demetria, Emily

wondered if she shouldn't have shammed it, played badly, and had done with the game of chess.

In the game room, Emily declined to play billiards, saying she rarely played at home, and watched while Val Lindsay tried to balance himself on one leg for a shot to the side pocket.

When they all said good night and had been lit upstairs by the gallant Mr. Jennings, Emily castigated herself.

She had nothing to read in her room. She'd meant to go back to the library and select something—anything.

Demetria finally fell asleep, after exhausting the topic of tomorrow's projected trip to Lindhurst, Val Lindsay's home.

Emily remained in her dress, telling her cousin she needed something to read and would slip down to the library after she judged everyone asleep.

A violent storm had blown up, and she went to the window. Emily could see the cloud formations when the lightning flashed. If only she could be in the tower when the storm broke, she thought.

More than an hour had passed since she and Demetria had come upstairs. Emily forced herself to wait a while longer, and it was almost two o'clock when she went down.

The night-lights were turned low, but even so, Ravencroft seemed more brightly lit than most houses at night.

Emily passed the latticed iron doors leading to the tower stairs. The stairwell was pitch black. Had there been a light of any kind available, she would have dared to ascend to the tower.

Regretfully, she continued down the long hall toward the library, the sounds of the storm muted by the thick castle walls.

Just as she reached the library door, it swung open and Holt Ingram stood there.

For a long moment, they stared at each other and Emily felt herself sway. At dinner, and during their chess game, Holt had been dressed formally. Now he wore riding clothes, his superbly tailored blue coat and buff pants revealing every masculine line of his powerful frame. His spurred, high-topped boots made him seem even taller than he was. He had

THE MUCH MALIGNED LORD 57

carelessly knotted a tie about his neck, and Emily dropped her eyes to his smooth bare throat. His pulse seemed to jump at her glance, and his lids came half down over his eyes, making them look drowsy and sensual.

On a heavy roll of thunder, he said, "I was thinking of you." His voice was low, imparting an added intimacy to their situation. They seemed isolated in the sleeping castle.

That sense of seclusion was one of the things Emily loved about the night hours, that splendid time after midnight when everyone was sleeping and she owned the world.

It did not occur to her to wonder why Holt Ingram was awake too. Never before had she shared the witching hours with anyone.

She stood still, barely breathing, held in thrall by his presence. He was so close she could smell him, a combination of horse and oiled leather. Had he been riding? His cropped black curls were a tangle across his brow. Emily could imagine him galloping *vent à terre* across the fields at midnight, defying the elements. How often she'd wanted to do that!

Before she could convince herself that she should utter some excuse and make her escape, Holt grasped her hand. Again she felt that sweep of warmth.

"Come to the tower," he said. "The lookout room. I want to show you the storm."

Emily went without the slightest hesitation. It simply did not occur to her to refuse.

She found herself on the stairs, Holt lighting their way with a candle.

The storm was imminent. They reached the top and the tower was buffeted by strong winds and filled with coiling, twisting light. Emily caught her breath as an incandescent phantasmagoria in brilliant blacks and whites leaped from horizon to horizon and back again. Such beauty she'd never beheld.

Holt had blown out the candle. The room was dark except for the merciless stabs of lightning.

Emily walked forward and pressed her palms against the glass. She felt vibrations from the rolling thunder. The wind, blowing even harder, shrieked and battered at the windows.

This sense of being at the center of a violent cataclysm was the experience she'd been seeking when she ran out into the storm as a child. That was dangerous, yes, but there was another kind of danger here as well.

She was caught between two charged forces, the man behind her and the storm before. She knew how lethal the storm was; the man—at this moment—seemed no less beautiful, no less lethal.

Desire, as she understood it, was a stranger to Emily; she'd tried to analyze that often fatal attraction between men and women. How much was emotional, how much physical? She could not comprehend passions so strong that people sometimes died of them.

What she felt for Holt Ingram must be akin to that sweet torment she'd read so much about. Even alone she couldn't be rid of the desire to be near him; indeed, she wanted more.

She wanted to touch him, to run her hands up his back as he held her. She wanted to trace his lips with her fingers. She forced herself to admit it—she wanted his kisses. Never had a man affected her so. She had begun to think no man could. It was beyond anything she'd ever imagined.

Not since their roadside encounter, when Holt Ingram had laughed and pulled her to her feet after she'd worked on Val Lindsay, had Emily been totally free of this—of *his*—domination.

Her senses responded to him in a rapturous, delirious rush. This condition called love—so sudden it could happen in one look, one touch—the combined physical and emotional relationship between lovers, the consummation, had always fascinated Emily.

Was it this the poets spoke of? Was she to understand at last, or was she destined to die without experiencing the joy of being held by a man she loved? Emily was certain Holt Ingram would have heard the beat of her thumping heart had not the crashing thunder surrounded them.

She kept her back to him and bowed her head, trying to control the suffocating warmth that swept her body. She felt pulled in Holt's direction, as if he were magnetized. She wondered if he was affected in any way.

THE MUCH MALIGNED LORD

The sudden flare of a tinderbox as Holt lit the candle cast the outer world in blackness, creating a mirror effect in the windows.

Emily could see her own face, white and strained. Behind her, looming tall, stood Ingram, his expression a mystery in the soft candlelight.

"I'll take you down," he said.

Emily couldn't speak. He sounded harsh, but controlled, as if he exercised some sort of restraint over himself.

She nodded, he took her arm, and they started toward the stairs.

A rippling crack of lightning split the air, bursting, crashing about the tower, as they were halfway across the room.

Unreasoning terror seized Emily. She whirled and threw herself at Holt, screaming his name, clutching him wildly.

He automatically opened his arms to receive her, dropping the guttering candle. They were plunged into darkness; the sky had opened and rain pelted the windows, obscuring all except the most dazzling flashes of lightning.

A shaft of fear such as she'd never known pierced Emily. She trembled violently, sobbed, and locked her arms about Holt's neck, bringing herself even closer to his body. His embrace, brutally strong, made her gasp, but she'd never felt so safe, held fast against the storm.

Holt loosened his arms to let her go, but Emily gave a little cry and clung shamelessly, burying her face in his shoulder. She couldn't bear to be separated from him.

Instantly, Holt tightened his arms in a vise that crushed her against him, bending Emily backward as he arched over her. He braced himself and enveloped her in a powerful hug that left her without breath.

After a while, as her heart slowed and she relaxed a little, he asked, "Better?"

She nodded, and although she was still shaking, Holt released her.

Picking up the candle, he lit it again, using the Prometheus Box he carried in his pocket. "Come," he said. "I have a small chamber below. A fire is burning on the hearth. We must warm you."

Six

Annora Ingram had heard Emily leave her room. Awakened by the storm, alerted to the latch clicking in the room next to hers, she had risen quickly and carefully opened her door a crack. She saw the girl hurrying along the corridor and descending the stairs. No doubt the little hussy was searching for her son, Annora thought.

Everyone knew of Holt's midnight habits. How Emily would pretend to blush when she bumped into him on the stairs, or in the library. How easy to contrive a tryst. And how like Holt to find a *convenient* under his own roof.

Squirming on her chair and thinking of her own position in the world, Annora decided to watch until the girl returned, hoping to learn something to use against Miss Emily Wilton.

She might be a mere dowager, Annora thought, but there were still weapons in her arsenal. Gossip was one of the more potent ones at her command. What she learned by spying on the girl's nocturnal activities would be well worth her loss of sleep.

Annora got a pillow for her chair and settled herself again. She wasn't quite without influence, she reminded herself. She had a few remaining friends in town, and she wasn't afraid to bend the truth if it served her purpose. Oh, if only she still reigned supreme here in Ravencroft.

Annora had first been obliged to step down in favor of her

daughter-in-law. One thing she had learned when Holt married Muriel: the moment a son took a wife, especially if he was heir to a title, his mother became superfluous.

She had regained some small stature when Muriel died, for her old position as chatelaine of Ravencroft was restored to her, including all the deference and respect that lofty position commanded. No matter how she hated the place, it was, after all, the great house she had come to as a young bride. That phase, unfortunately, lasted only a few years. It was a jolt when—at Holt's whim—she had to relinquish her authority once again and step down, leaving him in sole possession. When he came home from the Peninsula, and after she'd fought going for years, Holt had relegated her to that pile, Abbingdon Manor. An obscure dowager in a dreary dower house—what a comedown! Annora had found herself forced into the ranks of all the other relics, of no account in society.

It was all Holt's fault; how she loathed him. Annora had been powerless to fight him, and that was when she began truly to hate him. She did not find submission easy; it was infuriating. But that was the lot of women. They were merely pawns, first used by their fathers to make a good marriage, then by their husbands to provide heirs to their dynasties. Long and long had Annora known she was nothing to her father, merely an insignificant younger daughter among eight children. She was lucky she was fair, her father told her, when he announced that he had contracted a marriage with Lord Ingram's son, a young man she'd seen just twice. And the Ingrams were only interested in what progeny she could produce.

She had presented her husband with two before he withdrew from her bed. She had devoted her life to Ravencroft, and now she was thrown away like a piece of used furniture.

Annora knew many women who professed themselves pleased to step down and relinquish the reins of power. She never believed them when they claimed they were content to resign themselves to second place. She wasn't, and she would fight to her dying breath those who had treated her so shabbily. What did she care for tradition? Holt might very easily have allowed her to remain at Ravencroft. Now, if she could frustrate her son's ambitions in any way, she'd be delighted. No one obstructed Annora Ingram's will. If they did, they came to rue the day.

This girl Emily, Annora mused. Holt seemed very taken with her. She was a doctor's daughter, of all things, and had actually gotten down in the dust and worked on Val Lindsay with her own hands. That in itself—and she certainly intended to alert various of her friends in the *ton*—should have checked any interest Holt might have felt in the girl. Surely he was only trifling with her; he couldn't possibly mean marriage. However, if he did, it would afford Annora great pleasure to thwart those ambitions.

Questioning the aunt, Annora had learned Emily seemed to have thought nothing of smearing herself with young Renton's blood. Lady Hume insisted that Holt had stood by smiling while the girl washed herself. It was hard to believe.

Nicole Quimby seemed properly horrified by her niece's predilection for members of the medical profession.

"Where she will marry, no one knows," her ladyship had declared. "Only think, Emily had to be begged to accompany us to London for her presentation. One should think she'd jump at the chance. But Demetria pleaded, and Emily finally said yes. I love her dearly, but the girl is so blue, so interested in medicine and history and science, I shudder to think of her future. I daresay she shall be consorting with all those young medical students in London, especially that one her father has sponsored, young Dr. Travis, and the assistants, the dressers, whatever they call them—that lot. It's sad to contemplate, but perhaps she'll end marrying one of them."

Annora yawned and her eyelids drooped. It did not suit her to have Holt take another wife. She would be very glad if Emily Wilton married some doctor, so long as she stayed away from her son. She would do everything within her power to frustrate any plans he might have to marry anyone. Before Emily and Demetria came, Holt had seemed content to stay home and nurse that wretched leg of his.

Stifling another yawn, Annora roused her abigail, Cora White, who was sleeping in the adjoining room. She wanted to know when the Wilton girl returned to her room, but she was growing very sleepy. Warning Cora to stay alert, she made her sit on the straight chair facing Emily's door, and climbed into her feather bed. If she could, Annora would surprise her son in his tête-à-tête. If this were her house, she'd search it through and drag Miss Emily Wilton back to her room. When morning came the girl should find herself tossed out, bag and baggage—yes, and that cousin of hers, that silly Demetria, too. Annora never liked pert young women. The way Demetria threw herself about like a frisking colt was most unbecoming. Yesterday, Annora had intercepted a *look* the girl had cast at poor Cecil Jennings that one could only call sportive.

Tomorrow, thought Annora, she would decline the trip to Lindhurst they had all planned and keep Lady Hume here. She would warn Nicole Quimby of the danger of allowing her daughter such flirtatious habits and take her to task for permitting her niece to roam strange households at night. More importantly, Annora would tell her ladyship a calculated tale about her son that she'd been concocting for the past two days.

Annora smiled. She would say Holt wasn't to be trusted with women. She'd complain that he was without moral restraint—Annora could imagine Nicole Quimby's horror when she said that. She would tell Nicole he was a master in the art of seduction, making up various sordid and quite specific examples with which to regale her ladyship; that should convince Nicole to leave and take her precious charges with her.

Annora sighed. For all she knew, at least some of her accusations could be true. Who knew what sordid liaisons Holt had contracted, what illicit relationships he had carried on, or how many young wives he had deliberately ruined? Perhaps not that last, but her son was as repellently handsome as the rest of the Ingrams. Women seemed to throw themselves at him whenever he was in company, even if he was lamed by the war.

Annora snuggled her nose deep in her pillow and set herself to sleep after making sure Cora Whit remained on watch. Yes, she would pour a round tale in the gullible Lady Hume's ear and see if that didn't send Holt's guests packing for London.

If there was an ounce of decency in Emily Wilton, which Annora supposed there might very well be, the girl, when she had the story from her Aunt Hume, would cut Holt dead instead of casting him smiles.

Emily had previously noticed the heavy door built into the tower wall. Directly beneath the top floor, lit by a snug fire, the small chamber seemed quite comfortable. Furnished with an easy chair, a table—obviously used as a desk—and a narrow, hard-looking bed, the room looked well lived in. Books were scattered everywhere and overflowed the squat oaken bookcase.

Ingram placed Emily on a low footstool directly in front of the fire. He reached for a blanket and bundled her in it, his manner brusque and impersonal.

She didn't know why her teeth were chattering; she wasn't that cold. She tried to smile at him, then bent toward the fire, rubbing her hands together, warming them.

A tiny iron kettle sat half in the grate, bubbling gently. If only she could think of some unexceptional subject of conversation.

There were words in her mind, but Emily rejected them. How could she tell Holt Ingram she thought she was falling in love with him? She considered the notion ridiculous, having known him only three days, but that, more than anything, was what she wanted to say.

Holt had thrown himself into the large stuffed chair, his long muscular legs sprawled before him, the toe of one of his gleaming riding boots tapping restlessly on the slate floor.

Emily had noted this habit of his. She felt certain he was unconscious of it. It seemed to her he had an overabundance of energy, barely checked. Had he really wrapped his arms about her and held her hard against him? She would think about that later. Emily clenched her jaw to stop the chattering.

Holt watched the woman he'd brought into his personal hideaway. He'd long thought of this room as his sanctuary.

He knew Emily shouldn't be here with him, alone. It wasn't a good idea, but, oh! how he'd wanted her. He had slept very little since meeting Emily Wilton.

Emily reached to pull her long hair outside the blanket, shaking her head slightly as she tossed its length over her shoulder to hang down her back. A grosgrain ribbon haphazardly held the mass; Holt wished it would come undone. He wanted to see it flowing around her again.

Holt remembered that hair in his hands when he tied it out of her way, as Emily tried to stop Val's bleeding. Like a swatch of liquid silk, the lustrous tendrils had clung to his fingers with an energy that seemed to crackle. Now he found himself wanting to untie the ribbon, to bring her hair to his mouth; he wanted to kiss it and to kiss her. He wanted Emily over him in bed, her curtain of hair around them.

Emily blinked when Ingram rose from his chair in a burst of movement. She looked at him as he turned his back and reached toward a wall cabinet.

"Would you like some tea?" he asked, clearing his throat.

"Yes," she said. "Please."

"Afterward, I'll take you down."

"Thank you."

The words came soft to his ears, but he couldn't turn to look at her just yet.

Holt assembled a small tray on top of the bookcase. After a moment, he brought it to a low table beside Emily. He poured water from the kettle into the porcelain teapot, setting the tea leaves to steep, and leaned back in his chair.

"Are you comfortable?" he asked. "Would you like to sit here? I could bring my desk chair."

Emily straightened. "I'm fine. The tea is most welcome."

He reached to pour, his hands steady as he gave her the cup. "I'm afraid I have no cream. And no sugar. I take mine plain."

Emily shrugged out of the blanket and sipped gratefully. "Yes, I've noticed. So do I."

"Why aren't you married?" he asked, then apologized. "I'm sorry. I don't usually pry into the lives of—" He paused.

He'd almost said *strangers,* but he could never call Emily Wilton a stranger. "Into the lives of other people."

Emily took another sip of tea, reflecting that she had asked his sister Belle the same question. "My mother became terminally ill just as I turned seventeen. She died three years later. I mourned a year, and since then I haven't wanted to leave my father.

"Now Uncle Mursey wants me to be presented along with Demetria and have my Season. I suggested I was a bit long in the tooth for that, but there was no persuading him that I didn't desire to come to London. However, my father was much in favor of the scheme and urged me to come. Perhaps I shall sit with the dowagers."

Ingram snorted at that. "You're nothing but a green girl. I don't care if you are twenty-three."

"Twenty-four in twelve days."

He shrugged. "You seem a veritable baby to me."

Emily was stung. She thought he must be alluding to her moment of terror before the storm. "If you refer to my recent behavior, I assure you, I'm not usually such a coward. I can't think why I screamed." *Or threw myself into your arms.*

"No," he said. "Strong men have insisted on leaving the tower when lightning began. As for your reaction, that's forgotten. I meant that in London you shall find yourself in society for the first time. Now *that* is daunting!"

Emily tried to smile when he did, but she was thinking of what he'd said. Forgotten? she asked herself. Had Ingram already forgotten holding her in his arms? She suspected she wouldn't be so fortunate. She would remember the feel of his body against hers until her dying day.

When Emily refused a second cup of tea, Holt took her down the long stone stairs, walking silently, hurrying them along with his hand on her elbow. In spite of his limp, he set a rapid pace.

He seemed anxious to be rid of her, thought Emily, arriving a little breathless at her door.

"There," he murmured, leaning past her to throw open her door. He spoke in a half-whisper. His mother's door wasn't quite closed.

The long corridor was dimly lit, but Holt could see the expression in Emily's eyes. She was troubled. He steeled himself. He knew the danger in trying to comfort her. He must get away. All he could think of was snatching her up, crowding her into her room, and kissing her. Had Emily ever been properly kissed? He thought not. He wanted to be the man to give her that kiss. But not here, not in this house, where she was his guest and under his protection.

"Good night, Emily," he murmured, and could not stay his hand from one caress. He touched her lightly, one finger drawing the length of her jawline. Then he left her.

At breakfast, both Aunt Hume and Lady Ingram declined the invitation to Lindhurst, and Emily found herself breathing a sigh of relief. The more she knew of Annora Ingram, the less time she wanted to spend in her company.

Emily thought the dowager looked at her strangely as she said, "I'm sorry for it, but I must cry off today. There were comings and goings outside my door all night, until four this morning. I'd forgot how noisy Ravencroft can be after midnight. Lady Hume wants to stay here with me, and I have assured her that Isobel is of an age to act the chaperone. Besides, Mrs. Nesbitt—who has been with the Lindsays forever—shall look after you. I trust your housekeeper is in residence?" This was directed at Val Lindsay.

On the point of sipping his tea, Val scalded his lip at the unexpected question. "Yes, ma'am," he assured Lady Ingram. "My mama always leaves Mrs. Nesbitt at Lindhurst when she goes up to town or travels. Someone has to be there, you know. And old Reynolds, the butler; naturally, he's there. Must be going on for seventy-five, Reynolds; he was my grandfather's footman, you know."

Val smiled at Demetria and winked. What luck! The old dragon wasn't going. He didn't mind Lady Hume, but it would be nice without the older ladies. He grinned when Demetria returned his wink. The minx was thinking the same thing, he'd bet a monkey.

This trifling exchange between Miss Demetria Quimby and

Valerian Lindsay did not escape Mr. Jennings. Cecil gritted his teeth and fumed.

How could Renton be such a nodcock? The girl was playing him for a fish. Well, he wished the viscount might get caught and landed. No doubt church bells would ring as soon as the Season was over.

As for himself, he was immune to all the fluttering sighs and lingering looks Demetria Quimby tossed about.

Cecil gave Demetria an underlook as he trod to the buffet for more kippers. She had the most beautiful mouth in the world, and her laugh was a cascading tinkle that had, quite naturally at first, entranced him.

Mr. Jennings resumed his place at the breakfast table, attempting to concentrate on the small talk around him, refusing so much as a glance at Demetria Quimby. He was used to her now; he had Demetria's measure.

Seven

Emily sat in her aunt's carriage with Demetria and Isobel Ingram as they were driven up the oak-lined lane after turning into the gates of Lindhurst. Val Lindsay also rode in the carriage, his cast supported by half a dozen pillows which Demetria and Isobel had placed around him. Lord Ingram and Mr. Jennings, mounted on the beautiful horses they'd ridden the day of the crash, rode on either side of the rumbling carriage.

Emily gasped when she first saw the huge Lindsay home.

Val, noting her reaction, said, "Oh, yes. Lindhurst is a pre-Elizabethan house; what is generally known as a 'Wealden house.' Didn't anyone tell you? The central hall and the projecting wings are under the one deep roof," he said, pointing. "Or perhaps you've heard of a 'recessed front' house? Same thing. Are you interested in old houses, Emily?"

"Extremely. My father has many books on architecture, and has infected me with his love of fine buildings. He and Mama and I toured Greece and Italy, studying the great works of the old master builders. What year was Lindhurst constructed?"

Val shrugged. "1550 or thereabouts. Ah, here we are."

After traversing the home park, the carriage now stopped in the long curving drive, directly in line with the front doors. These had been thrown wide by an elderly butler.

When the steps were let down, Demetria tumbled out, followed by Isobel Ingram. Emily came more slowly, gazing in awe at the immense structure, staring at the great timbers which made up the house. Remembering her patient, she turned to urge Val to be careful when the footmen helped him out. "You must stay off your leg, Val. I'll get out, and then they can unload you."

She started to descend the carriage and found Holt Ingram beside her, offering his hand.

She gripped it briefly, ignoring the warm tingle his touch inspired, and stepped down.

"Thank you," she said. "Do they have a rolling chair for Val?"

"I believe the footmen are going to form a lady saddle and carry him between them into the house," Holt told her.

Emily's mouth opened slightly, as if she were going to answer. Her gray eyes, shadowed with dark, curling lashes, studied him calmly. After a moment, she nodded.

He would, Holt vowed silently, kiss her before this day was out.

In the solar at Ravencroft, Annora Ingram smiled secretly into her teacup. Beside her, Lady Hume wept, crushing her lace handkerchief.

Annora was reciting a list of Holt's transgressions, all pure fiction. She had made them up herself, averring that her son had started his lascivious behavior when quite young.

"He was sent down from Eton, not once but three times, for keeping girls in his room," Annora said. "He was a fiend for the company of loose women even then. By the time he was fourteen, he had ruined three of my upstairs maids, and he seduced the vicar's daughter the first year he was at Oxford. We had to buy the girl and her father off and send them out of the country. And my husband paid out thousands to the sluts of Oxford, and London, too. No telling how many by-blows Holt has scattered about. In bedrooms from Mayfair to Dover he brings ruin to the fairest of the beau monde, and when in the country, no farmhouse or shepherd's hut is safe from him. He is quite comprehensive in his tastes, you see."

Annora congratulated herself. That was a nice touch about the farm girls and the nonexistent vicar's daughter; she was glad she'd thought of those. But she mustn't get carried away. Her gaze slid sideways as she prepared to reveal her greatest inspiration. It had come to her with her morning tea. Holt had married young at the behest of his father. She could use that fact to lend validity to these tales she was planting in Nicole Quimby's ears.

"Yes, Lady Hume, my son has been a confirmed rake since the age of sixteen, and that's why his father and grandfather insisted that he marry so young. They thought it would settle him, cure him of his satyr-like propensities. Alas! It did not answer. The very night his wife and child died, Holt was visiting his mistress in Bristol."

Annora complacently sipped her tea. If Holt ever had a mistress in Gloustershire, she'd never heard about it, but there was absolutely no way Nicole could ever learn how Holt had stood over Muriel's bed, keeping vigil all through that fateful night, his dark anguish apparent for anyone to see.

Nicole could hardly believe what Lady Ingram was telling her. "How—how can you say such things about your own son?" she cried.

Annora smiled grimly. "Because I am a woman of principle; I feel that you should be warned. As much as I hate to say it, my son is a libertine. But then, I suppose he's no worse than many men. I see that your niece has fallen under his spell. She is quite naive, I believe. I only hope it's not too late and she isn't ruined. She was gone from her room almost two hours last night. I will wager Ingram enticed her to the tower and then to that eagle's nest of his up there. He has refused to let me up there since he was ten years old. His father, the late baron, upheld him in this."

When Nicole looked at her in astonishment, the dowager nodded. "And all over a tiny thing. Ingram was away, as he often was, and Holt disobeyed me. My son was down from Eton, you see. As punishment for his misdeed, I had the footman lock him in the tower with only a candle and a jug of water. A storm came up. I thought he would beg to be let out.

I waited, but no. The next day, his tenth birthday, I was sure he would plead to be released. I'd had them bake him a special cake, too, being quite tired of the whole affair. Well, Isobel wouldn't stop crying for one thing. In spite of anything I can say, she dotes on her brother, always has. But Holt wouldn't come down. He was waiting for his father, he said.

"Luckily, my husband came home. There was a terrible row, but instead of upbraiding Holt for his mutinous behavior, my husband threatened me—*me!*—with dire consequences if ever I chastised Holt again. Imagine, a mother not allowed to discipline her own son. You can see how the Ingrams used me."

Annora fell silent, brooding on the inequity of her husband. This last episode, the story of her locking Holt in the tower, for which she'd always felt justified, happened to be true.

"But Lord Ingram seems such a gentleman," protested Nicole.

Lady Ingram laughed shortly. "Yes, my dear. He has perfect manners, which he learned at the end of my strap. But can you not see that a man bent on seduction must always have coaxing ways? Be thankful his eyes landed on your niece, rather than your daughter, because he is worse now than when he was young. In his tender years, he confined himself to preying on the lower orders. Now anyone, no matter how young or innocent, is his fair game. As an example, I believe there is at least one earl in Sussex who must suspect that his heir might be Holt's. The child is said to have those dark Ingram looks, and Holt and the bride were seen in intimate conversations at Kew. Yes, and Holt lured the daughter of the Marquess of ... Well, never mind the name, but the girl was only eighteen and newly engaged. Holt coaxed her into a series of assignations at Brighton, causing her fiancé to demand the engagement be terminated. Her brother challenged Holt to a duel, but nothing came of it. My son joined the army shortly afterward, and I'm certain it was to avoid the scandal. Parents can't be too careful with their young daughters. Men like my son are constantly trying to seduce innocent girls.

"Which reminds me: I am very much afraid, my dear Lady

Hume, that Demetria has been allowed to become too free in her manners. Oh, through no fault of your own, I'm sure! No doubt this old uncle of Demetria's, the present Earl of Mursey, is to blame. It's too bad you must live with him. Men can never see what harm there is in encouraging children—especially little girls—to be saucy, never thinking it leads to impudence when they are grown up. But you shall find it impossible to launch Demetria if you fail to subdue her spirits. She is shockingly bold with her eyes. And that laugh of hers! Well, I can only say that such a laugh, somewhere between a gasp and a giggle, will never do! No, your ladyship. The *ton* must rapidly close you out if so much as a hint of fastness is detected in your daughter. As for your niece, I shudder to think she may already have surrendered her virtue to that rakehell the world calls my son."

Mrs. Nesbitt seemed delighted to have them at Lindhurst. Emily could see that Val Lindsay was the light of the housekeeper's life. She and old Reynolds, the butler, fairly beamed as they welcomed everyone in.

The housekeeper was Irish, motherly, and much given to clucking. "Oh, you poor boy!" she kept exclaiming as they tried to get Val into the Red Saloon.

When Val introduced her to Emily, the woman grasped both her hands and said with tears in her eyes, "Ah, you're the lass who saved our boy! God bless you, girl—er—miss, God bless you."

Immediately at ease with the woman, Emily smiled and said, "He's a very special young man, isn't he?"

"Oh, aye, he is at that." Mrs. Nesbitt bit her lip and her bright blue eyes overflowed. Lifting her apron, the good woman buried her face and gave way to a bout of weeping.

Ingram smiled at Emily over the dumpy little woman's head as he wrapped his arms about her. "There, there, Mrs. N. No need for tears, although I'm sure you'll feel much better for shedding them."

Sniffing, the housekeeper allowed Ingram to hold her a moment. Then she quickly finished her crying and wiped at her face. "Aren't you kind to an old woman, your lordship? Aren't you kind?"

"No, no." Holt grinned and patted her shoulder. "I remember running to you with a bee sting one time."

"That's right! Oh, what a brawny, brown little boy you were." Mrs. Nesbitt turned to include Emily, Demetria, and Isobel Ingram, all standing nearby, in the conversation. "Came to my kitchen white as a sheet, the child did. Not a whimper, but he looked sick as a wheelbarrow. And his black eyes round as two agates. But I fixed you up, didn't I, m'lord?"

"You did, then and several times after. I remember skinned knees and a broken arm. 'Tis you"—Holt fell into a teasing imitation of her Irish brogue—"who are kind, Mrs. Nesbitt."

At this, Val Lindsay demanded his fair share of attention. "Hi, Mrs. N.! Remember me? It's *my* broken leg. Reynolds was saying you've located an old Bath chair of my grandmother's in the attics. Do you think you might ask the porter to bring it in? And I believe we must postpone our picnic. It's coming on to rain."

They repaired to the Red Saloon, and for an hour, Ingram and Cecil Jennings (who had mechanical ambitions), with much advice from Val Lindsay, worked at tearing the top off the Bath chair. This was a rolling chair of the type made famous at Bath, with a hood and solid piece that latched across the front to protect the invalids from cold drafts and other noxious currents of air which might prove detrimental to their health. According to Reynolds, the ancient butler, it had been custom-made for the old lady. It did not fit Val at all.

"Belle," Val asked, "did you ever see my Grandmother Renton? Was she tiny? I can't remember her."

Isobel Ingram, who with Demetria and Emily was studying one of the Van Dycks, looked up. "Oh, yes, I remember her, but only dimly. I was very young that time she visited. Holt, did you meet the Dowager Countess Renton?"

Holt shook his head, taking a wrench from the porter, who stood by with a basket of tools. Trying to loosen one of a series of small nuts that held the slanted door on the bonnet of the chair, he said, "I must have been at school. I don't recall ever seeing her."

"Anyway, her chair is much too small for me," Val said, swiping the hank of dark hair off his forehead. Viscount Renton was ensconced in a wing chair, from which he could freely see what his friends were doing. "Cecil, do you think you could design me a chair that will bear my weight and be long enough for my legs? After we get to town, I mean."

"Don't see why not, Val," said Cecil, who, after apologizing to the ladies, had removed his coat. Holt Ingram was also in his shirtsleeves, which he had rolled up. At one point, he had ripped off his cravat and opened his collar. They finally had all the bolts off.

Holt nodded at Cecil and, together, they lifted the hood away, effectively stripping the chair to its seat and running gear.

They piled Val Lindsay on the framework and pushed him into the solarium when Reynolds said luncheon was ready.

A surprise awaited them. It seemed they were having a picnic after all. Quilts were spread in front of the fire in the large, fern-filled room.

Three large hampers stood in the middle of the quilts, stuffed to overflowing with good things to eat. Dozens of candles had been lit, casting a soft glow over the potted plants and hanging ivy. The rain had settled in to a steady drizzle.

Isobel laughed and clapped her hands together. "Oh, Mrs. Nesbitt—exactly like the picnics you used to make for Allegra and me! Thank you—this will be like old times."

Belle's eyes, Emily thought, were sparkling. Away from her mother, Isobel Ingram had an attractive liveliness that allowed her quiet beauty to shine through. Her coloring, a golden reflection of her brother's swarthy good looks, made her appear as if the sun had warmed her. Emily and her parents had toured the Mediterranean when she was eleven; she'd seen brunettes in Naples with complexions like Belle's. Could the Ingrams have Italian blood? However they came by their dark complexions, it made them—brother and sister—the most beautiful people Emily had ever seen.

Emily was pleased when Demetria insisted Holt and Mr. Jennings stay in their shirtsleeves.

"A picnic is meant to be informal," cried Demetria. "Val," she commanded, "take off your coat so your guests can be more comfortable. There!" she said, as Val divested himself of his jacket and, following Holt Ingram's lead, removed his cravat and unbuttoned his collar.

"You don't mind, Emily?" Val asked.

Emily did not mind in the least. "N-no." She ventured a look at Ingram. He was watching her in a way that made her drop her eyes. "I—I wish everyone to be comfortable."

"Yes, let's all enjoy ourselves," begged Demetria. "I'm not looking forward to the formal strictures of the *ton*. Although," she drawled, smiling slightly at Mr. Jennings, "I shall no doubt find something to keep me amused."

Mr. Jennings's mouth tightened and his ears turned red.

They seated themselves on the cushions provided. "Isn't this nice?" asked Demetria. "Oh, what have you given us, Mrs. Nesbitt? I'm frightfully hungry."

"Everything you like, my dear," said Mrs. Nesbitt good-naturedly. "Now you young folks serve yourselves, and ring if you need us." She smiled and went away, sweeping Reynolds and the footman with her.

Eight

With hearty appetites, the picnickers fell upon the feast. Roast beef and sliced chicken sandwiches, washed down with lemonade and hock, quickly disappeared. Rum cake and spice cookies were included for dessert.

Eating a boiled egg, Val Lindsay described the rolling chair he wanted, and he and Cecil became deeply embroiled in an argument over the size of the wheels.

Watching Emily as she sat beside him on one of the quilts, Holt rubbed his leg, almost unaware of what he was doing. Emily must have noticed, for she asked, "Does your leg pain you, my lord?"

"Sometimes," Holt said, glad he could discuss his injury with her again.

"How long since you've consulted your doctor?" she asked in a practical tone.

"Six months."

"Too long," Emily stated. "*Do* you suffer from low fevers? You didn't answer when I asked you before."

Holt smiled. "You withdrew your question, as I remember." The curve of her cheek was entrancing. A wave of heat went over him. He could imagine running his tongue just under her chin, kissing her pulse points, then her lips. He looked away.

"My lord?" Emily seemed concerned. "You *have* been having fever! Is—is your wound sometimes hot to the touch?"

She flushed when Holt turned his head and looked down at her. Her question had quite naturally brought an image of a hand on his bare thigh. Her blush betrayed her. She must be picturing what he was thinking.

Such a sweet innocent, he thought, as she valiantly tried to carry off what she'd been about to say.

"What I mean is, you are obviously not healing as you should. Fevers and—and warmth of the wound are indications that . . . Promise you'll see your surgeon when you get to town."

"Yes," he said, "if you'll remember to call me Holt."

Emily swallowed. "I will."

"Say it."

"H-Holt."

He nodded, his eyes roaming her averted face, tracing the curve of her brow, her soft hair, her breasts pushing against the pale blue, armure cloth gown she wore.

Holt realized how unfair it would be if he kissed Emily before she had a chance to become acquainted with anyone else. He didn't want her falling in love with him because he was the only man she'd ever met. He didn't count the young sprigs of country society. Holt understood how innocent Emily was. She was vulnerable. After she'd been presented, after she'd danced at Almack's, basked in the light of the beau monde and received her due of masculine attention, after she had triumphed in a few light flirtations, he would kiss her. When they married, Holt wanted Emily to come to him freely, choosing him over all others. To kiss her now would be to take unfair advantage.

He got to his feet and offered her his hand. "Come," he said. "Belle, if you're finished, let's take Emily and Demetria up and show them the Shell Room." He raised his voice. "Val, I'm taking the girls up to see the seashells."

Their host waved them away. "Yes," Val said, "I can't go. They might like to see the portrait gallery, too. Make yourselves at home," he told them, anxious to get back to his discussion with Mr. Jennings.

THE MUCH MALIGNED LORD 79

The Shell Room was found to be the lifework of one of Val Lindsay's great-aunts, a maiden lady who spent her time gathering shells and gluing them to almost every available surface. Cornice boards, door and window frames, bookcases, tables, and serving trays—all were covered with shells.

Emily was trying to imagine how empty one's life must be to devote it to such an endeavor, when Holt said he understood the lady had spent thirty-seven years at the task.

"Oh, dear," Emily exclaimed before she thought.

An amused glint in his eye, Holt nodded. "Yes, indeed," he said, understanding exactly what she meant. "The poor old thing must have been desperate for something to do."

"But then," Emily said, "I believe that most people in the *ton* live a life of idleness. That's why I doubt I'll ever marry. I'm so used to helping Papa, I can't imagine a life devoid of useful work."

She stopped, wondering if Holt would think she was criticizing his life-style.

Apparently he did not, for he said, "I agree. That's one reason I went into the army. I hope I know how to relax; I find my chess games engrossing. But I'm afraid I'm an unfashionable fellow; I enjoy having something to do. I don't pretend to be the expert on agriculture that Cecil is, but I try to keep abreast of the latest scientific methods. And I find myself spending more and more time with my breeding book. We've been raising Coteswold sheep at Ravencroft for almost three hundred years."

"Oh, really?" asked Emily. She was intrigued. Uncle Mursey had just bought a new bull and three rams. She gave Holt details about the Mursey flock and her uncle's special herd of cattle as they descended the stairs, leaving Belle Ingram to tell Demetria about the book she was writing.

The solarium was empty, Mr. Jennings and Val and the rolling chair having disappeared.

Mr. Reynolds, supervising the removal of the picnic by one of the footmen, said, "Lord Renton took Mr. Jennings to the potting shed. There are wheelbarrows and carts there; they've gone to study them. Would your lordship wish to take the young lady into the library? You'll find a lovely fire, and one on the second level, too."

The Lindhurst library was quite dark, the day being so closely overcast. Rain beaded on the mullioned windows as Ingram stoked the fire. One small branch of candles burned on an oak table.

Emily felt a multitude of needs. She wanted to fill her eyes with Holt Ingram but did not dare more than a glance. She found him more irresistible than ever in his state of undress. He had rolled down his sleeves, but left his collar open. She wanted him to touch her and knew that was impossible.

Emily never lied to herself. She'd developed a fascination with Holt Ingram, and whether it was love or not, she wouldn't be satisfied until he kissed her. She suspected the baron's kisses would be far different from those of the Honorable Parry Edwards.

Mr. Edwards, third son of Lord Twyford, had so far forgotten himself at Squire Dundee's garden party that he attempted to plant two chaste kisses on Emily's lips. One landed on her mouth, the other—when she violently shoved the gentleman backward into the hedge—glanced off her cheek. And of course Jeremy Norville's kiss didn't count. Jeremy was her cousin, and they had both been fifteen. He had been showing her what he'd learned at Eton. Jeremy pressed his lips tightly against hers and Emily felt nothing at all. "Well," said Cousin Jeremy, seeing her so unaffected, "perhaps it isn't the same with cousins."

Shifting her gaze from Lord Ingram, who lounged before the fire, Emily let her eyes drift about the room. The huge columns, the paneling, all the furniture, looked to be made of Italian walnut. The hangings of crimson and gold damask were embroidered with the Renton arms, and the burr walnut bookcases gleamed in the firelight. The rich colors of the leather-bound volumes, the objets d'art, a bronze or two, a large painting Emily didn't recognize (but which she was sure was from the Flemish school), all combined to make a gorgeous apartment anyone would admire.

The dimensions were impressive, too. Large and square, the library had a ceiling that towered twenty feet. A charming clerestory, a bank of windows built to admit light, was placed far up on each of three walls. A winding staircase rose to a loft on the second level which Emily imagined held almost as many books as this one did. The Rentons must have been collecting books for generations.

"I like this," Emily said, aware that Lord Ingram was still watching her.

"Do you enjoy books?" he asked.

"I—yes. Books are a passion of mine. Do you?"

Holt nodded. "Belle and I both love them. She writes, you know."

So he did know about his sister's writing. "I understand Mr. David Locke wants to publish her work," Emily remarked.

"Yes. I've met Locke once or twice. He—he's a special friend of my sister's. I intend to see this project of Belle's through, this year. She deserves to have a life of her own, to marry. And if Belle wants to see her stories printed, I mean for her to do exactly that, especially if her writing is good enough—and I suppose it is, else Locke wouldn't want it for his publishing company."

"I'm glad," Emily said. "Isobel is lucky to have you for a brother. I can't wait to see what she's writing. I love to read."

"Yes, you told me. What do you like best?"

"Oh, poetry, modern novels, old tales of chivalry. But other things, too. Aunt Hume suspects I'm blue—I enjoy anything of a scientific nature. Medical books and journals. Old books; any of those I can get my hands on."

"The Lindsays are famous for their antique book collection. Would you like to see them?"

"Yes," Emily murmured, pushing aside her self-consciousness. Here was something to take her mind off the baron.

They went up the narrow stairs to the loft and Ingram lit a candle they found on a Jacobean trestle table pushed close to a floor-to-ceiling window. Rounded at the top in a fanlight, the window afforded an excellent view of a rain-shrouded landscape, reminiscent, or so Emily thought, of an old Dutch painting. A fire burned on the hearth, adding to the snug atmosphere of the balcony-like room.

Holt joined Emily on the long bench at the trestle table, and for several minutes they silently perused the old books he'd located, until Emily noticed he wasn't staring at the books, but at her.

She didn't know how she must have looked, but Holt unexpectedly rose, stepped over the bench, and walked away to the window. He gazed out, his back to her.

A charged silence filled the room; Emily didn't know what had happened. She slanted a glance at Holt's tall figure, wondering what he must be thinking. He had his hands shoved deep in his pockets.

She was becoming uncomfortable.

"Queen's gambit," Holt said abruptly, without turning.

Emily felt angry; he was hiding behind a game. Her retaliation was immediate. "Queen's gambit declined."

"Pawn to queen four," he said.

"Pawn to queen four in kind," she snapped. In her mind's eye she could see the board.

It was Holt's move. "Pawn to queen's bishop four."

Emily tried to concentrate. "Pawn to—king three."

His response came quickly. "Knight to queen's bishop three." He continued to look out the window.

Emily moved to stand before the fire. "Queen to queen three," she said coolly, and he turned at this erratic, but perfectly effective defense.

It was new; Emily had worked out the remaining moves last month to please her papa.

Holt walked across the loft and placed his hands on the mantelpiece on either side of her, his long arms barring her escape. His breathing was uneven.

"Bishop to king's knight five," he said between clenched teeth. He watched her with narrow, slitted eyes.

"King's knight to king two," she whispered.

Emily was trembling. She could not go on. "I don't want to play anymore," she said miserably.

"Neither do I," Holt said, and, reaching out, drew her full against him.

Nine

He brushed his lips quickly across hers, a barely restrained tension gripping him. "Open your mouth," he said shortly. His deep-timbred voice rumbled in Emily's ears.

Instinctively, she complied, and when she did, Holt kissed her the way he'd wanted to in the storm, with the lightning crackling around the tower. He kissed her without mercy, again and again, to ease the torment he felt when he couldn't touch her.

Emily would have fallen without the support of his arms. Needing his strength, she strained closer, his fine cambric shirt no barrier to her grasping hands. She welcomed his invasion, his urgency. Without being aware of it, she'd lived her whole life for this.

Satisfied that she was clinging with her arms around his middle, Holt lifted his mouth from hers and took Emily's head in his hands. In a rush, he kissed her eyes, hair, brow, and the corners of her mouth.

Emily stood with her face upturned, eyes half closed. She panted lightly, her mouth a little open, waiting for Holt to find her lips again.

Wrapping his arms more closely about her, Holt took possession of her mouth, and now Emily kissed him back. Her tongue—a tiny brand—followed his, tentative at first, then boldly, greedily. Holt moaned, a burst of desire streaking through his belly.

Emily tightened her arms and strained upward. He was tall, so tall ... Swiveling her neck, she opened her mouth as wide as she could under his. She could never get enough of him ...

Holt tensed, went still, and lifted his mouth from hers.

Emily murmured a protest and opened her eyes.

Inexorably, he put her from him, steadying her as she swayed.

"Sorry," he said hoarsely, and swallowed. "I didn't mean to do that. I had decided I wouldn't kiss you."

He shook his head. When they came to the library, it simply happened. But if he were being honest, Holt must admit he was glad.

Now Emily looked flushed and confused—and not a little angry. If he didn't take her down those stairs immediately, he would begin kissing her again.

"Holt, where are you?" came Isobel's voice, calling her brother. "Holt, are you and Emily up there?"

"Yes, up here," he said, as Emily's eyes flew to his.

"Stay there, Belle," he called. "We'll come down. We've been looking at these old books."

For the remainder of their visit, Holt seemed content to fade into the background, leaving Emily's side to join Cecil Jennings and Val Lindsay for a visit to the Lindsay stables, inspecting Val's newest hunter.

Isobel entertained the cousins with tales of her visits to Lindhurst as a child and growing girl. "I can't wait for you to meet Allegra. She and I were together constantly when we were growing up. She's almost a year older than I, and her father gave her a miniature carriage, pulled by two ponies. She and I went everywhere in that contraption. Allegra was Lord Renton's youngest daughter, you see, and he positively doted on her. I'm looking forward to seeing her in town, and her mother, Lady Oralia Lindsay, too."

This conversation was interrupted by the entrance of the males of the party. When Emily looked up and encountered Ingram's eyes, she flushed. He looked at her steadily, his features perfectly sober, but she thought a smile lurked deep in his eyes.

The visitors left Lindhurst shortly after four in the afternoon. All the way home, Emily relived those enchanted moments in Holt's arms. His kisses had shaken her as nothing she'd ever experienced. As the carriage wheels rumbled along the roadway, she remained rather quiet, preferring to maintain her silence, listening to the conversation between Demetria and Isobel.

Val Lindsay had brought a sketch pad and lead pencil, and was busily drawing plans for his new wheelchair, admiring his designs and demanding that the women give him their opinions.

Emily, vaguely aware that Isobel had looked at her closely when they first entered the carriage, could spare Val little attention. She was puzzled over Holt's last words. He hadn't meant to kiss her, he said. How was that? How could anyone *accidentally* kiss someone? His words didn't make sense.

Arriving at Ravencroft as the sun slanted in the west, they found that a tempest had swept over the castle.

They were bowed in by Higgins, the butler.

"Where are their ladyships, Higgins?" asked Holt as they divested themselves of their traveling cloaks. "Are they at tea?"

Higgins bowed and said tonelessly, "Lady Hume has retired to her chambers. I believe she is indisposed. The Baroness Lady Ingram is gone. She found it necessary to return to Abbingdon Manor, my lord. She left this message for you."

Emily saw Holt stiffen and heard Isobel gasp as the butler, his stately manner unimpaired, handed over a sealed letter. Holt took it silently, and Emily thought a *look* passed between him and the butler.

That was no wonder, Emily thought. For a hostess to leave a house when there were guests was an egregious insult, unless there were circumstances so beyond the ordinary that her departure became an absolute necessity.

Holt's mouth was a grim line, and Isobel went quickly to his side and took his arm.

Throwing up his chin, Holt apologized to Emily and Demetria, who immediately excused themselves.

The porter had brought Val Lindsay's invalid chair, and Cecil indicated he and Val would retire to the game room. As Cecil rolled the viscount toward the back regions of the castle, Emily hurried Demetria away to consult with Lady Nicole.

Brother and sister were left standing in the great hall. Isobel threw Holt a troubled glance.

"Come to the library," Holt growled under his breath. "Let's see what she has written."

"She's done something terrible, I know it," said Isobel, when Holt had shut the great oak doors. "Hurry! What does the note say?"

Holt broke open the seal and read two lines. *I'm going to Abbingdon,* Annora had written. *Send Isobel as soon as the Mursey party leaves tomorrow.* It was signed as all her notes and letters were signed. *Annora, Lady Ingram.*

Isobel's lip was caught in her teeth. She looked at Holt and shook her head. "I can't imagine why she left, but I must go up to Lady Hume's suite and do what I can to repair the damage. You know Mama. She has done something outrageous, precipitated some quarrel or other, and has now gone her way, leaving devastation in her wake. How like her. And how utterly embarrassing."

"Belle," Holt said abruptly, "you needn't go to Abbingdon, if you'd rather not. You know I've long urged you to make your home at Ravencroft. I'm leaving for London next week. Why don't you stay here and we'll travel to town together? You—you haven't mentioned Locke lately, but I had imagined—"

"Yes." Isobel nodded. "I'm going to marry him if I can. The other night when Mama tried, indeed succeeded, in humiliating me in front of our guests—that decided me at last. It will be hard; many of the *ton* will desert me. If I didn't have you to support me, I don't know if I'd have the courage, no matter how much I love David." She looked up at him with swimming eyes.

Holt hugged her briefly and patted her shoulder. "You have that always, my dear sister. I'm glad you've finally decided to have Locke. I'm beginning to learn that love comes from unexpected quarters."

Something in his quiet tone made Isobel search his eyes, so like her own. Her soft lips curled in a little smile. "Emily?"

One of Holt's brows slanted upward. "Yes. And nothing or no one, save Emily herself, shall keep her from me. No doubt Mama will do her worst, simply to circumvent my happiness. It will avail her nothing. There is nothing I will not endure to marry Emily Wilton. I have decided to have the operation. I will not come to her a cripple."

"I'm sure a limp will not prevent Emily Wilton from loving you," Isobel protested.

Holt smiled tenderly, and Isobel knew he was remembering the girl he had come to love. "No, Emily won't mind my limp, but in her role as my *dear physician,* she gave me a solemn little lecture while we were at Lindhurst. She has convinced me that an operation, painful as it will be, is my only recourse."

He gave a deep sigh. "Go to Lady Nicole. Offer our apologies. Try to learn what happened." His frown deepened. "I'm going to ride over to Abbingdon. Not that I expect Mama to admit a thing. As usual, she will shrug and gloss over whatever she's done. Do you want me to tell her you're staying with me?"

Isobel spoke slowly. "No. I shall return to Abbingdon and ride to London with her. I don't want to raise any more of a storm in the *ton* than necessary. If she will go to London quietly, I shall go with her. If she uses some excuse to delay, I'll go alone. I must return to the manor in any case. I have some pages of my latest novel hidden there, in my maid's room. Gertrude has helped me in many ways, Holt. She can travel to town with me if I have to go alone. I may need one of the coaches from Ravencroft."

"Anything," he replied, squeezing the hand held out to him. "I will order a coach made ready for you. Ravencroft is your home, Isobel, and always will be. Go," he urged. "Make our apologies to Lady Hume. This will be an unpleasant evening, I'm afraid."

Just how unpleasant, Belle did not know. She went up the stairs. What would she say to Emily and Demetria? Or Lady Nicole? She only hoped her ladyship wasn't in hysterics.

When Emily and Demetria entered Nicole Quimby's bedchamber, they found her in a state bordering on delirium, crying and threshing about on her couch, pitifully grateful they had returned from Lindhurst at last.

"What is wrong, Mama?" cried Demetria, running to her mother's side.

"Everything! Oh, why have you stayed away so long? I thought you'd never come. That woman"—Nicole shuddered in revulsion—"has said the most horrible things. And then she went away, simply walked out of this dreary castle and left me alone. Demetria, she called you impertinent and said you were a terrible flirt, that you rolled your eyes, and—and she accused you of *laughing,* as if no girl ever laughed before.

"As for Emily!" Nicole turned to face Emily. "Oh, my dear, I can't bear to tell you what she thinks of you! Annora claimed that you went to the tower for an—an assignation with Lord Ingram in the middle of the night, and were probably r-ruined! Because Ingram . . ."

Emily went still with shock, and Demetria gasped, "No!"

"Yes, yes!" Nicole shrieked, and threw herself backwards onto the couch cushions, covering her face with her lace handkerchief. Suddenly she sat up again, emerging wild-eyed from behind the sodden handkerchief. She hiccupped and moaned. "Annora says Ingram is a libertine, a ravager of innocents. He . . . none of the maids are safe from him, and . . . his father had to pay off the vicar when Holt seduced—"

"Mama, compose yourself," interrupted Demetria sternly. "You mustn't say such things. Surely you misunderstood Lady Ingram."

Emily crossed to the table beside her aunt's bed and poured a very large dose of laudanum into a glass. Then she added another splash.

Bringing the medicine to Demetria, she said, "See if you can persuade your mother to drink this, please. I'll get a cool compress for her head."

When all this was accomplished, Emily pulled up a chair and took Lady Nicole's hand in hers. "Now, Aunt," she soothed. "Do strive for calmness. How long has Lady Ingram been gone?"

"Hours!" wailed her ladyship.

"Long enough for you to work yourself into a frenzy," pronounced Emily in a hard little voice.

"And so would you be, both of you," Nicole gasped, "if you'd heard what I did. Ingram is the worst kind of womanizer, a confirmed scoundrel. He has practiced the art of seduction from his youngest days—at Eton, at Oxford, here at Ravencroft. Yes, in London, too! And then throughout his marriage, even in the army!"

Nicole swallowed and her eyelids suddenly drooped.

The medicine, Emily thought. She'd given her aunt enough of the sedative to jolt her out of her hysteria. She watched as the effects began to take hold.

Nicole sighed and said more slowly, "All Ingram thinks of are schemes to bring about the ruin of any woman he comes across—bored young wives, girls just presented, respectable widows. From the beau monde to the demimonde, from earls' daughters to farmers' daughters—highborn or low, it makes no difference to him." Her words were a little slurred now.

Lies, Emily thought. All lies. Her heart was beating so hard it threatened to choke her. "What you're saying about Holt Ingram is ludicrous, Aunt Nicole. What purpose his mother had in pouring such filth into your ears can only be guessed at. Lord Ingram has acted the perfect gentleman since we first met him. I've never seen a man who seems less like a hardened rake."

Nicole peered at Emily through red-rimmed eyes. "And when have you ever encountered a rake?" she asked tartly, rousing a little. "As for his coaxing ways, well, his own mother said it in a nutshell. A man who is determined to wheedle himself into the affections of unsuspecting women must necessarily practice pleasing manners." She went into another bout of tears before saying, "Demetria, call the maids to help us pack! We must leave this instant!"

"But Mama," protested Demetria, "we can't go now; dark is coming on in an hour."

"In the morning then, early," insisted Nicole, wringing her hands. "Tonight, we'll shove furniture against the door and all sleep in my bed." Her eyes searched blearily for this piece of furniture, and she gestured with a wavering hand. She would be asleep in minutes, Emily thought.

At Emily's command, Nicole was constrained to walk to the bed, leaning heavily on her niece and daughter.

"There, Mama," Demetria said, pulling off Nicole's slippers and tucking her under the down comforter, "you must rest now."

Nicole's eyes closed, but she half opened them to mutter, "That—man is dangerous; I have it straight—from his own mother. Not safe—we're not safe here; I won't spend 'nother night—in Ravencroft." Then she fell asleep, snoring gently.

Emily gazed down at her aunt. "Demetria, Belle mustn't know the extent of this contretemps. She would be devastated if she learned of the infamous lies her mother has told about Lord Ingram." Her gray eyes held Demetria's. "And they *are* lies, you understand."

"I know that, Em," Demetria exclaimed. "Lady Annora is a gorgon. Poor Lord Ingram. And poor Belle. Oh! We must get our story together, what we're going to tell her."

"Yes." Emily was thankful Demetria realized what they must do. "Only listen, Deme. When Belle comes to us, as I'm certain she will, we shall leave Holt Ingram out of it. We'll report what she said about me. It's bad enough that the dowager should cast aspersions on me for leaving our room in the middle of the night—simply to visit the library. And she dared to criticize you to your mother's face, calling you a hardened flirt, and so on. On top of that, she left the castle, abandoning her duty as a hostess—"

Emily thought a moment. "Yes, Deme. Aunt Nicole probably would have flown into her fit even if Lady Ingram hadn't maligned Holt. Remember that Belle knows your mother is excitable and easily offended. All we have to do is keep mum on what she said about Holt. Hist! There's a knock. Let me do the talking."

Ten

At Abbingdon, Annora was just sitting down to a solitary dinner in her small Yellow Parlor when Holt stalked in. Without removing his riding coat, he proceeded to demand what she had done to precipitate such a crisis.

"You may as well tell me, madam. I'll discover it sooner or later. It must have been something out of the ordinary even for you, if it caused you to leave Ravencroft and sent Lady Hume to her bed. How could you prate of good manners and then be so lacking in common courtesy as to leave a house where you had constituted yourself hostess? How charming to bring my guests home and find that you had deserted Lady Hume to her prostrations and left the field of battle."

Annora's lips twitched behind her napkin. Well, well, so Holt was upset already. She could tell by his rapid breathing, by the fulminating gleam in his eye, that her little scheme was a success. Had Nicole Quimby worked herself into such a state that she had babbled the tales so carefully planted? Had she complained of the censure of her niece and daughter? Had she been insulted when left to fend for herself in the castle? And the little Wilton—had she already given him the cut direct? Annora certainly hoped so. She almost smiled.

"I have no idea what you are talking about, Holt. I decided to come home, told her ladyship I was leaving, and bade her good-bye. I believe this is where you have ordained that I shall live, is it not?"

Holt checked his next words and examined his mother's calm countenance. Had he jumped to the wrong conclusion?

Annora buttered her bread. "What did Lady Hume say? Have you talked with her?" she asked.

Holt slapped his boot with his riding crop. That was it: he hadn't stayed to hear what Belle could learn from Lady Hume. Nor had he talked with Emily. That was what he wanted to do most of all. He kicked one of the firedogs. "You admit some people might think it rude that you left so abruptly."

"I find it ironic that you, Holt, of all people, should have the effrontery to preach propriety to *me*. Now either go, or sit and eat. I hate you looming over me."

"Madam, I'll go. I expect to find little comfort at my own dinner table tonight; there is none here."

"Stay a moment. Does Isobel come to me?"

It was a minute before Holt answered. "Yes. She expects to come to Abbingdon sometime tomorrow. If you, as I suspect, have speeded our guests on their way, she should see you in the afternoon."

When he had departed, Annora called for wine. Taking it to her large wing chair by the fire, she arranged her bony figure comfortably and gave a contented sigh. She had plotted successfully. Emily Wilton would take fright at the thought of her narrow escape, and Holt would find himself balked in his pursuit of the girl. As for Isobel, Annora was glad to learn that her hold on her daughter was still in force. She would grill her tomorrow on what the guests had said.

Finishing her wine, Annora pulled the fur lap robe across her knees. Night had come on, and she could imagine Holt riding in the dark, that frown on his face. Let him suffer, she thought. Hadn't he exiled her from Ravencroft?

Emily's story had satisfied poor Belle, who had apologized most feelingly. They went into the Blue Saloon, and Demetria joined Emily in assuring Belle that they understood it was no fault of hers.

"Nor Holt's," said Belle. "He has ridden over to Abbingdon to talk to Mama. He will want to see you at dinner; we must muddle through this as best we can. And I quite understand that you must take Lady Hume away. The earlier you leave Ravencroft, the better. Her nerves won't sustain much more. Later, in town, when things get back to normal, we shall visit each other." Belle's smile was strained. "I'll see you at dinner, then. Holt should have returned by then."

Dinner was as uncomfortable as Emily had expected. Her first thought was that she and Demetria should have trays in their room, but she had realized that would only make things worse.

Conversation was an effort for everyone. Even Cecil Jennings's famous urbanity could not cover the awkwardness.

Emily had refrained from looking directly at Holt Ingram, except once, fleetingly, during the first course, and then she quickly averted her eyes.

Toward the end of the meal, Holt spoke directly to her. "I'm sorry you must go. However, if you feel it necessary—"

It was necessary, of course. "I believe my aunt was planning on leaving tomorrow in any event," Emily said.

"Yes!" Demetria leaped on this statement. "It's time we continued our journey to London. Although, I must say, it's been very pleasant—" Her voice faltered. "Very pleasant," she asserted more positively. "I wouldn't have missed seeing Ravencroft for anything. Belle, you and your brother gave us welcome indeed. Val, I feel I have a new friend in you, and Cecil, you must remember you have promised to dance with me at Almack's."

Dessert was over, and Emily said, preparatory to bidding everyone good night, "I'm afraid Demetria and I must excuse ourselves. We will finish packing and make an early night."

But Holt intervened. "I don't believe we've shown you the Armorial Hall, Emily. Belle reminded me, just before dinner. Shall we?"

His eyes demanded that Emily stay, and she nodded.

"This way, then," Belle said. "Val, the porters are prepared to transport you and your chair, if you want to see the armaments again."

THE MUCH MALIGNED LORD

Val looked at Belle, then shook his head. "No, I believe Cecil and I shall opt for some billiards. We've seen those old shields and suits of armor a hundred times. Isn't that right, old man?" he asked Cecil.

Agreeing wholeheartedly, Cecil rolled Val away.

Emily found Holt by her side. "You must see this," he said, tucking her hand into the crook of his elbow and leading her to the staircase. Belle and Demetria trailed behind as they made their way to the dungeons to view all the weapons of war the Ingrams had accumulated over the centuries.

The Armorial Hall was located deep in the castle. It was long and narrow, with undressed walls of rough gray stone. A series of side rooms lay just off the main chamber. A primitive fire pit marked the center of the room, and the high ceiling was blackened from the smoke of countless fires.

"But this is wonderful," Emily breathed. "This has all been kept in the style of the fourteenth century."

Holt agreed. "The Ingrams have a lively interest in the past," he explained. "Some of the wives—most of them—were avid collectors and excellent conservators. I hope you—I hope you have an interest in antiquities."

Emily snapped her eyes to his. He was looking at her with an intensity she couldn't mistake. His statement had been anything but casual. What did it mean? Did he plan to ask her to become part of the Ingram tradition? Was he intimating that he expected and hoped she might be one of those wives who "collected and conserved"?

As steadily as she could, Emily said, "I am fascinated with artifacts of the past. Museums of relics are some of my favorite places. I'm glad you wanted me to see this display before we left; I'd have hated to miss it. Did—did all these things belong to your family members?"

"Most of them. Some, a few, were won by my ancestors in battle; others were collected," Holt said.

Emily looked about. Old suits of armor lined the room: full suits; half suits; battle and jousting armor; parade armor, this last highly etched, guilded, and embossed, with classical myths depicted on the breast and back plates. Earlier examples of long ringed mail—hauberks—were preserved in glass display cases, along with mail hoods. The collection boasted many helmets of the type called by the Normans *heaumes,* as Emily knew. There were boiled-leather helmets, iron helmets with nasals, and assorted pieces of plate body armor, even horse mail.

Holt escorted Emily about the room as he pointed out various pieces and gave her their history. Her hand rested lightly on his sleeve. Such a tiny hand, he thought, looking down at it. *Does she know that she holds my happiness in it?*

They walked past cabinets containing hand weapons, lances, pikes, longbows. There were numerous swords, of a variety Emily had never imagined.

At last they came to what was obviously the showpiece of the collection. They stopped before a tall glass cabinet containing a particularly fine sword and shield. "These," Holt said, "were Rupurt's. He won his knight's honor at Agincourt."

The baron's voice dropped as he told Emily how it had happened. "Do you know that battle?" he began.

She nodded, and he said, "Henry V, you remember, was fighting in that muddy defile between Agincourt and Tramecourt. He fell—or was almost beaten down—at the crucial point in the battle. Rupurt of Ravencroft, a young squire, leaped to stand over his king, wielding his sword in the melee, fighting like a berserker until the French line was beaten back.

"Henry knighted Rupurt there in the mud of the battlefield, on St. Crispin's Day, 1415, and presented him with his folded glove as a gage, a wage, by which Henry promised his help and support."

Emily was looking up at him, seemingly transfixed.

"Do you know what that meant, Emily?" Holt asked softly.

"Yes." She was suddenly seeing in her mind's eye something out of the pages of an antique book she'd come across containing the ancient rules of baronial court procedure: *He shall wage his law with his folded glove and shall deliver it unto the hand of the other, and then take his glove back and find pledges for his law.*

She recited this verbatim to Holt, and added, "As I understand it, Henry's folded glove, *de son gaunt plyee,* his gage, was the symbol of his promise to be Rupurt's benefactor. Henry's wage was his pledge—his law that meant the promise was real and would be forever unbroken. The folded glove given and received was at that time a promise between two people. Isn't that right?"

Holt nodded, and she had a momentary feeling that his eyes were consuming her.

The silence stretched between them for so long that Emily became disconcerted, not knowing what to do or say. She turned half away, searching for Belle and Demetria, and saw them at last in one of the side rooms, bending over a long display case.

"Look at me, Emily," came Holt's command.

When she complied, he said, "I want to say again how sorry I am that my mother created this unpleasantness. You know how I feel about that. Now I want you to go to London and have your Season. Many of the things that happened during your visit here are best forgotten, or at least put aside. You know what I mean." His voice had become hard.

If he wasn't talking about his mother, Emily couldn't guess what he meant. Obviously, he did not choose to explain, for he terminated the conversation and steered her toward the others.

"Belle? Demetria?" he called, gathering the women for the ascent to the upper stories. "Are you finished looking? Emily wants to go up."

Emily felt confused as they climbed the stairs. Had Holt been telling her to forget the kisses they'd shared? Was he, in effect, telling her to get on with her life, and implying that she was to forget what had passed between them?

Emily and Demetria retired to their room shortly after Holt's abrupt good night. Demetria went off to check on her mother, and Emily slipped between the sheets. After the great bronze doors closed behind her, would Ravencroft be lost to her forever? Would she ever sleep in this magical place again?

Her heart went out to Holt Ingram. She tried to concentrate on the man instead of his kisses. She prayed he would never hear the lies his mother had told Aunt Hume. Emily did not believe for one moment that Holt was the hardened adulterer his mother said he was.

She went to sleep wondering if she would ever belong to him and to Ravencroft.

The next morning, as he and Belle came out to wish them good-bye, Holt seemed reserved. But there was one moment when he relaxed his guard and smiled at her. One moment, when he took her hand and pressed a kiss into her upturned palm, his lips warm and vital.

As they pulled away from Ravencroft, Emily closed her hand to retain that warmth, remembering it was only yesterday that he'd held her in his arms, moaning "Sweet, sweet" deep in his throat.

They made a three-day journey from Ravencroft, their reason for stopping twice being that Nicole Quimby had exhausted herself crying and gone sleepless the night before they left.

On that trip, Emily discovered that she was not the girl who had left Herefordshire five days ago. That girl had never dreamed of such wanton delight as she had experienced when Holt Ingram kissed her. She would never be the same. He had awakened the woman sleeping within her. When she gave him back his kisses, she knew some part of her innocence was lost. But how gladly she had given it. She would give it again and again. Now she yearned for a further, ultimate, most secret desire to be fulfilled. Emily wanted to belong to Holt fully.

Lying in bed in the inn at Bilbury, she buried her face in her pillow. She wanted Holt Ingram as all women have wanted their men since love began. Most of all, she wanted to feel Holt's child in her belly. She wanted him to take her to his secret room in the tower. Holt had brought her to life. He must feed this fire he'd started inside her.

Emily knew exactly how men and women joined; she had helped her father deliver babies since she was eighteen.

Before Holt kissed her, she had been aghast that women could allow themselves to be gotten with child. Emily rubbed her hand over her flat belly. A dull, warm ache had settled deep within her. Curling into a knot, she hugged herself. She understood those women now. Only a lover could cure this ache, and Holt was the only lover she would ever want.

Eleven

EVEN THOUGH Emily was consumed with thoughts of Holt Ingram, London, when they reached it, fascinated her.

The Lesters, with whom they were staying, welcomed them with open arms. Lady Jane Lester, Nicole Quimby's older sister, took Nicole in hand and pooh-poohed all her flights of fancy concerning the revelations of the Dowager Baroness Ingram.

"Holt Ingram?" her ladyship cried, turning quite red. "Never! You have fallen victim to his mother's tongue. The truth is very pliable to Annora Ingram. She goes everywhere, spreading gossip like wildfire, she and all the old tabbies like Lady Gimbald and Hortensia Butterworth, and in particular old Hetty Humfry. Don't believe Annora. Holt Ingram is one of the most eligible men in the *ton*."

Lady Jane was frankly middle-aged, a comfortable matronly woman who wore turbans, and was as plump as her sister Nicole was thin. She was very short, always trying to catch her breath, and constantly fanned herself.

Jane Lester's words were balm to Emily's ears. Now she could look forward to seeing Holt with unabated pleasure.

She and Demetria, between being fitted for new clothes and receiving gifts from their uncle, the Earl of Mursey, managed to get in a whirl of sight-seeing.

A week passed, and another. Emily kept waiting for the

Ingrams to arrive in town. She'd been watching for them expectantly.

Fourteen days passed and she didn't hear a word from Holt Ingram. Emily thought her stay at Ravencroft could have been a visit to another place, another time. The happenings there took on a feeling of unreality, although she lived and relived them in her thoughts every waking moment.

Climbing the steps to the Tower of London, she recalled Holt leading her to the top of the tower at Ravencroft.

The rain made her think of the Lindhurst library and Holt's kisses.

Taking tea, she grew pale remembering Holt's hand, strong and tan, offering her a cup in his small chamber.

She and Demetria visited an antique book store with Lord Lester, their courtly host, looking for old books on chess for her father, and the smell of those musty volumes brought back the moment Holt's mouth descended on hers. Two weeks had turned into an eternity.

The afternoon she saw Val Lindsay, Viscount Renton, being driven round the course at Hyde Park by Mr. Cecil Jennings, Emily's heart almost bounded out of her breast.

Val Lindsay, catching sight of Emily Wilton and Demetria Quimby, shouted, "Ho, Cecil. There they are! Was wondering when we'd fetch up with those two. Pull round, catch up to them.

"Demetria!" he cried. "Where did you get that spanking team? And that landaulette is all the crack. I never saw one so fancy."

Demetria smiled happily and told them the carriage and team were presents from their Uncle Mursey, all picked out and ordered, waiting for them at Lester House.

"Yes, isn't this a sumptuous rig?" she cried. "Emily and I were so surprised to think that our uncle had arranged such a wonderful gift for us. And he designed this landaulette himself. I love the maroon and gold fittings, don't you? And these seats! Whoever heard of baby blue seats? Uncle wrote that Emily and I both have blue eyes and they would all match up, except Emily's are gray."

"Well, that about tears it," Val exclaimed. "If I could, I'd climb over there and take a turn with you. Since I can't, why don't you get up here with me, and let Cecil drive Emily round a few times?"

This arrangement was speedily carried out, Emily welcoming Mr. Jennings more than he could possibly know. Now, if only she could bring the conversation around to Holt Ingram.

But first, it seemed Cecil Jennings must learn what she and Demetria had been doing since they arrived, whom they'd seen, the places they'd been, and what they planned for the near future.

Some twenty minutes were consumed in this way, Emily doing her best not to demand news of Holt. It was only when she had told Cecil that she and Demetria were being presented next week—their court dresses were finished—and that they had been going to antique shops trying to find a really wonderful old chess set for her father's birthday that she heard at last the name she'd been trying to bring to Mr. Jennings's lips.

"Something like that antique ivory set at Ravencroft?" inquired Mr. Jennings. "Now that is beautiful. And it's old. I believe—yes, I think Holt got that at a shop in Chelsea. I could take you there."

"Is he in town, then?" asked Emily, freeing the words from deep inside herself.

"Who?" asked Mr. Jennings. "Holt Ingram? Yes, came up right after you left Ravencroft. I've been round to St. James several times to see him. And Val and I have been busy manufacturing his rolling chair. You must see it when the lacquer is dry."

Two weeks, Emily thought, and Ingram hadn't bothered to pay a morning call. That must tell her something about how he valued her kisses.

Emily could barely speak. "You said Lord Ingram was living in St. James. Somehow or other, I thought he had a town house. In Albermarle Street, I believe he said."

"Does, yes indeed, just off Picadilly." Mr. Jennings nodded, expertly bringing the team to a standstill near the riding house. "Well," he said as they waited for Val Lindsay to come driving round, "not a town house, precisely. More a

THE MUCH MALIGNED LORD 103

mansion, I'd say. Been in the family for years. But Holt doesn't stay with his mother, you know."

Cecil glanced sideways at Emily. "Don't quite know how to say this, but there are strained feelings between Holt and the dowager. Poor Isobel. She's the one to bear the brunt of her mother's temper. It's common knowledge that Lady Ingram quarrels with everyone, sooner or later. Lady Hume must have been quite shocked to have Lady Ingram give her one of her infamous scolds. Holt didn't say a word to me or Val, but he looked a thundercloud after Lady Hume insisted on taking you away. As usual, his mama had done her worst and made off like a thief in the night. Val Lindsay said no good would come of leaving Lady Hume to the old dragon's mercy; said it before we left for Lindhurst that morning. Not that I think I'm telling you anything you don't know, Miss Wilton. Have you seen Isobel since she got to town? Arrived only yesterday, I understand."

"No, I haven't seen her; I haven't heard from anyone at Ravencroft," Emily said.

The news that Holt Ingram was in London and hadn't tried to contact her made Emily feel faint. All those tales of his mother's. Were they based, even a little, on the truth? Emily knew nothing of men on the town.

Had Ingram's kisses been a prelude to a practiced seduction? He had declared that she was a green girl. No doubt he thought she was a peach to be plucked and fall ripe into his hands.

She managed to pull herself together as they drew up to Cecil's coach and he exchanged places with Demetria. She said good-bye in an absent way that made Demetria look at her quite sharply.

Emily sat through a concert that night and went over every single word, every look, Holt Ingram had given her. His eyes had swept her from crown to feet when they first met in the road. What was it he'd said? *I've never met a girl like you, Miss Wilton.*

Emily couldn't help thinking her unusual actions must have spurred his rapacious appetites. Perhaps, even then, he was contemplating her ruin.

Emily had been in London long enough to learn that even so levelheaded a woman as Lady Jane Lester had been shocked at her running down the road and attending a broken and bleeding Val Lindsay.

"My dear Emily," she had said in her considerate, commonsense way, "only think. Such behavior would be thought very *coming* if it were known.

"Young ladies in the *ton* simply do not do such things. Nicole tells me you knelt in the dust and that your hands were covered with the young man's blood. I find that hard to believe—I know how Nicole exaggerates. Not only that, she swears she watched while Ingram gathered your hair and tied it back with his own hands. Surely she was mistaken. An impossibly intimate action! It does not bear thinking of," she said, fanning herself.

"You have lived too far from the world, my dear. You can't know how people will talk. They shall begin to think you're either fast, or an eccentric, and that would be fatal to all our plans. Emily," she finished earnestly, "I wish you will reflect. Such excessive behavior can never do, especially during your and Demetria's Season. If you don't care for yourself, at least think of her."

Emily had easily given her promise. The circumstance of attending Val Lindsay had been extraordinary. What were the odds of such a thing happening again?

As for her reputation, she cared only what one person thought, and that was Holt Ingram. Had he imagined her abandoned to all restraint when she asked him to tie up her hair? He hadn't seemed to. And Val Lindsay. Could Holt have saved him without her help? She remembered the blood spurting brightly just above Val's wrist. Her only thought had been to stop it. Not for any consideration in the world would Emily have let that bleeding go unchecked. Her papa would have expected her to act exactly as she had.

If others wanted to judge her for what she'd been impelled to do, let them. It was hard to imagine Holt Ingram in such a role.

From the moment of their meeting, Emily had known—thought she knew—him for a man of honor. Was she so poor a judge of character? But then, she'd never met a *libertine* before. What could she—a country miss bred in Herefordshire—know of men who habitually courted demireps and practiced seduction for a pastime?

She couldn't get Aunt Hume's words out of her brain. *"Wouldn't a hardened rake necessarily need attractive ways?"* her aunt had asked pitifully, after Annora Ingram's terrible disclosures. *"Wouldn't such a man develop coaxing manners?"*

Well, the answer to that could only be, he would. Emily seemed to have fallen for Holt Ingram's attractive ways and coaxing manners as easily as a fawn into a poacher's snare.

Oh, but she hated to remember how she'd tried to please him, playing that silly chess game. And that night of the storm. Emily winced. What a fool she'd been, following him to the top of his tower. Now she understood why Holt hadn't kissed her when she threw herself into his arms. That room below the tower held a bed. Obviously, the baron knew what he was about. She was at his mercy, but something—she didn't know what—had stayed him; had he taken pity on her?

And his words later at Lindhurst. *"I didn't mean to kiss you,"* he'd said. That probably meant he hadn't intended kissing her in that exact moment! In *that* place.

Emily could believe debauchers must play their games very carefully. Their strategy must be perfect, else they wouldn't be successful.

No doubt the reason his lordship hadn't called since his arrival in London was he meant her to stew, to worry, to build up her hopes and expectations, so when he did decide to come round, Emily would be so glad to see him, she'd fall into his arms, and he would have won the game in spite of his mama's telling all.

As for Isobel, well, can a loving sister ever know her brother is a scoundrel? Isobel worshiped Holt. Naturally, she would refute any *truths* she was unable to bear.

Emily still could not like the dowager baroness. Who knew—perhaps if Annora Ingram had been a loving mother, her son would have turned out differently?

She gasped at her trend of thought. Emily couldn't believe

she was picking at straws, trying to make excuses for Ingram. She'd heard of women so violently infatuated with some reprobate that they refused to listen to their families. Such women inevitably ruined themselves, living all their lives with their mistakes. She was not of that ilk! Emily hardened her heart, put memories of Ravencroft and its sinister master out of her head, and resolved to get on with her London Season.

Twelve

Lady Lester was delighted. The *ton,* in that unaccountable way society had, and which it evinced only on the rarest occasions, took Emily Wilton and Demetria Quimby to its collective heart.

"The Cousins" they were called, and from their glittering presentation ball, which lasted until dawn at the Lester mansion in South Street just off Hyde Park, Emily and Demetria were in constant demand.

Never, declared Lady Maitland, one of the old-guard society dragons, had two girls since the Gunning sisters so captured the imagination of the beau monde.

Almost everyone was delighted with their success. Lady Lester's mail delivery was quadrupled, the crested invitations piling up on her breakfast tray each morning.

No less than three of the patronesses of Almack's called in South Street to grant the girls vouchers to the hallowed precincts of society's most prestigious subscription club.

Lady Sefton, of course, was a childhood friend of Jane Lester's, and Ladies Castleraugh and Cowper proclaimed themselves diverted by the pair.

Not to be outdone, Lady Jersey, upon the occasion of their very first attendance in the Assembly Rooms, had been pleased to present Emily to the Earl of Wainfeld as a very desirable partner for the waltz.

Demetria, presented at the same time to the extremely eligible Mr. Moulton, laughed and thanked Lady Jersey, saying she'd long promised her first waltz to Mr. Cecil Jennings and went off to find that gentleman.

Tully Moulton, present only because his sister had coaxed his attendance, gulped at the way Demetria's dancing eyes engaged his, took himself in hand, and hurried through the crowd to demand the girl's second waltz. He proposed a week later, was gently refused, and vowed his lifelong devotion. He became one of Demetria's court, all of whom had proposed and been turned down, and who—while never giving up hope—considered themselves her joint protectors.

The cousins' looks, style, and elegance made them much sought after. Demetria's stunning blonde radiance contrasted pleasingly with Emily's quieter, classically beautiful features. Their clothes, many of them imported directly from Paris by Madame Fanchon, were the envy of every mama who of necessity rigged their darlings from a pinched purse.

It was well-known that the girls, even Emily Wilton whose mother had married some country doctor, had respectable fortunes, and their uncle, the Earl of Mursey, constantly delighted in surprising them with gifts. Only think of that splendid Arab filly he'd sent for Miss Emily Wilton's birthday.

The cousins dazzled onlookers as they tooled their famous lavender and gray low-perch phaeton—another gift from their doting uncle—in Hyde Park each afternoon, taking turns driving, and with a small boy dressed in Mursey livery perched behind them. If the cousins didn't drive their phaeton or landaulette, they rode, their Worth habits perfectly complementing one another.

When the weather was splendid, they drove in a group to Kew Gardens or Richmond Park, even Windsor, the laughing, animated center of the Season's gayest, brightest set. Their manners, said Society, their charm, were what must always please. Nothing or no one could eclipse the fame of "The Cousins."

Val Lindsay stood in the middle of Lady Lester's Grotto Room, surrounded by admiring females, balancing on the new crutches Emily and Cecil Jennings had designed for him. His dark hair fell over his forehead, making at least two of the morning visitors, both young ladies in their first Season, sigh with rapture.

"Emily," Val said, "when did you say this dashed cast could come off? I'm tired of being tied down. It almost makes me wish we hadn't had that wreck."

Emily, appreciating the irony of young Viscount Renton's statement, said, "I believe you should consult a physician for that information, Val. Do you have one here in London?"

"My sister does. A surgeon at Guy's Hospital. Allegra," he called, "that doctor of yours. What's his name?"

Allegra Haddon, née Lindsay, who had married into an ancient though untitled family, looked up from her conversation with her mother, Oralia Lindsay, Lady Renton. Nicole Quimby, Lady Hume, sat nearby, with their hostess, Jane, Lady Lester.

"Dr. Oreton, Val," Allegra answered. "And he's Mother's doctor, not mine. I'm never sick."

Lady Allegra was a tall, vivacious brunette, the mother of two girls at school in Bath; her husband, Mr. Frederick Haddon, a career diplomat, was in the Foreign Office.

Allegra yawned behind her hand. Their ball the previous night, honoring the survivors of the 4th Division's Forlorn Hope, that disastrous assault on the Badajos breaches, had been a tremendous success. Exactly what one always hoped for and dreaded, a veritable squeeze.

Only one dangerous moment had occurred. Demetria Quimby almost precipitated a duel between a young captain in the Horse Guards and the honorable Julian Hinchley. If Cecil Jennings hadn't intervened and danced off with Demetria, things could have come to a nasty head, something, Allegra thought, a diplomat's wife must avoid at all costs.

"Dr. Oreton, you say. Hi, Emily," Val said, "will you go with me to see this doctor fellow? I don't understand all their long-toothed medical gabble. I'd like it if you came along. Do you have any idea what he'll say?"

Emily snipped the thread on the needlepoint she was working and nodded. "Yes, I'd be happy to. I should imagine by this time next week, you'll be free of the cast. How long has it been? Five and a half weeks?"

"Six weeks tomorrow," fretted Val, awkwardly lowering himself between Miss Meredith Longley and her friend, Miss Caroline Colby.

"Can't be too soon for me." He sighed, allowing the adoring young ladies each to take a crutch and tenderly bestow it alongside the gnarled oak settee they occupied, beside a leering cast-iron statue of Pan. Various other statues of fauns, some in plaster, but mostly painted iron, decorated Lady Lester's famous Grotto Room.

The rustic furniture—gnarled wooden benches, settees, low tables, and chairs in fantastic shapes—was arranged around a softly bubbling fountain. Lady Lester had grouped plants everywhere, tall ferns and overflowing pots of hanging vines, to create the atmosphere of a leafy forest glen.

Relieved of his crutches, Val smiled impartially at his most fervent admirers. "Thanks, Meri. You, too, Caro. You're very kind, but I never intend to break another leg."

Laughter exploded at this ingenuous statement, but Emily was hardly attending. Six weeks and it seemed a lifetime.

Had it been so recently that Holt Ingram came into her life? A thousand years couldn't seem so long!

There had been enjoyable times since Emily came to London, especially since she determined to exorcise Ingram from her mind. But she could never totally forget him, nor Ravencroft.

The man and his home—that ancient fortress she returned to in her dreams—continued to hold a fascination for Emily which she despaired of ever losing. Like Val, she almost wished that wreck hadn't happened.

If Val Lindsay's horse hadn't bolted, she wouldn't have met Holt Ingram or stayed at Ravencroft, and—most of all— never lost her heart to a man who carelessly bestowed such unforgettable kisses on country girls that they were affected for a lifetime.

Emily had come to acquit Holt Ingram of nefarious intent. No, he'd been lightly amusing himself, she decided, dallying with her. She had taken him seriously. It was unfortunate for her, but at least no one knew. The scars, though painful, did not show.

What hurt Emily most was to think that those kisses she'd returned so trustingly had meant nothing to the baron. Men were always a favorite subject of women. Allegra had given it as her opinion over tea only last Thursday that creatures of the male persuasion were apt to indulge in vagrant moments of passion without a second thought.

Emily pressed her lips together. Since Lord Ingram was known to be in London, and since he'd never contacted her, she must conclude that such was the case with him. He probably didn't remember he'd kissed a green girl at Lindhurst one rainy afternoon.

Mr. and Mrs. Horace Norville were distant cousins of Emily's on her father's side. From Stropshire, they were in their early sixties. Mr. Horace Norville was short, fat, and hard of hearing. He spoke, as the deaf are wont to do, loudly. Mavis Norville wore her white hair in a tight frizz and possessed a charming style of elegance that Emily always admired whenever the Norvilles visited them in Hereford. Mavis was as good-natured and as expansive as her husband. Emily had spent several summers at their country seat when she was a child, and the families still visited back and forth. The Norvilles were great favorites of hers.

Norville House was located in the heart of Mayfair, in fashionable Green Street. Mavis and Horace were delighted when Emily brought Demetria to call.

The Norvilles insisted on hosting a ball for Emily and Demetria. They had rearranged their schedule to accommodate this new event after receiving Emily's letter that she was coming to town.

"Oh, Emily!" Mavis cried, kissing her. "I was so glad you wrote. I do wish I'd known sooner. A really important ball takes at least six months to plan. However, we shall muddle along as best we can."

Emily had no doubt that Mavis, famous hostess that she was, would manage quite well. She expressed her thanks for the trouble her cousin was taking, glad to visit these kinfolks of her father's once again.

She saw them many times in the next few weeks, for Horace and Mavis Norville were very popular members of the beau monde. Mavis took the cousins under her wing. "How glad I am to have two beautiful young ladies in and out of the house," Mavis told them. "Make no mistake. My sons are wonderful. Will and Jeremy are young men any mother could be proud of. But every woman should have a daughter to present to Society, and here I have two!"

During the second week in June, on the night of the ball, the Lester carriage pulled up to the Norville mansion in Green Street. Mounted police were directing traffic, and linkboys ran everywhere.

"Your cousins did well to expect a large crowd, Emily," Jane Lester remarked. "Horace Norville told me at Lady Romsey's salon on Tuesday last that they'd sent out over two hundred invitations. Looks like they've all accepted."

Inside, standing in the receiving line, Emily and Demetria shook hands for what seemed like three hours but was only one.

Emily stood between Jeremy Norville on her left—Jeremy who had kissed her at fifteen—and his older brother, Colonel Sir Robert Willoughby Norville, who had been through every military campaign since the Denmark Expedition.

Holt Ingram arrived with Isobel on his arm, looking stern, his features set in exacting lines. He still limped. Isobel greeted them warmly, but Holt bowed formally, barely touched Emily's hand, and passed quickly down the line and out of sight.

Emily lifted her chin and swallowed, trying to preserve her countenance after his cool greeting.

At last Mavis Norville gave a brisk nod and said that they might as well join the crowd. "I have the dancing set to start in ten minutes."

Mr. Horace Norville looked up fondly at his wife and spoke loudly. "Yes, yes, m'dear. You go on; I'll stay here a moment. I'm expecting—" Horace stopped and peered at the stairs where his special guests were just arriving.

THE MUCH MALIGNED LORD 113

"Ha!" he boomed. "Here they are now, and on time." He stepped forward to shake hands with Frederick, the Duke of York, and their mutual friend, Lord Alvanley.

"Your grace," Horace said, beaming. "And Alvanley. Allow me to present my young cousin, Miss Emily Wilton. And this is Emily's cousin, Miss Demetria Quimby."

York was the king's second son, Wales—Prinny—being the first. This royal duke was as corpulent as the rest of his family. His stance, his sloping forehead, and most of all his bulging eyes revealed at once his Hanoverian lineage.

The most accessible member of the royal family, York smiled at the girls and cried, "So you're 'The Cousins'? M'mother was telling me about your presentation. You're the Wilton girl, I take it?" he asked Emily. "Yes, I shall never forget your mother. Alvanley, you remember Clemmy Quinby, old Mursey's daughter? Oh, Clemmy was beautiful, a breathtaking girl. Broke my heart, if you want to know the truth." York laughed loudly, as if at a great joke. "Broke a lot of hearts in that Season of hers. My brother Wales was one of her admirers. You look like her, you know."

The duke turned to Demetria, lifted her hand, and kissed it. "And this pretty thing must be Hume's daughter. He was a friend of mine—sorry he's gone. Your Uncle Mursey stays at Carlton House when he's in town. You must say everything proper to Mursey for me. Last time I saw him, he had a horse I wanted."

York passed on down the line with a word for everyone, especially Colonel Norville, who had served under him in Germany. He and Alvanley then strolled into the Venetian Saloon, Horace Norville and one of the members of the German legation trailing them.

Bemused, Emily had just assured a waiter that she wanted nothing, when she accepted her dance card from Cousin Mavis.

"Here you are, my dear," Mavis said, handing over a printed card with a tiny pencil attached. "You see, it's more than half-filled. You must look at the top line. Holt Ingram was here last week, insisting on signing it. Mr. Jennings signed it too, and also Demetria's. And there's Wainfeld's signature. Poor Wainfeld made a special trip up to town to put his name on your card, Emily. Wanted the honor of leading you out in the first dance; can you imagine? Seemed disappointed. I'm certain he doesn't remember that only a girl's nearest kinsman or her host—even her betrothed, if she has one—may lead her out. Wainfeld is a good fellow, but his mother was rather too kin to his father, if you know what I mean. Our family, thank God, has never married cousins. However, that's not what I wanted to talk about. When I explained that your Cousin Will must lead you out—just as Jeremy should lead Demetria—Wainfeld seemed to understand. Then he expressed his dissatisfaction that he wasn't first after Will, Ingram having nipped round and gotten that dance."

Why had Ingram bothered? Emily asked herself. She couldn't believe he had gone to so much trouble to dance with her. He had barely spoken in the line. She felt exasperated that she never failed to be affected by his presence. When he touched her fingers in greeting, his eyes had briefly roved her face and hair. Would she be able to meet him in the figures of the dance without betraying herself? Vowing to appear as cold and controlled as the baron, Emily went to look for her Cousin Will.

Colonel Will Norville, a bluff and hearty soldier of forty, with long military sideburns, led his cousin out, and the first dance was over before Emily knew it. She must have conversed with Will, but couldn't remember having done so.

When the dance was finished, Emily, trying not to be obvious, searched the crowd for Ingram. Where was he? She could see Wainfeld hovering about the sidelines, but the baron seemed to have disappeared, or perhaps he'd left already. Would Lord Ingram go to the trouble of signing her card just to desert her and leave her to wilt among the wallflowers?

Chiding herself, knowing very well that any number of men would step into a breach left vacant by the baron, Emily turned and almost bumped into him.

His eyes were as black as ever. She hadn't noticed before, but he seemed a little pale. And ... had he lost weight?

"I want to talk to you." He was austere. No greeting, no smile, but he narrowed his eyes and murmured, "You're just as I remembered."

Emily raised her brows. "I've been at Lady Lester's, my lord, on South Street. You could have seen me anytime." She was angry, but preserved a fatalistic calm.

"Yes. We shall discuss that and various other items, but later." Ingram grabbed her hand and they started toward the country dance that was making up. He stumbled a little, grunted, and recovered. Was his leg worse?

"Why did you say you didn't want to kiss me?" Emily asked, and could have sunk through the floor. The question had been burning in her mind for two months; that was her only excuse for voicing it.

Ingram jerked his head around, frowned at her, and, abandoning the dance, dragged her rapidly off at a tangent toward the long back hall. Intercepted by Colonel Norville, Ingram barely slowed. "Will." He nodded.

"Holt! Stop a moment. How's that leg of yours? Not dancing, I see. Emily, don't let him stand on it too long. Where are you off to?"

"I need to talk with your cousin." Ingram then did a surprising thing. He pulled Emily against his side and stood with his arm around her. "Where can we go?"

A small grin appeared on Will Norville's mouth, then deepened. "Like that, is it? Emily, you have my blessing, for what it's worth. I've served in battle with this fellow. Couldn't stand beside a better man. Come with me."

Will showed them into a small back parlor, the tiny room his mother used for sewing. "No one will find you here," he promised, and left them, closing the door.

Emily was fuming. She was sorry about Ingram's leg, but he—and Cousin Will—had dragooned her into coming here. At least she would have the riddle of Holt's *accidental* kisses solved.

"Well?" she asked dangerously. "Are you going to answer my question?"

From across the room he came to her. "I never said I didn't want to kiss you, dammit! That would have been a lie. I said

I didn't intend doing it that day in the Lindhurst library. No, I planned on doing it now, after you'd been out some weeks. Like this."

And once again, Emily found herself in Holt Ingram's embrace, being ruthlessly kissed, exactly as she remembered.

Thirteen

Even as Emily pushed against him, her mouth shaped itself to Holt's lips. Her body—traitorous body—molded to his, and that familiar rush swept over her. After one perfidious moment, she forced her arms to push him away instead of curling about his neck as they wanted.

"Let me go." At least she could command her voice. "Let me go!" She wrenched herself from his arms.

Emily scrubbed her lips with the back of her hand. "What are you trying to do?" she cried. "Don't bother answering—I know! It's a matter of conquest, isn't it? You're trifling with me again. You want to see if you can make the little country mouse fall for your dalliance."

Holt clenched his teeth and said tightly, "As a matter of fact, I've fallen in love with you. I want you to marry me."

He stopped speaking and raised one brow, his gaze level, as if assessing her reaction.

Emily went utterly silent, astonished that he could say such a thing. To what *lengths* would Ingram go? He had toyed with her emotions since first she encountered him on the road to Ravencroft. At Lindhurst, he had kissed her so well that she couldn't bring herself to contemplate other men's kisses. After that, for two whole months, he had ignored her. Not a word, nothing!

Emily's eyes lit with suppressed anger. "Let me give you

a piece of advice, my lord. You should be careful whom you kiss. As for love, well, I'm afraid you and I must disagree on its definition. And your proposal: if this is your modus operandi, I should be wary, my lord. Some poor girl might believe you—then where would you be?"

Holt stiffened. A flash of surprise crossed his face, succeeded by a thunderous scowl. Eyes blazing, he opened his mouth to say something, but Emily cut him off, throwing up one hand in a swift gesture of exasperation.

"No, my lord! Enough! We are finished. I shall discuss this no further, if you please." And before Holt could protest, she whisked herself out the door and slammed it behind her.

Emily did not understand how she got through the rest of that evening. She danced with Wainfeld twice and rejected his proposal for the third time; she waltzed with Mr. Cecil Jennings, who seemed distracted, watching Demetria's every move.

Cousin Horace Norville took her arm and escorted her to the game room, where, much against her will, she sat with him, Lord Alvanley, and the Duke of York, and played a game of whist. Unfortunately, her perturbation was such that Emily absentmindedly helped her cousin set the other two.

Whist was a particular enthusiasm of her Uncle Mursey's and Emily had been trained to watch every move closely, to remember what everyone played. Now she mechanically did so, automatically storing each move in her brain, tagging who played what card. Only half attending, she couldn't rid herself of the sight of Ingram's face, puzzled, angry and ... hurt?

Yes, she recalled how he jerked up his head when she repudiated his declaration of love, and something—she didn't know what—flickered in his eyes. Emily did not dare think his offer genuine.

Bringing her mind back to the game, still reflecting on her disastrous interview with Lord Ingram, Emily saw a chance to finesse. This was a thing she would ordinarily disdain to do, but it would take the winning trick, and she wanted to end this game and get away and think.

Brought to herself by York's genial shout of congratulation, and his telling her he'd never been beaten by a beautiful

THE MUCH MALIGNED LORD 119

young girl before, Emily remembered her company. She started to apologize, tried to say it was an accident, but Alvanley—a member of the bow-window set at White's—roared with laughter and told her it was the neatest thing he'd ever seen. "What a story this will make in the clubs, eh, York? Two old hands like us rolled up by a slip of a girl from the country!"

"Oh, please, no," Emily begged, horrified. Her face burned; she must be crimson.

"Modest, too! Horace, this is a delightful girl, your young cousin." Alvanley took snuff, but liberally, as was his wont, sifting a cloud onto his chest and, after a hearty sneeze, ending with a dusting of dry snuff on both cheeks, his eyes dancing merrily.

Eventually he and York took themselves off to Carlton House, laughing and teasing Emily fondly.

She felt quite sunk. What had she done? She would be the subject of one of those *on-dits* that swept the *ton*. The last thing she'd wanted was to figure in the gossip of the tattle-mongers. If she could get herself home, she decided, she would hide in her bed for weeks.

Demetria bounced about their room at dawn, throwing open the windows. "Emily!" she demanded. "Get up. I want to ride in Hyde Park."

Emily groaned and burrowed her head under her pillow. So much for her plan to hibernate for the rest of the Season. She needed sleep, having roamed the picture gallery until half past four.

Demetria laughed and unceremoniously dragged her cousin from the bed. "None of that," she warned. "You can sleep later. Hurry! Put on your gray riding habit, and I shall wear my blue."

Tully Moulton, Cecil Jennings, Val Lindsay, and the assiduous Lord Wainfeld made up their escort. Near the gate, they encountered Lord Ingram, who was riding with Colonel Will Norville.

Emily felt herself go pale. She had told herself over and over in the midnight hours just past that she was perfectly happy to have broken with Ingram. She had paced up and down before the Lester portraits, trying to banish the memory of his lips on hers. Angry or not, she had melted when his mouth descended on hers. Ingram's strength, his passion, were what she longed for. Exasperated, she had flung herself down the hall and, undressing in the dark, reminded herself that she must have convinced him at last that she wanted no part of him. She would never think of him that way again. But the moment she slept, dreams of Ingram kissing her invaded her sleep, explicit dreams, graphic in every detail. Now Emily looked at the man who had provoked those dreams.

Bowing from the saddle, his expression perfectly cryptic, the baron and her Cousin Will generally greeted the party and turned their horses to ride in the same direction. The talk was of the Norville ball the previous night, but Emily heard none of it. She felt Ingram's glance, but she refused to respond. Once around the park they rode, and when they reached the gate, Ingram and her Cousin Will left. Emily did not see them again that day or the next.

In his rooms off St. James, Holt sat his teacup in the saucer, and said, "Belle, for some reason Emily thinks I've been trifling with her. I can't imagine what gave her the idea that I'm some kind of licentious rake. She as much as accused me of using my proposal as a tactic to lure her into my bed."

He shook his head. It was a relief to discuss his problems, but then he and his sister had always supported one another.

Isobel bit her lip. "It's my belief that she was very hurt when you let so much time go by before contacting her here in town, simply because you wanted to present yourself to her whole once again, the successful operation a fait accompli. That's what you said, wasn't it? How could you have failed to tell Emily, when she was the one who urged you to have the operation in the first place?"

"Perhaps," Holt conceded. "Yes, I made a mistake in not telling her. Oh, I've handled it all wrong. But Belle—I've never been in love before!"

Rubbing his chin, he declared, "I want her, Belle. I refuse

to believe she doesn't—that she feels nothing for me. When I kissed her—"

"Then you did kiss her at Lindhurst," Belle said. "I thought as much. But never since?"

Holt shrugged. "At the Norville ball. Something has made her distrust me; something more than my not contacting her for eight weeks."

"Maybe not," Isobel said. "I know that Emily is a novice at love, as are you. You must have hurt her deeply. If I were you, I'd try to explain at the first opportunity that presents itself."

"I keep wishing I could win her somehow," he said, wistfully, "and carry her off to Ravencroft. Isobel, do you think I can bring her to care for me?"

Isobel nodded, murmuring, "I'm sure of it. It's my opinion that she cares for you now."

"I'll do anything." He ran his fingers through his hair and tried to smile. "Enough about me," he said. "When have you seen Locke?"

"I've seen him at his office twice, and tonight, I'm seeing him at Admiral Tilley's. I've just about got him worn down. He's going to want to talk with you."

"Any time," Holt promised. "Oh, I must tell you. I'm driving into Kent tomorrow to escort Mrs. Constance Ridley and her little son Gerald to town. She and her mother, a Mrs. Emmett, are bringing the boy in for treatment. I have arranged for a doctor to look at him. I'm putting them in rooms in Panton Square."

Isobel looked puzzled, and Holt said, "Ridley was my batman, remember. He got killed in the gunfire that broke out just after truce was called ending the second siege of Badajos. I knew Ridley had a wife and child living on her father's farm in Kent. I sent them his effects and what money I got after selling his horse and gear. Naturally, I added a little, hoping to make it easier on Mrs. Ridley and the boy, and I pledged them a modest yearly allowance. In addition, I promised to educate the boy. Now the child needs a doctor to examine his leg. He has been dragging it since a bout of fever last summer."

"You are a good man, Holt," Isobel told him, going to his side and sliding one arm around his middle.

Holt hugged her, but shook his head. "I only wish Emily thought so."

The world of the *ton* was too small for their paths not to cross. Now that Ingram had decided to come out of hiding, it was inevitable. Emily saw him everywhere.

The Season was drawing to an end; glittering affairs from morning to night must be attended. Venetian breakfasts, luncheons on the water, a dance on the Earl of Rotham's yacht. Dinners, late suppers, the theater. Emily tried to keep herself exhausted so she could sleep at night and not roam the house thinking of Holt Ingram. She was unsuccessful.

Wherever she went, Ingram was there, leaning against the wall or sprawled in a chair, watching her with those black, unfaltering eyes. He never seemed to smile, and when anyone spoke to him, they soon moved on, finding his mood irascible. Why did he insist on appearing in company? It obviously afforded him no pleasure. Emily refused to believe he was actually suffering. Had she wounded his pride when she balked at being drawn into his game?

Surely the man was of an age to have suffered reversals in love. Love—there was that word again. As Emily had told Ingram, his idea of that tender emotion must differ greatly from her own. She refused to become some nameless conquest Holt Ingram could rack up like a number on the wall.

Striving never to be alone, Emily desperately resisted the memory of his kisses. Those fatal kisses at Lindhurst, and that lingering one at the Norvilles', had made her fall in love with him, of course. Not that she was in love, no indeed! Infatuated, more like. She couldn't eat, and she had trouble sleeping.

Emily found herself thinking of Ingram every waking moment, even now, when she was sitting in a sunny corner of the breakfast room in South Street, doing her needlepoint and forcing herself to listen as Jane Lester discussed Lady Jersey's ball last night with her sister Nicole and Oralia Lindsay, Lady Renton. Oralia, who was Val Lindsay and Allegra

Haddon's mother, was a fat, grandmotherly woman. She had conceived a great liking for Emily, and for Demetria, too. Emily liked Lady Oralia in return, but she wished the lady would stop trying to feed her. Oralia was convinced that if only Emily would eat more, she might grow. "You're so tiny!" Oralia never failed to exclaim whenever she encountered Emily.

But Emily had never felt less like eating. What she needed most was rest. Even when she could woo sleep, she dreamed of Ravencroft! One dream in particular had begun to haunt her. The scene was always the same: running, running from some unknown horror, Emily stumbled up the great stone steps of Ravencroft, pounding on the bronze doors, demanding sanctuary, only to find upon entry that the danger was within. Holt Ingram waited there, and he was surrounded by a white-hot light—such as she'd seen limning him that first morning at Ravencroft. Except this light was a nimbus of the night, erotic, intensely seductive, drawing Emily to be consumed forever.

Damn Ingram! Why had that fox run across the road in front of Val Lindsay's coach?

Such tiny happenings one's fate hinged on, Emily mused. If Val's horse hadn't bolted and swerved into her aunt's carriage, she and Holt should have passed and never met until they came to town. And she wouldn't have fallen prey to Ravencroft and its master. The man, the place—when would she get them out of her mind?

In desperation she let Dennis Gouverneur kiss her at Vauxhall. Dennis—the second son of Lord Asnor—had only lately come up to town. Immediately he became one of Emily's most ardent admirers, assiduous in offering his escort and contriving to go wherever she happened to be invited.

Dennis was a Corinthian of the first stare, a Nonpareil whom everyone, including Emily, liked. If anyone could make Emily want to kiss him, Dennis should have been the man. He was tall and sandy-haired and handsome in a way Holt Ingram could never be.

When Mr. Gouverneur clasped her to his bosom, Emily thought his kiss—though pleasant enough—was exactly as thrilling as Jeremy Norville's so many years ago. She was forced to explain why she was turning him down, that she hadn't really meant to kiss him, but would think of him as a brother always.

Mr. Gouverneur humbly begged pardon, meekly accepted her explanation, miserably said he would always cherish her friendship, and took himself off to the King's Arms to drown himself with gin in Cribb's Parlour.

Emily was rather ashamed of herself for that episode, but she'd been desperate to learn if she could be stirred by another man's kisses. She had her answer.

What was to be her fate? Emily despaired. Would she slink home and continue playing chess with her father and Uncle Mursey until they died . . . and she was old? She hadn't wanted to fall in love when she came to town; she proclaimed herself pleased enough to go, after they persuaded her, but entertained no hopes of meeting anyone like Holt Ingram. What terrible luck that she had fallen into his clutches at Ravencroft. He was precisely the sort of man she found most attractive.

Emily thought her tastes must be rather eccentric, for she knew others found Ingram somber, even forbidding.

Oh, but they'd never seen the sudden flash of his smile, nor heard him laugh; never felt the force of his arms, the urgency of his passion.

Impatiently, Emily jumped to her feet, startling the older ladies at their quiet coze. They looked at her in astonishment.

"I—I just remembered. I must write a letter," Emily explained, and made her escape.

Perhaps she'd lie down for a few moments. Demetria was gone to ride in the park with Val Lindsay and Miss Meredith Longley, Emily having declined.

Her head ached, and she felt more agitated than at any time in her entire life. She thought she'd die if she didn't see Holt Ingram this instant—which was impossible because she never wanted to see him again. Ever!

Demetria returned from her morning ride just as Emily's father arrived in London. Sent upstairs for her cousin, she found that Emily had fallen into an exhausted sleep.

"Emily!" Demetria shook the smaller girl. "Wake up. You'll never guess—your father is here. I didn't know Uncle Amos was coming, did you?"

"N-no," Emily stammered, trying to clear the sleep from her mind. "My father, you say. At Lester House?" She rubbed her hand over her face and smoothed her hair. "I—I must go to him."

Once awakened, Emily stumbled down the stairs and stood in her father's warm embrace, clinging with her arms round his neck.

"Papa," she cried, needing the feel of his solid bulk. "I'm glad you've come. Why didn't you let me know?" Then she surprised them both by breaking into a bout of weeping.

Amos Wilton pulled away and searched his daughter's face, asking what in the world.

But Emily could not tell him; what, after all, was there to say?

Amos Wilton smoothed his neat gray beard, walking about his suite in Fenton's Hotel, St. James. He sipped a glass of wine, speculating on the cause of Emily's tears.

He had expected to find his daughter happy. Her letters had been full of the success she and Demetria had so kindly—as Emily termed it—received in their reception at the hands of the *ton*. He had been sure she was on the way to finding someone to marry at last. Ingram, perhaps, if his Cousin Horace Norville's letters could be believed.

He was glad when Horace suggested that his presence in London was desirable. And when the letter came from Holt Ingram, Lord Ingram of Ravencroft, asking Amos's permission to formally address Emily, Amos had known he must come. He would see what he could do for his only child, but he also had business of his own.

Now he could tell Emily he wanted to marry Squire Cheney's sister, Dorinda. Dora Cheney, a spinster in her early fifties, a friend of his late wife's, had surprised Amos by admitting she had been in love with him for years. Amos had long considered Dora a special friend. He had fallen into the habit of visiting her and the squire, and playing penny loo with Dora for hours. He enjoyed her conversation.

Those hours he spent at the Manor, he and Dora reading together in the squire's pleasant parlor while Cheney snored in his chair, were increasingly dear to Amos. Sometimes he and Dora simply talked for hours on end.

Amos Wilton loved his daughter, but a man had needs, and he was still vigorous. Not only that, Emily's mother Clementine had made him promise he'd marry again. He was eager to do so, had been ready for months, but knew he must tell Emily, something he'd been dreading to do. He would take her to dinner and break the news. But first, he had several appointments. At least one of which, that with Lord Ingram of Ravencroft, he anticipated with the liveliest curiosity.

Fourteen

"SHE'S MAD to dance and laugh and flirt," blurted Mr. Cecil Jennings, fiddling with the riding whip in his hands. He had called at the baron's rooms in St. James.

Holt snapped up his head. Dressed in a purple-striped dressing gown over his riding pants and Hessians, he'd just sat down to breakfast when Cecil walked in.

"Emily Wilton?" he demanded. Holt had watched Emily dancing, laughing, and—yes—flirting for hours last night at Sally Jersey's.

"No." Cecil Jennings's mouth drew down in a pursed grimace. "I'm talking about Deme Quimby, of course. Who else? Did you see how she danced with Moulton three times? And after she'd turned him down. When I raked her over the coals for it, she laughed and said she never could count, and Moulton was a very good dancer."

Amused, Holt remarked, "I saw her waltzing with you. Seems to me she reserves all her waltzes for you."

Cecil frowned, refusing to be mollified. "Yes, and she went into Jersey's library and played at whist with Jeffery Sloan. We both know Sloan is a rake of the worst inclinations. I can't see why he's suddenly taken with a girl that age. He must be forty if he's a day."

Irritated, Cecil moved his shoulders in his superbly fitted

riding coat and tugged at his spotted neckcloth, a Belcher to be sure, but subdued.

"Perhaps Sir Jeffery has fallen in love at last," speculated Holt. "Or is under the hatches again. I've heard they've refused him the book at Tattersall's. White's, too. And they haven't let him hold the bank at Brook's for two years."

"The man's an out-and-outer. To see Demetria Quimby laughing into his eyes makes me ill," fumed Cecil. "I'll tell you what it is, Holt. She's playing with fire; the girl's going to ruin herself, mark my words."

Holt Ingram laughed. He refused to worry about Miss Demetria Quimby. "But how can she, Cecil, when she has you to watch out for her? You *are* watching her, are you not?"

Mr. Jennings departed in a pucker, for once out of patience with his friend.

Just as well, Holt thought. He had more than he could think of, deciding how to make Emily Wilton fall in love with him. The Quimby chit did not interest him at all.

Sitting at his dressing table, arranging his cravat in the Oriental, Holt lifted his chin and then carefully lowered it, creasing the starched neckcloth and quickly tying the ends.

Timmons, his valet, stood nearby with a dozen freshly ironed neck pieces at the ready. His master hardly ever needed a second one, so expert was he in achieving the desired effect. Today, Timmons thought complacently, was no different.

Holt stared at his reflection in the mirror, sought Timmons's eyes, nodded, and allowed himself to be helped into his black riding coat. He declined fobs, stickpins, and other jewelry except for his signet ring.

Holt looked forward to meeting Dr. Amos Wilton. He had sent Wilton a letter to his Herefordshire home, and the doctor had answered that he would be happy to take luncheon with the baron at Fenton's. He would send round a note when he arrived in town.

That note had arrived last evening, and the time for their luncheon was set for today. The doctor had written that he had reserved them a private table, and would be pleased to receive the baron at precisely noon.

THE MUCH MALIGNED LORD

Holt allowed Timmons to hand him his walking stick and kid gloves, and set his beaver solidly on his head. He ran a finger inside his cravat and eased the neckcloth. It wasn't every day a man asked for the woman he loved, he thought as he came down the steps of the London rooms he kept in order to avoid sharing his house in Albermarle Street with his mother. It was not unusual for the male members of the beau monde to keep rooms in St. James—Clubland, some dubbed it, being the location of White's, Brook's, Boodle's, and others. Even when they married, most noblemen simply rented houses or suites of rooms for the Season, regarding these temporary domiciles as their pieds-à-terre. Few of them actually owned town houses, considering their homes in the country as their seats.

Fenton's Hotel was just a few steps from Ingram's door. He entered and found the large dining room crowded to capacity. The maître d'hôtel spotted him and attentively escorted him to Dr. Wilton's table, bowing all the way.

As they introduced themselves and shook hands, Holt found himself examined by a pair of cool, assessing gray eyes. That's where Emily got hers, he thought, liking the looks of Amos Wilton immediately.

The doctor was medium tall, trim, and precisely dressed. He affected a neat, close-cut beard. He still had a full head of dark brown hair, although the beard was shot through with gray.

"Won't you sit down?" asked the doctor. "I was talking with my cousin, Colonel Will Norville, about you last night, Lord Ingram. He was more than complimentary; said you and he served together in the Peninsula."

"Yes," Holt said. "Starting in Albuera, probably the bloodiest battle we were in. I—I thank Will for his generous comments and can certainly respond in kind. We fought side by side several times. I believe he saved my life the night I was wounded."

"I should like to hear about that," said Amos.

"Will and I were in Colborne's command when he took Renaud redoubt by a coup de main. The whole thing lasted only ten minutes. We moved round to the gorge of the works.

We had just forced the postern gate and rushed in when I was shot in the thigh. At that moment, the French capitulated and the attack was over. Will personally brought me to the attention of the surgeons, and later I learned that he stood by while they got the bleeding under control and did emergency field surgery."

"And that surgery," said Amos. "Was it successful?"

Holt smiled. "Not according to your daughter, sir. Emily gave me her opinion as to why my wound hadn't healed properly. She said I probably had a pocket of infection along the bone. She urged that I come to town and let my doctor operate again."

At Amos's amused expression, Holt went on, "She is a remarkable girl, sir. Brilliant. Her memory is amazing."

"Yes," Amos agreed. "And did you follow Emily's advice concerning your operation?"

"Yes, I did. Seven weeks ago Dr. Slocum operated and found Emily's suspicions correct. I am well now, and he reports my prognosis excellent. My recovery should be permanent."

"I'm glad for your sake."

"It was for Emily's sake also, Dr. Wilton. I couldn't bear the thought of coming to her a limping cripple. I was fully determined to go home to Ravencroft if the operation hadn't cured me. That's why I kept it secret from Emily. The only people who knew were Will Norville, Val Lindsay, and Cecil Jennings, and I swore them to silence."

"You waited until you were sure the operation was successful before writing to me for permission to marry Emily?"

"Yes."

Amos took a sip of his wine. "I believe you should have trusted my daughter. A limp would not stop Emily from loving you."

"My sister Isobel is of the same opinion. If I've made a mistake, I must rectify it. However, Emily will hardly give me the time of day. When we meet, she barely looks at me. Still, I cannot believe that she is indifferent to me. If you have no objections, I still intend to convince her to have me."

THE MUCH MALIGNED LORD   131

Amos regarded him steadily. "Perhaps you'd better tell me what is going on between you and my daughter."

"I came to love Emily immediately I saw her," Ingram assured Amos.

"And Emily?" Amos asked. "She hasn't written a word about you. At least, not to me."

"No, she wouldn't," Ingram said. "I rushed my fences, kissed her at Lindhurst. At the Norville ball, I kissed her again. That was the first week I was out of bed. At that time, I told Emily I wanted to marry her, but she has taken it into her head I can't be serious. She refused me, said she wouldn't discuss it again. She needs time, sir. Don't imagine I'm giving up. I—I was married once, when I was very young, but that was arranged by my father and grandfather. The marriage was unhappy. We weren't at all suited . . . and my mother interfered. Muriel died, you know, having our child. And she hated Ravencroft. Emily, I believe, loves it almost as much as I do. I want your daughter as my wife, Dr. Wilton. She means my life to me; I've never loved before."

Amos Wilton, newly in love himself and remembering his own young passion for the Earl of Mursey's daughter Clementine, understood. Clementine, the darling of the London *ton*, was unattainable for a young doctor, even one of gentle birth and distantly connected to some of England's oldest families. Amos thought he'd never have Clementine, until she walked into his surgery at Beacon Hill and laughed and kissed him on the mouth.

"I must talk with my daughter," Amos said, smoothing his beard. "She and I are dining here tonight. My decision must be based upon what she says. As for you personally, sir, with Horace and Will Norville vouching for you, I can have no objection. If Emily wants to marry you, you have my sincere blessing."

Holt went away heartened, and more determined than ever to speak with Emily as soon as she'd let him.

"Surgery?" Emily choked and reached for her water glass. She and her father were dining tête-à-tête in the spacious dining room at Fenton's. Her father always stayed there when he came to London.

"Holt—Lord Ingram had his leg operated on when he came to town two months ago?" she asked when she regained her voice.

Dr. Wilton, leisurely inspecting his sirloin, darted a glance at his daughter. "Yes, Slocum did it."

The doctor chewed a moment, then said, "I know Slocum. A good man. I'm working with him now on a case—a little boy with a withered leg. I'm glad you suggested the surgery to Ingram. He was in bed almost six weeks, you know. Said he was determined to stay off his leg and give it every chance at recuperation. He was wise to follow Slocum's prescription."

Emily's heart was beating rapidly. Ingram hadn't been *able* to see her. He'd been trying to get well; no wonder he'd looked so drawn that night at the Norville ball. What had Cousin Will said? Emily remembered him cautioning Ingram to stay off his leg. Obviously Will had known about the surgery, but he was a special friend of Ingram's. Cecil Jennings and Val Lindsay—they must have known too. Emily could only suppose there was a conspiracy of silence. To what purpose? She found it difficult to eat; her appetite had evaporated. Speculating on Holt Ingram's silence, she was only dimly aware when her father began telling her something about Dora Cheney. Emily rather liked Dora Cheney—she'd been a friend of her mother's.

When Emily could grasp what her father was saying, that he had asked Miss Cheney to marry him, Holt Ingram flew out of her mind.

Her father had fallen silent and was watching her apprehensively. Emily forced herself to smile, then her smile became genuine and she exclaimed, "But that's wonderful, Father. I never had a clue. I shall welcome dear Dora into our family with heartfelt good wishes. Congratulations." She offered her hand across the table.

Releasing his breath in a rush, Amos Wilton grasped his daughter's hand and kissed it. Tears rose in his eyes. "God bless you, Emily. You never fail me. You are exactly like

THE MUCH MALIGNED LORD 133

your mother. She said—Clementine wanted me to remarry, you know, if ever I found someone. Whoever thought it would be dearest Dora?"

"One finds love in the unlikeliest places, Father," Emily said, thinking of that dark pile called Ravencroft. "Yes, I remember what Mama said. She wanted you to be happy. So do I."

"No one could possibly take Clementine's place," Amos said.

Answering tears pooled in Emily's eyes. "No, indeed," she forced herself to say brightly. "But Dora must be made to feel entirely welcome. I shall move in with Uncle Mursey and give you the house, of course. I'm sure of my welcome with him."

This happened to be the truth. Her Uncle Mursey would be delighted to have her at the castle. Thankful she at least knew where she was going, Emily added, "You and Dora deserve to have time alone." Only lately had she realized how precious were the moments spent alone with one's love.

"Emily," Amos said gently, "do you love Holt Ingram?"

Her face flamed, but Emily looked straight at her father. "I—I don't want to love him."

"Do you not? He seems to care a great deal about you. He asked for your hand today in this very dining room."

Emily could only stare at her father, until he said they would discuss it later, and pressed her to drink her soup.

The dining room at Fenton's Hotel was large and crowded that night, as Emily dined with her father. It wasn't to be expected the Wiltons should have noticed a table in the far corner, holding Annora Ingram, the dowager baroness, along with Agnes, Lady Mallory, and Mrs. Mehitable Humfry, two of Lady Ingram's oldest friends.

Like Annora, Lady Agnes was a widow, an extremely large old woman with raddled cheeks. She always dressed in tight black satin and jet jewelry. These past few years she had dedicated her life to making her daughter-by-marriage miserable. Lady Mallory was one of Annora Ingram's more steadfast satellites.

Mehitable Humfry was also a widow, a tiny bird of a

woman addicted to bright colors and tall turbans with swaying feathers. She had a habit of blinking her eyes and peering quickly about, as if she were afraid of missing something. Hetty Humfry spent her days and nights collecting items of gossip, which she then dutifully wrote in her journal, adjusting facts and figures to her own satisfaction, making the happenings ever so much more interesting. She was a veritable one-woman source of misinformation.

"Stop a moment, Hetty," Lady Ingram begged her friend, in the middle of that lady's crimson confidence story, some malicious tale learned at Melbourne House concerning the latest antics of Byron and Lady Caroline Lamb.

"You must forgive the interruption," Annora said, "but isn't that the Wilton chit? There, by the windows. Turn slowly and look. You too, Agnes. Yes, it's she, and dining alone with a man old enough to be her father.

"Well, what a scandal! How my son Ingram will want to learn of this. Yes, the Wilton girl stopped at Ravencroft on her way to London, you know. She had her Aunt Hume and cousin, Demetria Quimby, with her. I told you how Deme Quimby threw herself at my son and Cecil Jennings. As for her behavior with Valerian Lindsay—that is to say, Lord Renton—I hesitate to recount the details. No, indeed.

"Who imagined the cousins would take this Season by storm? One should have thought Emily Wilton's erratic behavior at the time of young Renton's wreck might have alerted the *ton* to the type of woman she is. I certainly spared no efforts to let the beau monde know what a queer nabs the girl is, but they were all so taken with her—

"Look! Oh, look again," cried Lady Ingram, who had an unimpeded view of the Wilton table. "The man has taken her hand across the table. Now he is kissing it! Shocking, very shocking. Anyone behaving in such a wanton manner must be given the cut, and so I shall tell my daughter Isobel. She is not to associate with that girl again."

Fifteen

Admiral Tilley's house was in Hampstead Grove. When David Locke took Isobel there, she was fascinated to learn that it had been built for a wealthy merchant in the 1600s. It was a jewel of a house, red brick in the William and Mary style, the only flaw being the rather small rooms.

"But the secluded garden," David told her, showing her around, "more than compensates for that lack."

Isobel smiled and said coaxingly, "I'd like a house like this, David. Wouldn't you?"

They had stopped in the library, and David paused before he remarked, "I have a perfectly good house in Soho."

"But you won't invite me to visit it," said Isobel.

She had been lightly teasing, but David growled, "You know the reason, Belle." There was nothing he'd like better than to have her in his home, permanently. He had told her so, many times.

"What I know is that I wrote you the minute I reached town telling you I'd made up my mind to seek a life of my own. I refuse to stay with Mama much longer."

"This is an old argument, Belle." David sounded weary. "You were born to the *ton*. If you marry me—"

"Yes, yes! I'll be forced to give up the beau monde." Isobel snapped her fingers under his nose, her anger and frustration overcoming her. "I think that's just an excuse, David.

You won't ask me to marry you because, in reality, you don't want me!"

David had been lounging against the tallest bookcase, his lanky figure graceful in his finely tailored evening clothes. Now he straightened—like a stretching leopard, Isobel thought, golden and dangerous—and his blue eyes lit with hot flash points as he glowered at her.

"Isobel," he breathed. His thick blond hair, worn in a rather long cut called the Turk, had fallen over his brow. He gave the characteristic jerk of his head that he used to toss it back and said explosively, "Dammit, Belle! You—you *can't* believe that!"

Hopefully Belle stared up at him, her dark eyes willing him to snatch her into his arms. If only she could provoke him into action, make him reach for her. More than anything she wanted him to hold her, to feel his kisses. David was right: she knew he wanted her. But she could never get him to touch her, except when they were dancing in a country set at a ball given by some of his friends. She almost stamped her foot. She'd been so sure her decision would make a difference, and now it seemed he was as adamant as ever in his opposition to their marriage.

Dinner was announced just at that moment, and they had, perforce, to join the other guests.

Isobel, seated between Admiral Tilley on her left and Mrs. Carmichael, a prominent doctor's wife, watched David as he talked with one of his fellow journalists. An artist, a woman who wore a Spanish shawl, sat on David's right, admiring him with her eyes, laughing whenever he made a comment. Oh, yes, Belle thought. No wonder the woman finds David fascinating. He must be the most beautiful male creature alive.

The women left the gentlemen to their cigars when dinner was over. Exactly like the *ton,* thought Isobel, but much more interesting. It was a mixed crowd, ranging from famous army and navy men to foreign ambassadors. She had enjoyed meeting them all, especially her hostess, Mrs. Tilley.

"David is special to me," Mrs. Tilley said, when she took Emily to a small alcove for a private conversation. "I met him when he published my husband's memoirs." Her eyes were warm and friendly.

Isobel knew she'd found an ally, and as they waited for the gentlemen to finish their cigars and brandy, she began telling the woman of her troubles in persuading David Locke that they should marry.

Mrs. Tilley folded her fan and took Isobel's hand, her blue eyes serious. "My dear, there will be many difficulties—I agree with David on that. But if you truly love him, and are absolutely certain you are prepared for those in the beau monde who will take a positive delight in snubbing you, then I suggest you go ahead. I have seen how he looks at you, my dear Isobel. If he is not a man in love, I've never known one. Here come the gentlemen now. Oh, David," she called. "Isobel has never seen the garden. Why don't you show it to her?"

David Locke strolled through the dark garden with Isobel, taking her to the bench farthest back against the vine-covered brick wall. As they walked, he glanced sideways at her, remembering that first day she stepped into his newspaper office. He would never forget how she looked. She was dressed in a dashing scarlet and blue riding ensemble, her jacket frogged, and with the lapels buttoned back and unhooked, allowing her white waistcoat to show. Her riding skirt was split in the latest mode, and worn quite short, and her Hessian boots had tassels of silver. Later, David had tried to sketch her. He never could capture her, but he spent hours remembering her golden brown eyes, peering up at him from under a rakishly tilted shako. He hadn't had a chance, he thought. He had lost his heart in that first moment of meeting. When he learned that she wasn't married, and never had been, he could hardly believe it. His surprise was all the greater when he discovered that she could really write.

Tonight, she had on a pale peach dress that looked white in the moonlight. It was high at the throat, but cut so that it revealed her lissome figure in all its perfection. She had straight shoulders and beautiful arms. He placed her on the bench and moved away, standing against a tree. If he came near her in this setting, he would kiss her, something he'd been aching to do for a long time. "Did you get my letter?" he asked.

"Yes. David, why will you *write* that you love me, but never *tell* me?"

"I don't think I could bear it if you said you loved me in return," he said. "I might take you in my arms and kiss you until you begged for mercy. That mustn't happen, for when we say good-bye, the memory of those kisses would be burned inside me. I do not want to live on memories."

"Then marry me," Isobel said. "We are agreed that we love one another."

"Sometimes love is not enough."

Belle's heart froze at the finality in his voice. She threw back her head, straining to see him in the shadows. Perhaps she'd been hoping foolishly, thinking that somehow all would turn out well for them. But if David had such strong apprehensions—

Suddenly she sobbed and buried her face in her hands. Her grief bent her like a slender reed as she cried wrackingly.

David had never seen Belle cry before, and the sight was more than he could bear. He slid onto the bench and held her, and then she was clinging to him, saying his name as if her heart would break.

Her tears burned him where they touched his skin. His only thought was to comfort her, action serving where only thought had gone before. He covered her mouth with his, kissing her deeply, searching out her sweetness, finding that her quick response fed the flames leaping in his body.

When sanity returned and he tried to lift her arms from around his neck, Isobel resisted and said strongly, "You will never be rid of me now. We love each other, David. You cannot show me just cause why we shouldn't marry and cherish one another. Holt has given us his blessing. You have only to speak to him to know how wholeheartedly he wishes our happiness."

David sighed and took her into his arms again. "Belle, I'm tired of fighting this battle. I'll talk to your brother. Perhaps we can work things out—"

"I want you, David. Only you," whispered Isobel, lifting her lips.

David still had all his old doubts, but he couldn't resist kissing her again.

Riding in her chair from Fenton's Hotel, Annora congratulated herself that she had just won in her little game against Miss Emily Wilton. Discovering Emily in a most flagrant indiscretion, Annora had the weapon she needed to destroy the girl. The gossip would send Emily slinking back to Herefordshire with that physician father of hers. Hetty Humfry would make the rounds today. By night, Emily's misconduct would be on every tongue. She would never be able to show her face in London again. Good riddance, Annora thought. Holt would be devastated.

Climbing the stairs at Ingram House, Annora's thoughts turned to Isobel. Try as she might, she couldn't quell her fears that Isobel was disobeying her; was in fact completely out of control.

As she prepared for bed, she began planning the strategy she would use to bring Isobel to heel.

Annora knew her daughter was writing again, scribbling those novels of hers day after day and far into the night. If one wished to carry on a little civil conversation, even at the dinner table, Isobel's mind was always off in the clouds, rendering up visions she could write about when she got back to that desk of hers. And she kept the manuscripts hidden; if Annora could have found them, they'd have ended in the fire like the others!

It seemed impossible that Isobel continued to dream of publishing a book with that nasty Mr. Locke. Locke was an ambitious parvenu; his family had owned a publishing house forever, back to his great-grandfather's time, if Isobel had her facts straight. And one of those morning newspapers, besides. As if a man in trade, no matter how wealthy he was, or how ever many royal warrants he held, could do for an Ingram of Ravencroft, *barones regis* from the twelfth century!

When Annora had been left alone at Abbingdon after Isobel abandoned her for London, she'd spent days imagining wild carousings, with that ramshackle Valerian Lindsay encouraging Isobel in every dissipation. Annora knew that Val's sister Allegra Haddon was always ready for a bacchanalia of the worst sort. Annora had pictured those revels—orgies, really—at Allegra's home. Allegra Haddon, a girl she could never like, had always urged Isobel to defy her. Haddon House, with that fast political crowd, was alleged to host parties that would put Carleton House to shame.

And Oralia Lindsay, Lady Renton. Val and Allegra's mother was exactly the kind of complaisant fool Annora detested. One must constantly wonder what the *ton* saw in Oralia, for Annora believed the woman was quite popular. If she thought to encourage Isobel in that connection with Locke—no, even Oralia wouldn't do that!

Since she could do nothing in Gloustershire, Annora had traveled to London posthaste, arriving in Albermarle Street and opening Ingram House in a great flurry.

A letter sent round to Oralia Lindsay's address in the Crescent failed to bring Isobel until late the following afternoon, when her undutiful daughter finally presented herself. Isobel did not seem to welcome her mother's arrival with any particular joy.

Using that futile surgery of his as an excuse not to come, Holt had neglected her, and Annora had been forced to write him a letter complaining that he was needed at home, insisting that it looked strange for him to live in rooms in St. James when he had a perfectly good house in Albermarle Street. To no purpose. Ingram stayed adamantly away.

Finally, when *Isobel* begged him, Holt came to dinner. Annora saw at once he was still rubbed over that tempest the Murseys had stirred at Ravencroft.

At that time, he was still limping from his operation, and Annora felt it only proper to tell him that she was certain all the pain would avail him nothing, that he might as well reconcile himself to being lame for the rest of his life.

Now she knew she must apprise him of Emily Wilton's behavior at Fenton's Hotel. She could imagine how Holt would look when he learned the girl he had so assiduously entertained at Ravencroft had dined alone with an old man who did not hesitate to paw over her hand and kiss it in public.

Annora sat at her dressing table and rapidly composed her letter, giving Holt all the details she'd observed in Fenton's dining room.

She also wrote Emily Wilton a letter, unburdening her mind of her outrage that someone who had been welcomed into the *ton* could dine alone with an older man, and in a public place, flouting the prescribed rules laid down by the lady arbiters of the beau monde.

Annora drew a breath of pure contentment. A task well done, she thought as she climbed into bed. She'd send the letters round by hand at first light.

Sixteen

Annora arose, dispatched the letters, and leisurely ate her breakfast. When Isobel left the house for some shopping, taking her maid Gertrude with her, Annora struck.

Calling Cora Whit, her henchwoman and abigail for thirty years, Annora ascended to Isobel's sitting room and proceeded to ransack her daughter's ormolu-mounted desk, sifting through papers, searching for manuscripts or any incriminating evidence that Isobel might be carrying on a clandestine correspondence with Mr. David Locke.

One of the largest drawers of the beautiful desk was locked, and shake it as she would, Annora couldn't get it open. She was in a fury now, certain that she had found her daughter's secret cache and determined to destroy it.

"Cora, open this. I will see what's inside."

Stolidly, the woman tried to pick the lock with a crochet needle, and then with a long hat pin. "I can't do it, madam. Perhaps we'd better leave it alone. Miss Isobel is going to be very upset."

"Fool!" shrieked Annora. "Get me an instrument of some sort. Hand me that fire iron."

"Madam, she will certainly see that you have forced the drawer open," cautioned Cora.

"I care nothing for that!" grunted Annora. She was trying

to pry the drawer open. When that failed, she said, "Stand back; I'm going to break it in."

Her hair had come undone, the long braids writhing about her perspiring face like two white snakes. Her mouth was a tight line. Awkwardly she struck at the delicately inlaid desk drawer, banging at it wildly until the front splintered.

Dropping the fire iron, Annora dragged the broken drawer from the desk, falling to her knees as she spilled the contents on the floor. In a frenzy, she pawed through several handwritten pages, scattering folded letters, invitations, a withered rose, and so she discovered what she'd been dreading all along. She came upon a letter from David Locke that told her just how far this sickening affair had progressed.

Several of Locke's letters were discovered, but one in particular, written only yesterday, almost threw Annora into a fit of apoplexy.

My dearest love, the scoundrel had written. *Tonight I shall take you to Admiral and Mrs. Tilley's rout party. I agree; we do need to talk. My darling girl, in spite of all my misgivings, please remember that I do indeed love you, and remain, Your own David.*

"I knew it, knew it!" Annora screamed, clutching the letter to her thin bosom and staggering to her room, followed by the phlegmatic Cora.

Sinking upon a chair, Annora cried, "The blackguard! The—the lowborn cur! To think that a daughter of mine could stoop so low. Get that thing away from me," she snarled, when Cora began waving a small ornamental vinaigrette bottle in front of her nose.

Almost at once, she started out of her chair and began dressing. "I'm going to see Mr. David Locke, Cora. Right this minute. And we shall see what he says when I thrust this—this *odious* letter in front of his face."

It was late morning when David Locke heard the disturbance in his outer office. Someone was yelling—an angry woman's voice. He'd been trying to concentrate on the newspaper article he was editing; he kept thinking of Belle Ingram's lips. He stood up just as his door was pushed violently open and Lady Annora Ingram swept in, her face indignant.

"Locke—if you are Locke—tell this—this *person* that he can't keep me out," she demanded.

The woman's indignation was plain, and David nodded quietly to Mr. Parsons, his clerk, and signaled that he close the door behind him.

David had recognized the old harridan. He'd seen her at the opera many times, ensconced in the Ingram box. Poor Belle. To think that she faced this woman every day. Her ladyship seated herself without waiting for an invitation. He almost smiled. Maybe Belle was marrying him to get *away* from the *ton*, if Annora Ingram was any example.

"You *are* Mr. David Locke?" questioned Annora, eyeing him up and down. "Well, I can't say I'm impressed." This was a lie. David Locke had just the sort of looks to appeal to certain types of low women. She only regretted that Isobel seemed to be one of them.

"I am David Locke, yes. And you, madam?" Perversely, David refused to admit that he knew her. Let the old tabby introduce herself.

Annora's mouth dropped open. "Why—I am Annora, Lady Ingram," she said, recovering from her surprise. "And I am here, sir, to tax you with this!"

Reaching into her reticule, Annora produced David's letter and brandished it in the air.

"You may recognize this, sir. It was written by your own hand, and sent to my daughter Isobel. How dare you, sir? What kind of a despicable creature are you to prey upon the emotions of an innocent young girl?"

When David's brows flew up at this description of Isobel, who freely admitted her age, Annora flushed. "I have never condoned unequal marriages; you must realize that my daughter's world will never admit you, if that's what you're hoping for. I can only say things have come to a pretty pass when some cit has the crass impertinence to look at the daughter of Ravencroft. Neither Lord Ingram nor I shall ever countenance such a connection. If you manage to marry

Isobel, she shall find herself disowned, erased from the family rolls, and banished from Ravencroft forever."

David looked at her for a long moment, then coolly asked, "Where did you get that letter? I cannot believe that Isobel would voluntarily surrender it."

His implication was plain. Her face flushing purple, Annora jumped to her feet. "That matters not. Only remember what I have said. You are to stay away from Isobel." With one last malevolent glare, she marched from the office.

Slamming the doors of Locke Publishing behind her, Annora mounted her carriage. She drove home to wait until Isobel might return. She would tell her sly daughter what she'd done. Thirty-four years old, and Isobel could still be cowed. Oh, yes. Telling her daughter that her grand scheme was shattered would afford Annora much satisfaction.

She hadn't long to wait. Isobel came into the foyer and Annora ordered her into the blue withdrawing room at once. Silently, she eyed her daughter up and down. Her voice full of contempt, Annora said, "You may as well know, Isobel; your little secret concerning Locke has been discovered. I found one of his letters in your desk. It sickened me, reading his absurd babblings. Let me tell you that I do not appreciate your going behind my back and consorting with persons of his class. It must revolt every feeling."

"Mama—" Isobel was shaking. "You had no right—"

"No right in my own house?" Annora laughed. "You are as disgusting as your Mr. Locke, who had the temerity to sign himself 'your own David.' You may imagine with what pleasure I threw that repulsive missive in his face."

"No, Mama! You didn't—you didn't go to David's office? Pray tell me you did not!"

"Certainly I went. You don't imagine I paid the man a *social* call?" she asked, avidly watching her daughter's ravaged face.

Belle closed her eyes as if to shut out the sight of her mother. But she couldn't shut out Annora's voice.

"I hope," Annora said, "that I'm not entirely powerless to protect my children, when they are embarked upon some folly. I have sent Mr. Locke about his business. Yes, and rid us of that Wilton baggage as well."

"Mama," Belle asked in fearful tones, "what have you done to Emily?"

Annora laughed, unable to refrain from boasting of her own cleverness. "First, I sent her and the rest of the Mursey party packing from Ravencroft."

"Yes, Mama. We know all about that. What else—"

"You don't know the half of it. I was certain that silly Nicole Quimby would go into hysterics if I made her think Holt was a vice-ridden rakehell. And she did. Oh, I spun her a fine tale. I was up half the night inventing scandalous escapades for Holt. And it was so ironical! He has always been so stilted and proper. Never, not that I heard of, has a breath of scandal touched him. But I told Nicole that from the time he was in school, up to and including the present, he deflowered and ruined every girl he came across, from vicar's daughter to the naive young wife of an earl."

"Lies, Mama. How could you tell such lies about poor Holt?"

"Lies? Of course they were lies." Annora sprang from her chair, her breast heaving. "Why should that little fool Emily marry my son and usurp my place as mistress of Ravencroft? Why should any woman? Holt thought to be rid of me when he expelled me from the castle and sent me to the dower house. Damn him! *Damn* him, I say! No matter who he tries to marry, I swear I shall prevent it somehow."

Belle stared with horrified eyes, shaking her head, looking as if she was about to be sick. She tried to speak, but apparently could not. Then she dashed out of the house in a way her mother could not understand.

Annora did not know, but she imagined Isobel must be going to Holt. Well, her daughter was upset now, but she would thank her mother later for saving her from a misalliance too terrible to contemplate.

Annora's letter staggered Emily for hours.

"Yes," said Jane Lester, when Emily showed it to her at the

luncheon table. "The woman truly writes with a venomous pen."

They were eating in the small dining room at Lester House. Lord Lester was at his club, and the only ones present were the cousins, and Jane Lester and Nicole Quimby.

Lady Jane tapped the letter with a finely buffed fingernail. "Annora Ingram's poor children have suffered such terrible invective all their lives. How dreadful for them."

Jane looked at Nicole. "Do you see, sister? The woman can't be believed. I told you that. Now do you see how she twists the truth? Apparently, Annora has never learned that appearances can be deceiving. She puts the worst possible construction on everything. That scene with Emily and her father at Fenton's Hotel is just one example. Emily, my dear, pay her no attention—ignore the miserable creature."

Deciding that Lady Lester was right, that there was really nothing she could do, Emily tried to put Annora and her abusive letter from her mind. Instead, she thought about what her father had revealed last night.

"Holt Ingram seems to care a great deal for you," Amos had said. Was it true? Had she been mistaken in thinking Ingram indifferent to her? He had hidden his feelings very well.

Now, against her will, Emily's hopes had been reanimated, and all morning she had expected Holt to come. He did not appear.

Just before dinner, as she was dressing for Lady Felbridge's musicale, one of the maids brought up a note that carried Ingram's seal.

Emily's hands were shaking so badly she could hardly open it. It was the first letter she'd ever received from him. At last the seal was broken, and she unfolded the single sheet of heavy bond. *Emily,* the baron had written in his fine slanted hand, *I have tried all day to come to you, but there is an affair that is demanding much of my time, if not my attention. I wanted you to know that I shall be unable to see you until Allegra's ball tomorrow night. I have spoken to your father about us. He has no objections. If you will come to an agreement with me, he and I can work out the settlements. Until tomorrow night—Ingram.*

Emily burst into tears when she read this, partly from relief and partly from frustration.

They were still in their dressing room, and Demetria came swiftly to her. Emily handed the letter to her, and she perused it quickly. "Well, Ingram certainly hasn't given up."

"He takes too much for granted! How does he *know* what I might say if he should propose again? Besides, that sounds like a b-business letter," wailed Emily, whose nerves had given way. "Oh, why did Papa go to Lambeth at this precise moment?"

"Lambeth? Why on earth would your father go to Lambeth?" inquired Demetria, diverted.

"A friend of his—Dr. Ellis, I think—lives there."

"But that's across the river," Demetria said.

"I know. Dr. Ellis has a small hospital and invited Papa to visit it. That's why he's staying over there for several days—two days, at least."

"Everything will be all right," Demetria soothed.

Emily had her doubts. "Oh, Deme! I haven't waited twenty-four years to marry a man who speaks of getting engaged as an 'agreement'! And I know there must be marriage settlements, certainly I do, but I want—I want to be wooed and won!" She collapsed again, crying as if her heart would break while Demetria held her. Where, Emily wondered later, trying to repair her tearstained face, has all the romance gone?

Holt had just reread his mother's letter condemning Emily when Dawkins brought Isobel to his tiny library.

Isobel, more hysterical than Holt had ever seen her, seemed unable to talk. He understood their mother had precipitated this crisis. As for Annora's letter concerning Emily, Amos Wilton had had a dinner appointment with his daughter last evening. Holt knew precisely what his mother had seen.

Holt opened his arms, caught Isobel in a bear hug, and simply held her until she had her emotions under control.

THE MUCH MALIGNED LORD 149

"What has she done now?" Holt asked, hoping to bring a smile to his sister's face. But his grim humor failed.

"Mama just returned from David Locke's office and triumphantly recounted all she said to him—that he was unfit to seek my hand, he should find his bride banished from the family, and so on! Everything is ruined!"

Isobel struggled to control her voice. "I have been trying to persuade David ever since I got to London that I want to marry him—that I care nothing for the beau monde. Only last night he relented somewhat and said he would meet with you. I had hopes that when he found you truly in favor of our marriage, he would formally ask your permission to pay me his addresses.

"Holt, I would marry him out of hand, except that David wouldn't do it. He is an honorable man; I've always told him that you and he would like one another when you got acquainted.

"Mama has done everything she could to wreck my life before, but this time she has succeeded! David may never forgive me for what she's put him through, and never ask me to marry him, not after Mama's performance. I assure you, Holt, he himself has felt all the things our mother threw at him quite keenly—the difference in our stations, and so on."

Holt held her while she cried again. When she had dried her eyes somewhat, Isobel took a deep breath and said, "But that's not all Mama has done, Holt. I must tell you—put you on guard. She has done you injury as well."

Holt shrugged, feeling no great alarm. "When has she done differently?"

"Yes, but this time, Emily was her target."

Holt stiffened. "Tell me," he rapped out.

"At Ravencroft, Mama said some horrible things to Lady Hume concerning you, to frighten her so she'd take Emily and Demetria away."

"What were these lies?" He was austere.

"You can't imagine, Holt. She said you were a—rake and—a libertine. When it became apparent that you were interested in Emily, she decided to get rid of her. Mama made up things—terrible things. I only learned about this today."

Isobel bit her lip and looked at him, her eyes filled with regret that such a thing could happen. Holt's face was a bitter mask.

Isobel continued, *"That* is why Emily thought you were trifling with her. It's no wonder she threw your proposal at the Norville ball back in your face. Mama's allegations, coupled with the fact that Emily felt you were giving her the go-by when—well, we've talked about you keeping your operation a secret and remaining incommunicado."

Holt rubbed his chin, a rueful expression on his face. "Go on—what else?"

"As to that, I'm afraid I didn't stay to learn."

Holt passed her the letter Annora had written about a "tryst" with an older man.

Belle read it, frowning.

"That," Holt said, indicating the letter, "can't hurt Emily. It was her father, Dr. Amos Wilton, who dined with her at Fenton's last night. I know, because I ate luncheon with him yesterday and he told me he would meet Emily for dinner."

Isobel caught her lower lip in her teeth and looked thoughtful. "Then Mama will only make herself look bad when the truth is known."

"And, when my engagement to Emily is announced, vindictive. I asked Dr. Wilton for Emily yesterday."

A rush of joy spread over Isobel's face. "I shall love having Emily for my sister. Congratulations, my dear brother."

Holt shook his head. "Don't congratulate me too soon. Nothing formal has been decided. I wrote her a note today that I would see her tomorrow night at Allegra's ball."

"I know everything will turn out for the best," Isobel said. "I'm thankful that *you,* at least, can be happy. On the other hand, I—" Belle's face broke and tears flooded her great eyes again. She slumped on the couch. "Oh, Holt, I love David so!"

"Stay here, Belle," Holt said. "I'm going to Locke to see what I can do. I'm sure I shall return with good news. Then you and I must see our mother. She has gone beyond the limits of what even I will stand for."

Seventeen

DAVID LOCKE had known for a year that he loved Isobel Ingram. Considering their case hopeless, he had admitted it to her only recently.

Everything old Lady Ingram said had brought home the truth. When she was gone, he told his staff to deny him for the afternoon. He locked his door and sat at his desk with his feet propped on top, his hands clasped behind his head.

The explosive rattle of the doorknob, the pounding of a hard fist, brought Locke out of his chair. He threw open the door, frowning, ready to vent his temper on the unfortunate person who stood there.

Holt Ingram was easy to recognize, of course. David had spoken to him several times. He'd even observed Ingram in battle once, when he was working in Fleet Street as a war correspondent and went out to the Peninsula. That was before David's papa died, and he took over the business.

David stepped back and with narrowed eyes said, "My lord." Although he'd promised Belle he would meet with Ingram, he certainly did not want to see him now, not after old Lady Ingram had rent him limb from limb.

What surprised David was that Ingram held out his hand and said, "Mr. Locke, I'm very glad to see you. I've just had a very interesting—ah—talk with my sister. I know my mother has been here, and for that I apologize. What I'm here for—sir, I must ask you: exactly what are your intentions concerning my sister?"

Locke shook Ingram's hand briefly and said, "I'm going to marry her, with or without your permission, my lord."

Holt's grin transformed his face. "Mr. Locke—David—you can't know how happy you've made me. My sister assures me her intention is the same. Now, if you can persuade Belle that my mother has failed to make you take a dislike to her, everything should be all right. I left Belle moaning that you'd never forgive her. She is lying prostrate on my couch in St. James this very minute."

"I must go to her," David said, grabbing his hat from the ornate rack by the door. "Poor Belle, as if I'd let anything—anyone—"

"Wait a minute." Holt grinned. "Allegra Haddon is having a ball for the Russian ambassador tomorrow night. Here's my invitation. Present this at the door. Allegra is a special friend of Belle's; she'll help us."

Holt shook David's hand again. "I must return to Ingram House. I shall insist that my mother apologize to you before leaving for Abbingdon Manor."

A grim expression crossed Ingram's tight features. "Henceforth, she will live in Abbingdon Manor—or some private villa in Italy. That's an option I hadn't thought of. Might be better for all of us if she's out of the country. She will never darken your door; that I can promise."

David Locke flushed. "Belle may see her mother when she wants to. As for me—"

"I know: never is soon enough. Terrible as it sounds, I feel the same. But I know what is best for the woman who bore me and my sister." Holt's voice sounded bleak, then he seemed to shake off some burden.

"Now," Holt continued, "about the ball. Belle, of course, will know you're going to be there. Do you imagine, given the time and a secluded spot, that you can convince my sister you still want her?"

David nodded and smiled. "You can depend on it."

"That's settled then; Isobel and I shall see you at Allegra's Russian ball."

THE MUCH MALIGNED LORD 153

* * *

Annora did not understand what was happening. She sat huddled in the drawing room after Isobel passed her in the hall, refusing to speak, and continuing up the stairs. Holt muttered that he would talk with Annora shortly and went inexorably toward the nether regions of the house.

A quake shot through Annora's breast. She knew Holt had learned of her visit to David Locke. What had gone wrong? He should thank her for taking care of an ugly situation. Apprehensively, she waited for his return.

Arrived in the servants' hall, Holt gave Mr. Caulkins a hundred pounds in notes and asked the butler to have the staff vacate the house for twenty-four hours.

"By that time, Caulkins, my mother will be departing for Abbingdon Manor. Do you understand that not one single servant is to remain in the house?"

Caulkins, who had been butler in Albermarle Street for fifteen years, bowed and indicated he understood perfectly.

"When Lady Ingram has departed, I shall take up my residence at Ingram House," his lordship stated.

"Very good, sir." Although Caulkins kept every inflection out of his words, he did allow his eyes to touch Lord Ingram's for one pregnant moment.

Holt nodded and took himself off to the confrontation with his mother. Something was numb inside him; this would be the final break.

Standing in the middle of the room, Holt crossed his arms over his chest and invited Annora to impart her version of her visit to Mr. David Locke.

He listened in silence while his mother blustered her way through her tale, then he cut her short.

"I have just come from Locke Publishing Company. Yes," he said, when Annora started nervously. "As head of the family, I have assured Mr. Locke that he has my permission to seek Isobel's hand in marriage."

Allowing this news to sink in, Holt paused a moment, walked to a settee, and deposed himself on it. He couldn't pity his mother; too much bitterness had passed between them. Holt realized he was restlessly jiggling the toe of one boot; he stopped and rose to his feet in one fluid motion.

At the fireplace, he leaned his elbow on the mantel and laid down the first of his demands. "You will apologize to Mr. Locke, madam; I think it only proper."

Annora glared at her son. "I shall never apologize for trying to save my daughter from a ruinous marriage."

Holt's mouth tightened. "I thought as much. Tomorrow you will return to Abbingdon Manor."

"I won't go!" asserted Annora. But a knot of dread had settled in the pit of her stomach. She had never seen Holt like this before. Fear spread its dark wings over her like some pall.

"I believe you are unwell, madam. You need complete rest. You shall be alone in this house for the next twenty-four hours—"

"My servants—" Annora began.

"What servants? You have no servants, madam. They are all mine. I hire them, pay their wages, fire them when needful. Those who have served you will be replaced."

His mother stared at him with an awful comprehension. She began to understand at last.

Holt continued. "You will remain here alone until this time tomorrow. This period of solitude should give you time for a little reflection, madam. You must plan what you want to do with your life. Isobel will no longer be tied to your side; she is to have a life of her own. You may retire to Abbingdon Manor or live quietly in some foreign country, guarded by servants loyal to me. There is an unpleasant alternative. There are private hotels on the Continent—"

"Asylums, you mean," Annora said dully. She rubbed at her throat. Her world had dissolved and she had lost everything.

Holt nodded slowly. Belle did not believe a sane person could have acted the way their mother had all these years, but Holt had long thought that Annora, who was selfish in the extreme and with a sadistic nature that craved dominance, was only too sane. What she did was calculated; Holt had been convinced of that all his life. She would never change.

Poor Belle, he thought. And what had Annora done to his own life? Until Emily Wilton came along, Holt had thought he would never be able to love.

Now that he had a chance to marry Emily, he wasn't going to let this woman who had borne him continue to impede his happiness.

"You know," he said conversationally, "I did wonder what happened at Lindhurst—what you'd done that was so terrible you were afraid to face me. Of course, if I'd learned of the tales you'd poured into Lady Hume's ears, I might have been tempted to lock you in the tower with—what was it?—a tiny candle and a jug of water?"

Annora shook her head. She seemed to have lost the ability to speak.

"Why not?" Holt seemed perfectly calm. "That's what you did to me."

"That was different; you were—"

"Yes, a little boy. And you a woman grown. Can you imagine the terror of total darkness? The candle lasted only an hour. I never called you mother after that. Did you notice? I made up my mind, in that absolute blackness, that you would no longer have power over me. It was simple—I would no longer love you."

Annora closed her eyes, shutting out her son's face.

Holt brushed his hand through his hair. "There in the dark, madam, I learned never to love. To love is to make oneself vulnerable; refuse love, and one becomes invincible. People can no longer hurt you. Oh, they can have the servants beat you. But if you don't care, well, it doesn't hurt so much. Where are you going?"

"Upstairs," Annora said, "to lie down."

"Don't think you can speak to Belle. I've sent her to Allegra's. We are alone in this house."

"No." Annora shook her head. "Just—let me go to my room."

"Understand me, madam. You shan't ruin Belle's chance at happiness. And I intend to marry Emily Wilton. That was her father she was with at Fenton's, you know."

Annora, who seemed withered, and older and thinner than

Holt had ever seen her, lifted her head at this. She had gained the stairs, turned from the third step, and stared into his eyes. Finally she nodded.

"I'm—I must get to bed."

Holt couldn't stop himself from calling, "Do you want something before I go?"

"No, nothing." Annora waved as if dismissing him. "I want to lie down. Leave me, Holt.

"Oh, Holt—" She stopped, sounding preoccupied. "I believe I will go to Abbingdon tomorrow, and then— Tell me, will my mail be censored? May I write letters?"

"Madam, you may write, but we know what a weapon your pen is. I suspect you sent Emily one of your scorching letters after you saw her dining with her father."

Annora jerked her head up and he said, "Yes, that was inevitable. From now on, your mail will be opened and scrutinized. And I warn you, be careful what you write, and to whom, lest even that small privilege be taken from you. We have no reason to trust you, madam, wherever you go. Servants will watch you day and night, without ceasing."

Annora closed her eyes and turned from him. She must get out of England; she wouldn't live where everyone knew she had keepers. Dry-eyed, she climbed the stairs.

Holt walked into the library, rubbing the back of his neck. His mother's reaction had been strange, not at all what he'd expected. But then, despite the fact that Annora Ingram had borne him thirty-six years ago, he did not know her at all. He sat for a long time, staring into the flickering flames. After a while, when the fire was almost ashes, he left Ingram House, walking from Albermarle Street to his rooms in St. James.

Eighteen

EMILY, ROAMING the Lester mansion in her night-owl hours, decided that Holt's letter was, after all, tantamount to a proposal. She was a little ashamed at her first reaction. She couldn't wait to corner him at Allegra's Russian ball, tax him with keeping things from her, warn him never to do so again, and then—just possibly—she'd let him kiss her once or twice or a dozen times.

She felt much better when she had it all sorted out, and slept deeply until Demetria woke her next morning. She went cheerfully with her cousin to Madame Fanchon's for a fitting of the superb ball gown she had selected.

Throwing caution to the wind, Emily had ordered a brilliant red dress, severely cut, of silky crepe de chine with a shocking décolletage.

No more playing ingenue, Emily thought. She wanted to look like a flame for Holt Ingram tonight, to remind him she was a woman. She was, after all, twenty-four. Her mother's diamond bracelet, the diamond drop necklace resting between her breasts, and the diamond stars in her hair should cap the picture. Two hours before the ball, Emily was dressed and ready.

David Locke was also dressed early for Allegra Haddon's ball. He descended the wide stairs of his town house in Soho, arrayed in the smartest evening dress designed by Weston. David had a box at Drury Lane, another at Covent Garden, and entertained quite often; he had need of the best evening clothes.

He stepped off the stairs and headed for his library. Reaching into his pocket, he pulled out a plush ring box and carefully opened it. Resting on a satin bed was the diamond solitaire he planned to give Isobel. He'd bought it last year, never knowing if he'd have a chance to put it on her finger. If his plans worked out, the details he and Ingram had agreed on, he would propose to Isobel tonight. And he swore that he'd love her so much she would forget the unhappy years with her mother. He would never let her regret she'd married him. Before this night was over, he would be a betrothed man.

Haddon House was large, even for a mansion in Mayfair, and currently one of the great diplomatic houses in London. Only Melbourne House and Holland House eclipsed it in political influence.

Holland House was down past Kennsington. Lady Holland was divorced and therefore shunned by many of the *ton*, although her husband, an uncle of the late Charles James Fox, was highly popular. Many of the great men went to Holland House, but they did not take their wives. Melbourne, Palmerston, Charles, 2nd Earl Gray (who had succeeded Fox as leader of the more conservative Whigs), Peel, Rockingham, Grenville—all were frequent guests at Holland House, where one could always find good talk and good food, even if Lady Holland's supper tables were so crowded that a man must sit with his arms clamped to his sides in order to avoid his neighbor's soup. Lady Holland herself—seeming to forget that she was never invited anywhere—complained that women did not visit her. But the men, who were free to go where they pleased in society, came in droves. Her house was the most important political center of the Foxite Whigs.

Carlton House was no longer comme il faut—Prinny's company there, styled the Carlton House set, was thought too fast to be good *ton*.

THE MUCH MALIGNED LORD 159

Devonshire House, once reigned over by Georgina, the famous Duchess of Devonshire, had grown sadly flat since the duchess died in 1806.

So, for several years, Haddon House had been the acknowledged headquarters for the new Whigs. Few houses could approach it in popularity and Allegra Lindsay Haddon's balls were always terrible squeezes.

The Lesters arrived shortly after eleven, their carriage blocked in the street for almost an hour by all the traffic, which crawled along until they finally reached the brilliantly lit portico and were let down.

Entering, Emily looked about, her cheeks hot as she ignored the stares caused by her red dress. There were many people, but she couldn't spot Ingram.

As soon as they were through the receiving line, she went with her aunt and Lady Lester to the Crimson Ballroom, Demetria having disappeared with Miss Meredith Longley and Val Lindsay.

Ingram wasn't in the ballroom, either, although she saw Isobel talking with George Gordon, Lord Byron.

Emily didn't particularly like Byron; she thought him dreadfully affected, though she had decided this might be an overcompensation for his clubfoot. One could certainly understand that. And Emily could admire his poetry, although she enjoyed that of the Lake poets better.

Isobel, dressed in the most exquisite gown of creamy jonquil peau de soie, came to Emily, abandoning Byron and his friend Hobhouse. "Emily, how different you look! Is this a new image? What a stunning dress—only wait until Holt sees you in it." Isobel's brown eyes were soft and warm, and she took both of Emily's hands in hers. "I am so thrilled to think we may become sisters. My brother is very lucky," she said, and swiftly bent to kiss Emily's cheek.

Emily smiled, glad that Isobel seemed so approving, but a tiny well of anger was growing inside her. Had Ingram announced to everyone that they were getting married? And without first receiving an answer from her?

Not seeming to notice Emily's constraint, Isobel's eyes roved the crowd, obviously searching for someone.

"Where is Demetria, Em? I need her."

"I believe Demetria is in the Oval Room with my Aunt Hume," Emily said, aware that she spoke a little stiffly.

Isobel did not seem to notice, but merely thanked Emily again and hurried away.

Watching Isobel thread her way through the mob, Emily decided Ingram's sister looked more beautiful tonight than she'd ever seen her. But what was Isobel's air of excitement all about? What was happening? And where was Ingram?

Emily had refused to ask Isobel where he was. That question had been uppermost in her mind—but no matter how badly she wanted to see him, she would not inquire after Holt Ingram.

The ever-faithful Lord Wainfeld appeared, and, bowing, asked, "Miss Wilton, may I take you for some lemonade?"

Emily was eager to move about. "Yes indeed, your lordship. That would be most welcome."

But Wainfeld had discovered her red dress, and seemed overwhelmed by her appearance. He raised his quizzing glass and subjected her to an up-and-down appraisal, which was certainly admiring but hardly flattering, Emily thought.

Wainfeld, a short, stolid man, seemed to have been thrown into a fit of unaccustomed enthusiasm, for he suddenly ejaculated, "Oh, I *say,* Miss Wilton! You *do* look incredible. You—yes, you really *must* marry me, you know, and wear red morning, noon, and night."

Emily couldn't help but laugh. "No indeed, Wainfeld. Variety is what lends enchantment. I'm afraid that you'd soon be quite bored with me if I should wear only red. I thank you for the compliment, although I thought we'd agreed, had we not, that you wouldn't propose again?"

"Can't help it," admitted the single-minded peer. "Words pop out before I think. Told m'mother I wanted to marry you; she said to persevere. Might wear you down, she said. Must keep trying. Know I promised; can't break the habit. Shall we go for that punch?"

Emily took his lordship's arm and accompanied him to the long refreshment table. After drinking her punch, she sent

Wainfeld off to talk to Colonel Sawbridge, and eventually ran into Mr. Cecil Jennings.

She had just spied Holt Ingram, standing with Isobel in conversation with the Turkish ambassador, when Cecil walked up to her and demanded, "Emily, where the deuce has Demetria got to? I saw her a moment ago with Holt and Isobel; now I can't find her—I say, what's all that buzz about?" He turned in the direction of the noise and craned his neck to see what was happening.

Straining to see over the surging crowd, Emily caught sight of Holt Ingram again, flanked by his sister and Val Lindsay.

Holt paid no attention to Emily, however, apparently not seeing her. He seemed in no great hurry to find her, she thought. A smile had appeared on Ingram's mouth and he was threading his way through the murmuring crowd.

Had Lady Caroline Lamb done something outré again? Emily and the entire beau monde were tired of Caro Lamb's antics to draw attention to herself and reanimate the affair between herself and Lord Byron.

No, Ingram wouldn't be glad to see Caroline Lamb; he detested the woman. And Belle—why was she looking so self-conscious?

Lord Wainfeld, who had drifted back, raised his quizzing glass. "Who is that fellow?" he demanded. "Never seen him in my life."

The crowd shifted and Emily was able to see at last.

Holt was shaking the hand of a tall, blond-haired man, impeccably dressed in severe black and white. His evening attire would have done Brummel proud.

"No reason you should have seen him," Cecil replied. "He's that publisher of Isobel's; he isn't part of the beau monde. Locke, I believe his name is. Well, all the society dragons will wonder at Allegra entertaining a cit!"

Someone moved in front of Emily and blocked her view. So that was Isobel's Mr. Locke! Aware of the stir in the crowd, and listening to the comments, she was afraid that Isobel had been right. Several people had turned their backs, refusing to shake hands with someone in the commercial world. Poor Isobel. And poor Locke, too. How must he feel?

But Emily knew he was prepared for rejection. He had warned Belle that he probably wouldn't be accepted and she wouldn't, either, after they were married. Oh, Emily thought, it was so stupid. The Americans were right. Nobility came from the soul. If she could, she'd walk right up to Isobel and Locke and give them her best wishes. She would certainly find an opportunity to do so later. Wanting nothing so much as to be alone, she stepped behind the American ambassador and lost herself in the crowd.

Emily paused beside a great potted fern, trying to decide if she should go to her aunt in the Oval Room.

Val Lindsay spotted her, strode across the floor, and said, "Good God, Emily, what did you make of that? I wonder if m'sister knew Holt was bringing Locke to her ball? Fellow makes a good appearance; haven't come across him before. Well, he and I don't move in the same circles."

Mr. Jennings arrived at that moment, still in quest of Demetria. "You got away before you could tell me, Emily. Have you seen your cousin? Demetria was with Jeffery Sloan earlier, and that will never do. Tell me where she is. She's not with her mother or aunt. She promised Lady Lester she wouldn't consort with Sloan again; I want to make sure she doesn't sink herself."

However she might agree that Sir Jeffery Sloan's influence must be deplored, Emily was unable to point Cecil in Demetria's direction. She had no idea where her cousin had got to.

All conversation was suspended as Holt Ingram rushed up and grabbed Cecil's arm.

"I want you to help me do something," he said, looking a trifle harried.

Ingram glanced at Emily, raked her with his eyes, nodded, and looked away.

That red dress, he thought. Emily was a distraction he didn't need right now. In that dress, she was a crimson flame, beckoning him. And ah, God—her hair! Holt clenched his fingers. He wanted to tear into that artful tangle—

Emily always affected him this way. If he didn't have her soon, he wouldn't be able to appear in mixed company.

"Cecil," he said imperatively.

Emily said in a low voice, "Holt, could I—?"

He cut her off. "No," he said, "not now." He couldn't stay and talk with Emily. He would ask her to supper.

They could eat, and then he'd take her where they could be alone. He wanted to hold her and slant her mouth across his. He would propose to her, and do a better job of it this time. But first he had to take care of this business between Isobel and Locke.

Unaware that he was frowning, he shook his head and said it again: "Not now." And he dragged Mr. Jennings away without so much as an apology.

Not now? Emily felt paralyzed. Holt had actually told her *Not now?* She couldn't believe it. She'd never heard anything so rude.

Excusing herself to Val Lindsay, moving away from the sounds of the small string quartet tuning up, Emily walked as fast as possible to Allegra's powder room on the third floor. Staring at herself in the large mirror, her mouth quirked in a bitter smile.

How carefully she'd dressed for Holt Ingram this evening, in this scarlet dress. How painstakingly she had endured her hairdresser's professional ministrations. The Frenchman had arrived carrying a bag containing his crimping irons, combs, pomantum boxes, and vials of gum arabic. When he was finished, Emily had breathed a sigh of relief.

Pulled up, held out, brushed, combed, braided, curled, her long dark hair had been caught high in a heavy bunch of braids and tight curls, and arranged *en masse* at the back of her head. Rid of the coiffeur at last, Emily had placed her mama's seven diamond stars over her crown and left temple, wishing that Clementine could be here tonight to share her daughter's joy.

In the mirror, Emily's eyes had sparkled like the diamonds. *Holt Ingram loves, loves, loves me!* That refrain had kept singing through Emily's mind, over and over, as she readied herself for him.

But that was before Ingram's cruel words dropped between them. Emily was beyond embarrassment; she felt decimated at his public set-down. Holt Ingram's discourtesy—was it deliberate? It seemed totally inexplicable.

Summoning what courage she possessed, she lifted her chin and went sweeping down the stairs. She would rescue Demetria from Sir Jeffery Sloan. Then she'd call a chair and return to Lester House.

In the back garden, David Locke lifted his mouth from Isobel's. He braced himself against the low wall and held her against him. "I want to be married very soon, Belle. We've waited much too long." He had his ring on her finger; that was the first step.

Isobel's low laugh made him kiss her again. "I'll leave with you tonight, David. You know that."

Holding her face so the moon could shine in her eyes, David said, "I find that very tempting. I believe you mean it. No, we shall do this in the proper time, and at St. George's, Hanover Square. Let's go inside. I want to dance with you."

"Yes," Isobel agreed. "And we'll let Allegra announce our betrothal after supper."

Deme Quimby had watched Isobel and her handsome Mr. Locke leave through the French windows. Just as she and Holt and Isobel had planned earlier, she thought. That was a good twenty minutes ago. Isobel had taken David Locke to the garden, and now he must have proposed, for they were entering again, smiling.

Demetria's task had been to create a diversion, and she had hit on Sir Jeffery Sloan as the perfect, although unknowing, accomplice.

All the old tabbies had protested when she took Sir Jeffery up in the new landaulette that time. Emily had accused Demetria of idly amusing herself. One could carry amusement too far, her cousin had said.

And the night Demetria had played cards with Sloan, her Aunt Lester had been scandalized.

Yes, she thought, tonight Sir Jeffery would serve her purposes admirably, and she would explain to Aunt Lester later.

Demetria's plan was to flirt so outrageously with Sir

Jeffery that everyone would watch her and not Isobel and David Locke. Everyone, including Mr. Cecil Jennings, would be properly shocked. Then she would confound them all by rising from this sofa where she and Sloan were sitting. She would walk away from the profligate who had been attempting to insinuate himself into her affections this past month in order to win her hand and her fortune.

Demetria was under no delusions about Sloan. He was on the lookout for a rich wife and had decided she would do. She felt a little sick when she thought of all the innocent young girls falling each year before the cynical courtship of older men like Sloan.

"Will you let me take you to Richmond next week?" Sloan asked her. He was tall and rather thin, his body—even carelessly deposed upon the couch beside her—long and graceful. His eyes roamed over her hair, and Demetria felt a little shudder of distaste. She couldn't think why she'd ever considered him attractive. He'd been handsome once, she thought. She could imagine how good-looking he'd been when he was young. Now the lines of dissipation were etched deeply in his face and his eyes were utterly cold.

"I've been to Richmond," she said, glancing about, wondering where Cecil Jennings was.

"Where would you like to go?" Sir Jeffery asked. "I'll take you anywhere."

"Yes, and my mother would have a fit of the vapors," Demetria said flippantly. "You're a dangerous man, Sir Jeffery."

"Maybe that's why you like me," he suggested, smiling a little.

"Who said I liked you?" demanded Demetria. "How do you know I'm not using you for my own purposes?"

A shuttered look came into his ice-blue eyes. "Demetria, we are all users. It's human nature. As for dragging me here to sit with you tonight, something tells me you're trying to make someone jealous. Mr. Jennings?"

Demetria stiffened. "Leave Cecil Jennings out of this. Beside, that's not the reason."

"What then?"

Demetria shrugged. "If you must know, I'm making everyone watch me instead of a friend of mine."

"Miss Ingram, perhaps? She and her newspaperman have just returned from the garden." Sloan nodded his head in the direction of Isobel, who was standing in front of the French windows, holding Locke's arm and speaking with her brother.

Stifling a yawn, Sloan said, "She'd better stay with her own class. Locke will ruin her. If they should marry, by this time next year Isobel Ingram and her tradesman husband will find themselves beyond the pale. Too bad, little one. But that's the way of the world."

"I—I think it's monstrous," Demetria said, a mutinous light in her eye.

Sloan, whose family had been English peers for four hundred years, laughed. "Behold the little egalitarian. Do you want to immigrate to France and be called *citoyenne?*"

"Don't be ridiculous," Demetria snapped. "I just think it's unfair that Isobel should be ostracized for marrying Locke."

Sir Jeffery raised one lazy brow. "Yes, my sweet. But that's the way of the beau monde—there are no exceptions. Exclusivity is the only weapon we have. My ancestors, and yours, have been guarding themselves against the social climbers for centuries. Marriage is a delicate matter, even between members of our tight little world. Don't tell me they haven't warned you against me."

"Lord, yes." Demetria grinned. "They all have cats whenever I'm seen talking to you."

Only last week she'd been forced to reassure Val Lindsay that she knew what she was about, although she did not tell Cecil Jennings a thing, a malicious little thrill going through her at Cecil's thunderous scolds.

Deme didn't know what to make of Mr. Jennings. She felt safe with him, she loved to waltz with him, but flirt as she would, he never made a move to kiss her. As for compliments, he had none. All she got from Cecil Jennings were strictures on her behavior, her dress, her driving in the park. Mr. Jennings seemed to have taken on the role of an exacting older brother, with nothing to do except criticize.

Judging it time to bring this little game with Sir Jeffery to an end, Demetria rose to her feet just as Emily came walking up on Mr. Jennings's arm. Apparently, they'd been hunting her.

Out of the corner of her eye, Demetria saw Holt Ingram laugh and say something to his sister. He hugged Isobel and shook David Locke's hand.

Several things happened simultaneously. Sloan had risen as Demetria did. Now he seemed to move closer to her, as though to guard what he deemed, or at least hoped, was his. He placed his hand on her elbow, holding her as if he would bar her escape.

Emily, her face set in unyielding lines, looked quite resolute. Her eyes swept Sloan, and she did not seem to appreciate the way he was holding Demetria's arm. She gave her cousin a minatory look. "May I have a moment of your time, Demetria?" she murmured through clenched teeth.

It was at this moment that Mr. Jennings, apparently with an agenda of his own, wrenched Demetria from Sir Jeffery and dragged her out the French doors, far back into the garden.

Beside Emily, Sloan straightened, looked grim, and started after Demetria and Cecil Jennings.

Emily, who thought Mr. Jennings should have his moment with Demetria at long last, said, "Sir Jeffery. So nice to see you." Her expression was grave, and she laid a detaining hand on his sleeve.

Something in Emily Wilton's eyes, so cool and gray, gave Sloan pause. He actually had no interest in young girls and had been courting Demetria only from financial necessity. He had thought Emily the more beautiful of the famous cousins from the first.

In this red dress, she was delicious. The diamonds scattered in her hair and that chunk hanging between those sweet little breasts, the fabulous bracelet, plus other jewelry he'd seen her wear, would get him out of the River Tick and keep him in the style he considered his due, at least for a while.

He had never seriously considered stalking Emily. He understood she'd had several proposals in this glittering, if belated, Season of hers. Sloan lived in daily expectation of hearing she'd become engaged. And, at her age, Emily Wilton couldn't be cozened into marriage as easily as young Demetria Quimby. Demetria, if he could sweep her off her feet or compromise her in some way, might be persuaded to fly with him to Gretna Green.

Emily's fingers still clutched his sleeve. Jeffery Sloan placed his hand over hers and bent toward her. She was such a little thing. Breathtaking really; a perfect pocket Venus. Sir Jeffery felt his jaded senses stir. It would be easy to accommodate oneself to a Golden Dolly as beautiful as Emily Wilton.

Emily was hardly aware of the glitter in Sir Jeffery's eyes. All she could think was that Isobel and David Locke, accompanied by Holt Ingram, had approached and gathered around her and Sloan.

Trembling, Emily held fast to the only arm offered. Holt Ingram glared at her and she couldn't think why. *He* was the one who had been so rude. She swept him with one killing glance and said, "Isobel, is this your Mr. Locke?"

Belle Ingram gladly introduced David to Emily, and to Val Lindsay, who had joined their circle, and even—after hesitating—to Sir Jeffery Sloan.

Emily was happy for her friend, for although nothing was said of what had transpired in the garden, the gleam in Belle's eyes told the tale.

As for Ingram, it seemed he could think of nothing to do except issue a command: "Dance with me, Emily," he said. Whereupon he had the *audacity* to smile. She went stiff with fury.

Dance with him? After what he'd put her through? She tightened her fingers in the crook of Sir Jeffery Sloan's elbow.

Spacing her words for effect, enunciating as clearly as possible, Emily shook her head and said: "Not now."

She watched as Holt seemed to recoil. After a measured pause, she added, "I'm promised to Sir Jeffery."

She turned away, presenting her back. A most willing Jeffery Sloan went with her as she moved away. Emily deliberately leaned on Sir Jeffery's arm, bringing her body close to his.

Nineteen

As Emily walked away on Jeffery Sloan's arm, Val said, "Ha, she certainly paid you off there, Holt. Tit for tat, I'd say."

Emily in that dress and walking away with any other man would have maddened him, Holt thought. But Sloan! And she was clinging to his arm.

Holt dragged his eyes to Val's laughing face. "What in the hell are you talking about, Val?"

Whereupon the diverted Val Lindsay chortled and proceeded to enlighten the baron of his latest iniquity.

"Exactly what *you* said to her, Holt. Remember? Emily asked to speak to you when you were busy trying to arrange a rendezvous for Isobel and David Locke. *'Not now,'* you said. And now she's paid you back—in spades. Oh, you are in a coil."

In the long walk to the ballroom, Emily had time to think. Glancing at Sloan through her lashes, she was suddenly ashamed of the way she'd used him.

She slowed and finally stopped, Sir Jeffery obligingly matching his steps to hers. He said nothing, merely watched her with drooping lids.

"Sir Jeffery," Emily began, and looked fully into his eyes, "I—I owe you an apology."

He inclined his head, and murmured, "Oh?" It had been fifteen years since a girl had looked at him as candidly as Emily Wilton. "What are you trying to say, Miss Wilton?"

"Just this. In that little scene back there, I used you. For— for reasons of my own, I did not want to go with Lord Ingram, and I—used you against him. I think there might not be a great deal of—of *liking* between you and Ingram, and I thought, or at least I imagined—"

"That he'd rather see you walk off with almost any man rather than myself?" Sloan smiled slightly.

"Yes." Emily had no doubt she was blushing dreadfully. "I'm sorry."

"You're forgiven," Sloan said instantly. "However, I do believe I should extract a small penance."

Emily's eyelashes fluttered, but she continued to look at him. "A penance?"

"Quite small. The favor of that dance you *said* you'd promised me. Do you think you might grant me that?"

Emily nodded, and that was the reason Allegra's guests were treated to the sight of Miss Emily Wilton being sedately handed through a country dance by one of society's most hardened roués.

Demetria had been kissed many times, but never to such purpose as by Mr. Cecil Jennings. Dragging her furiously to the gazebo, he shoved her inside and pulled her against him. Then he proceeded to ravish her lips, bruising her most painfully.

For a while Mr. Jennings held her wordlessly against his thudding heart, trailing kisses up her throat in a dilatory manner, until he no longer seemed able to deny himself. He kissed her mouth again and again.

It was different—quite different—being kissed by Cecil Jennings, Demetria thought. Young men from Oxford and Cambridge, visiting the country assemblies, had much to learn, in her opinion.

Cecil looked so precise, so collected at all times, she had only been able to imagine the fire lurking beneath that restrained exterior. Demetria was not disappointed.

THE MUCH MALIGNED LORD 171

But after a dozen kisses, Cecil pushed her from him, saying sternly, "There, that should teach you a lesson."

Demetria sighed and dropped into the wooden swing. Languorously, she stretched. Rocking herself with one toe, she sighed again. "Cecil," she said, "why have you waited so long? I've been trying to make you kiss me since the Season started."

"Yes," exclaimed Cecil. "Me and everyone in Mayfair who wears trousers."

But this Demetria would not allow. "Not at all," she murmured, rising and leaning against him, putting her arms around his neck. "I haven't kissed a single man since Ambrose Wiley—Lord Silkwood's son, you might know the family—at May Day last year. And he could kiss *nothing* like you. None of them can."

Her lips almost touching his, Deme begged, "Please, Cecil. Will you do it again?"

Cecil Jennings, never reluctant, complied. Rocking her in his embrace, he said huskily, "Oh, Demetria, I do love you."

"Yes, I'm glad to hear that, except it's terribly inconvenient, don't you know?" Demetria leaned back in his arms to see his face. "I'd expected to have several adventurous Seasons before I contracted marriage. It *is* marriage you have in mind, isn't it, Cecil?"

"Will—will you have me?" he asked in wonder.

"Well—I might—sometime—when I'm ready." Demetria grinned. "Cecil, you goose, why do you suppose I wouldn't waltz with anyone else?"

In another part of the garden, Holt lit a cigarillo, sat on a bench, and smoked. He tried to think rationally. It wasn't easy with the blaze of fury that raged inside him. What had possessed her? he asked himself. Women were totally illogical, he thought, calming a little.

He knew Emily would come to no harm dancing with Sloan. In a few minutes, he would go back inside and drag her into some dim room and kiss her until she agreed to marry him.

But when he went to find her, Holt discovered that Emily was gone.

Emily was in bed when Demetria came home, long after midnight. Pretending sleep, she hoped her cousin would climb straight between the sheets.

But Demetria shook her callously. "Open your eyes, Emily. I know you're shamming. Why did you leave so early? Did you ever talk with Holt Ingram? And why did you dance with that nasty Sir Jeffery Sloan? Don't you want to hear about me and Cecil?"

Emily smiled tiredly. "Are you betrothed, Demetria?"

"Not yet. Cecil Jennings has his work cut out for him." Demetria twinkled, showing her dimples. Then she grew serious. "Emily," she asked, "has Ingram ever kissed you? I thought he did at Lindhurst. You looked so—you looked like I felt when Cecil got through with me in Allegra's garden."

The blood rushed to Emily's face. "Demetria! Please!"

"Well, if you don't want to talk about it, we won't, but I've kissed many boys, and not one affected me like Cecil. Perhaps that's why. They were boys and Cecil is a man."

"I think you're in love," Emily said quietly.

"I'm afraid you're right. But"—Demetria shook her finger—"I'm not giving up. I don't want to be married yet."

"Are you afraid of—of being a wife, Deme?" asked Emily.

Her cousin was quite young. Perhaps, despite her many kisses, Demetria was unable to face the reality of actually giving herself to a man.

The marriage bed could be frightening. Or alluring beyond imagination. Emily closed her eyes against the bright picture of Holt carrying her to his bed in Ravencroft. Tears welled in her eyes. In view of his behavior tonight, there seemed little chance of that ever happening. Not only was he lost to romance, he was the rudest man she'd ever come across.

"I'm not afraid of any of it," asserted Demetria. "But I wanted at least two Seasons. Oh, drat Cecil Jennings, I think I really love him."

Emily took her cousin's hand. "Uncle Mursey will be so pleased."

THE MUCH MALIGNED LORD 173

Just how pleased, Emily and Demetria discovered at breakfast when the earl himself, old Leland Quimby, came round to tell them he'd decided to come to town for their masquerade ball.

"Staying at Carlton House, don't you know," Mursey said. "Dear old Prinny wrote and asked me to come, you see. Fatter than ever, George is. Man gorges himself day and night. Goes about in a silk dressing gown the size of an Arab's tent. Poor man; I was in his regiment, you know. Those were the days. Yes, got into town late yesterday. York was at Carlton House; dined with us last evening. Said he'd seen you two. Told me Emily beat him at whist. Did you?" Mursey asked, quizzing her with a grin.

"I didn't mean to, Uncle," Emily assured him earnestly. "We were at Norville House and Cousin Horace insisted I play. I was distracted, simply not attending. But you trained me well, Uncle Mursey. I remembered every card played."

"That's my girl. Wales wants me to bring you to see him, and you, too, Demetria." He swallowed his tea and looked at Emily in an assessing way. "But perhaps Ingram won't approve your going, even under my chaperonage."

A spot of color riding on each cheek, Emily said, "Uncle, what Ingram approves or disapproves has nothing to do with me; I shall be more than happy to go to Carlton House and play cards or chess or even cross-straws with the prince. And as far as I'm concerned, the sooner the better."

Holt Ingram sat in his chair in White's, hiding behind his paper. If Emily was angry at him, and Val Lindsay said she was, it was only because he'd been so careless as to hurt her feelings.

She had refused him all day. He had risen at dawn, anxious to take Emily's hand and explain he hadn't meant to be so abrupt. She avoided him in the park. When he called in South Street shortly after ten, his card was returned to him. The Lester butler informed him Miss Wilton was resting.

This afternoon, after he'd seen his mother off to Abbingdon Manor, he had persuaded Val Lindsay to plead his case again. He would apologize if Emily would let him. When that might be, he had no idea.

Holt looked out the bow window of White's. They were lighting the lamps all along St. James Street. Darkness was descending, and here was Val, still not come. If Renton had forgotten—

But it seemed Val hadn't, for he came into the long reading room at that moment and headed straight for Ingram.

"Holt," he said, "you'll never guess what I learned today. Yes, yes, I went to Lady Lester's—a little late, I'll admit, but Meredith Longley and I—"

Val grinned and threw himself into an overstuffed club chair. "Never mind that. The girls were at Allegra's to take her up in their phaeton for a drive at five. I went there and Emily refused to take your note.

"Did you know Mursey has arrived in town? Yes, he's here, staying at Carlton House. And the girls have been invited there tonight, and the Lesters, and Lady Hume. Allegra and Haddon are going, too, and so am I, I guess. I came here as soon as I could because I thought you'd want to know."

At his friend's dark look, Val protested. Though well aware that the prince's residence in Pall Mall was considered beyond the proper limits, he said, "But Holt, only consider. Mursey is her uncle. Lady Hume is going, and the Lesters, and that's not to forget m'sister Allegra and her husband, Haddon. They dine at Carlton House quite often. And I'm not exactly nobody. I wouldn't let anything happen to Emily."

Ingram left White's and walked along Picadilly toward Albermarle Street, feeling frustrated and tense.

There would be a time, he swore it, when he would have his ring on Emily's finger, when he would take her to his bed and love her as he wanted.

There was a depth of passion within Emily that he must cherish to full flower. Holt felt a tightening about his chest when he thought of kissing her, of her instinctive response to his practiced caresses.

Holt counted the times they'd been alone. That first morning in the tower, he had watched Emily with an awakening heart.

No, it began before that, when he first took her hair in his hands, there, at the site of the wreck. Something had happened to him then, in that very instant. He'd conceived an obsessive desire for Emily, and not just physically, but for her mind, and soul, and for her sweet spirit, striving so valiantly to save his young friend's life.

That desire had grown and grown, and he'd discovered that it wasn't this constantly aching state of arousal, this physical need, that haunted him so much when he was away from Emily. No, it was the softer, more gentle need to simply hold her against him and smooth her hair. True love, both physical and spiritual, was what he felt for Emily Wilton, Holt thought—love such as he'd never expected to find, thinking as he had that his heart was dead inside him.

Holt remembered how, during the storm, she'd thrown herself into his arms. That was the first time he'd held her. Only by a superhuman act of will had he been able to put Emily from him.

And in his chamber, that tiny room under the tower that had seen him grow into the man he was meant to be, Holt had given Emily tea and knew this was the woman he would love until he ceased to exist.

The urge to take her on his lap and taste her lips had been almost unbearable, but he had resisted and rushed Emily to her room, keeping her safe from him. Sleep had eluded him during the remainder of that night. At dawn he had walked the rim of the tower wishing he were a poet so he could write verses extolling Emily's lips, eyes, hair.

And then he'd kissed her in the library at Lindhurst, and later at Norville House, where he blurted out he wanted her to marry him.

Now, entering his house, Holt wondered why he hadn't said he loved her. Sometimes he thought he had, but he could never remember his exact words. That proposal had surprised him as much as it had Emily.

Holt poured himself a brandy in his study. As planned, he'd moved home when his mama left. Isobel was gone with David Locke to visit friends in Russell Square. He was in the house alone, except for the servants. Sitting before a solitary fire, he tried not to worry.

He was desperate to see Emily, to talk with her. He would see her at the Heathcote ball tomorrow night, and she would have no choice except to let him explain away this *malentendu* that surrounded them.

Holt sipped his brandy. At Heathcote House, he would hold Emily and dance with her. He'd take her to a small anteroom and explain how much he loved her and that he wanted her for his wife—that his intentions had been strictly honorable from the first. Emily must understand that he hadn't contacted her during the time of his surgery and convalescence because he was waiting to learn if it was successful; he would promise never to keep secrets from her again and apologize for his uncivil manners at Allegra's, claiming as his excuse his distraction with Isobel and Locke. He would be most explicit, Holt thought. And then he would kiss her until she made him stop.

Twenty

At Heathcote House, the Lester party separated. The Lesters and Lady Nicole retired to the Green Saloon to play whist with Commodore Dillard. Demetria and Cecil Jennings seemed eager to seek some nook where they could be alone, and Emily was on her own.

Drifting from room to room, greeting special acquaintances, she could not refrain from searching for Holt Ingram. Refusing him all yesterday had been the hardest thing she'd ever done. But she had thought that if she talked with him, she'd cry. Emily didn't want that. Now she found herself more than ready to see him. His letter had stated that he would be here.

Eventually, she was hailed by Val Lindsay and Meredith Longley, and went with them to watch the dancing. Her card was practically empty. She hid it in her reticule, assuring Val and Meredith that she did not want to join the country dance that was making up. The Season was over; most of the *ton* had already left London for the summer.

Feeling solitary and miserable, Emily wandered into the rout room, accepted a glass of wine from a waiter, and walked about, wishing her father were back from Lambeth.

At last, she established herself on a folding chair near the dowagers' corner. She didn't know whether it was her imagination or not, but there seemed to be intrigue in the Heathcote mansion tonight.

Everyone was watching Lady Caroline Lamb stalk George Gordon, Lord Byron. Caroline was as thin as a fence rail, her eyes dark patches in her face.

Byron did not dance, due to his crippled foot. Caroline, who adored to dance and was referred to in the press as that "correct and perfect waltzer," had renounced dancing for her lover's sake all the while their affair was in bloom. Now it was over, and she had walked up to Byron earlier, saying, "Now I suppose I may waltz," to which the poet had replied in an insulting manner that he cared not what she did.

The *on-dit* recounting that incident buzzed round the crowd, and all eyes, some merely curious, many malicious, tracked Lady Caroline and Byron as they went their separate ways.

Only five minutes ago, Emily had been standing near a doorway conversing with Lord Byron when Caroline passed through.

Byron, impelled by Emily knew not what, had leaned forward and murmured in Caroline's ear, "I've been admiring your dexterity."

Emily thought it unforgivable in Byron to taunt her after what had passed between them earlier. Especially since he must know Caroline's emotional state was highly precarious.

Still sitting with the dowagers, Emily had a thought. She would go to the supper room—perhaps Holt might be there. Acting on her impulse, she had just walked in and was standing by the long serving table when Lady Heathcote herself brought Ingram to her, saying she should like to remind Miss Wilton that his lordship was a particular friend of hers.

Their hostess excused herself, and any doubt engendered by his terse letter and abrupt behavior was soon dispelled as Holt took Emily's hand and brought it to his lips. He grinned, his white teeth gleaming in his dark face. He was breathing a little fast, as if he'd been hurrying. His eyes roved her features, and his mouth smoothed into the intimate smile of a lover. He stood very close. An aura of masculine hunger, sensual and compelling, emanated from him—a latent desire so intense that Emily blushed, thrilled to think it was directed at her. Her fears and hesitations of yesterday seemed ludicrous and absurd.

"At last!" he murmured. "I'm sorry I'm late, my love. I had to go to Panton Square. I've lived for nothing all day, except to see you. However, there were things I had to do—people who needed my attention. As for yesterday, I don't believe I could survive another like it. If you misunderstood my letter, I apologize. When I showed Isobel a copy, she seemed to think that it would have made her mad as fire. You must teach me to be more tactful, my darling." His voice deepened as he said, "Emily, I wouldn't hurt you for the world."

Emily must have answered him with her eyes, for he nodded.

She was trying to say something when his voice altered and he spoke even more softly. "Mama is gone, Emily, first to Abbingdon Manor, then to Italy where she will live permanently. Her lies can't hurt us anymore." Holt shook his head, as if to dispel the image of his mother lingering there.

He smiled again. "Isobel and Locke are engaged. Did you know?"

"Yes," Emily said. She felt the force of his body. Not since she'd sought the sanctuary of his arms in the tower had she felt so powerless before him. She needed him, needed his strength. She wanted to lean into his embrace, but stood rigid, aware of the eyes around them. There were many who must be watching.

He looked about them and said, "Come; let's find a place of privacy. I have something to ask you, and—I want to hold you." His voice roughened. "Emily, I want you—I must have you."

"Yes," Emily told him. She was perfectly willing to answer any and all comments, apologies, or admissions that he wished to shower upon her in a positive way. "Yes," she said again.

She had just placed her hand in the crook of his arm when shrill screams rent the air.

Emily and Holt turned, and there, a wild look on her face,

stood Caroline Lamb, slashing at her arms with a wineglass she'd smashed, intent on a silent, terrible self-destruction.

Lady Melbourne, Caroline's mother-by-marriage, long used to Caroline's horrid tantrums, stepped forward and grabbed the young woman's wrists, forcing her arms down to her sides.

Without thinking, Emily grabbed a stack of damask napkins to staunch the blood.

Holt caught Caroline as she swooned, crunching the broken glass under his evening slipper.

"How bad?" he asked Emily.

"Not—I can't tell," Emily said, trying to see if the cuts had gone deeply or were superficial. Blood was everywhere.

Caroline lay perfectly limp in Ingram's arms as he carried her to the small anteroom indicated by Lady Heathcote.

He laid Caroline on a sofa, and Emily inquired of their hostess whether a physician was in the house. "If not, one must be got immediately." She was brusque, without time to be polite.

The scandalized guests crowded around, trying to see, and Emily had to push one dowager aside to get to the injured woman.

Trying to stop the bleeding, Emily decided Caroline's wounds weren't serious, but she worried that glass might have gotten in some of them. "I need some warm damp cloths, Holt."

Ingram thought later that she had seemed perfectly ready to command him, as if her reliance on him was the most natural thing in the world and to be taken for granted. She looked at him the way she had when they first met.

He ordered the servants to bring whatever Emily wanted and stood by, a great red smear on his white shirtfront. Her dress, a white tissue silk, was streaked and probably ruined, he thought.

When Emily could give over her ministrations of Lady Caroline, Holt pulled her away and took her up the stairs, moving, Emily was happy to see, with a vigorous agility, and without a limp.

As they passed the second floor, he said, "Emily, I know

THE MUCH MALIGNED LORD 181

you need to wash and so do I. After that, we'll find a room where we can be alone."

Holt's words seemed to spur his passion, for suddenly he crowded her into a dark ell in the shadows of the stair landing. His mouth descended on hers as he pulled her against him. He seemed to be snatching at life, as if he couldn't wait to possess her or take the time to restrain himself.

Emily abandoned herself to his ardor, returning his kisses as well as she was able, her heart fluttering in her breast. He kissed her deeply, moaning a little, then slackened, releasing her but still holding her with his hands on her shoulders. He ended with a series of swift openmouthed kisses, his lips clinging as if he couldn't bear to let her go.

Emily was dazed as he hurried them up to the powder room. "Get in there and do what you need to," he said. "That looks like a small withdrawing room down the hall; we'll meet there. Don't be long."

A tremendous golden bubble seemed to envelop Emily as she entered the powder room and let a maid help her remove the worst of the spots from her gown. Her happiness was such that it frightened her. She had just washed her hands when a little old bird-like woman entered and told the maid to get out.

"Miss Wilton, I am Hetty Humfry," this lady said. "We have spoken once or twice, I believe."

Emily tried to smile at the tiny woman. Her towering headdress seemed too large for her, the long feathers curling and bouncing as she talked.

"I remember you, Mrs. Humfry. How are you?" Emily could think of nothing except getting back to Holt.

"Quite desolate, Miss Wilton, if the truth be known. You must realize that my dearest friend has been constrained to leave her home and country."

"I—are we speaking of Lady Ingram?" Emily asked. "I didn't know you were friends."

"We were," stated Hetty. Her anger seemed to spill over into her words. "Friends of forty years, Miss Wilton, do not desert one another. I'm the only one who knows the full extent of poor Annora's tribulations. However, this is one secret

I shall carry to my grave. You may be sure that I would take no pleasure in seeing Annora's shame broadcast to the *ton*. Oh! that ungrateful son and daughter of hers! Who could have imagined they would turn on her like this ... Here!" Hetty thrust a letter into Emily's hands. "Poor Annora—forced to send this communication to you by stealth. Ingram dismissed all her servants, you know, before he sent her away. She was alone in that big house, Miss Wilton, when by the merest chance I rang the bell. But noble being that she is, she was thinking of others, rather than herself. She said she must save you from marriage with her son, if she could. She thought she should tell you that even if her son were to marry you, it would only be to gain a legitimate heir for Ravencroft. His mistress, a handsome woman known only as Mrs. Ridley, has lately been installed in Panton Square."

Emily gasped. Panton Square. Hadn't Holt just come from there?

"Ah! So you've heard rumors, too?"

"No," said Emily. "Just—"

"You should know that the woman has a small son who is said to look suspiciously like Lord Ingram, Miss Wilton. The child is dark—"

"Stop," Emily cried.

"For the sake of your future happiness, I urge you to listen."

Emily, feeling her heart shrivel inside her, asked, "How did Lady Ingram come by this information?"

"Cora Whit, Annora's abigail, spotted Ingram driving the woman and child in his curricle in St. James Park. Cora observed them closely for several days, and noted that it seemed a regular practice. She managed to hire a linkboy to discover where the woman lived and learned of the Panton Square address. Annora never actually saw the pair, but Cora reported that Ingram was very attentive to the woman and seemed fond of the child."

"I won't listen," Emily said.

Hetty shrugged. "Then read this letter from Annora. Read the truth and think of my dear friend as she lives out her life in cruel exile, far from England's green and glorious shores."

THE MUCH MALIGNED LORD 183

Hetty's exit was triumphant. She hurried down the staircase leading to the picture gallery. She had seen Ingram lurking down the hall, obviously waiting for Emily Wilton. Much good it would do him. Hetty could imagine what the girl would say when she emerged from the powder room. Annora was revenged!

Against her better judgment, Emily broke the seal and scanned the contents of Annora's message. It contained nothing beyond what Mrs. Humfry had told her.

Miss Wilton, Emily read. *I feel that I cannot leave town without warning you against my son. I have it on good authority that he has lately brought a woman and child to Panton Square and installed them in rooms there. The child is dark-haired, and is thought to resemble Holt to an amazing degree. My son may marry you to gain a legitimate heir for Ravencroft, Miss Wilton, but if you imagine he loves you, or will honor his marriage vows, you are sadly mistaken.*

Emily stared at Annora's strong handwriting until the words blurred. They could *not* be true, and yet—

Slowly, almost dragging her feet, she walked to meet Holt. He straightened away from the wall when he saw that all the animation that had previously lit Emily had faded, leaving her dull and listless.

She wouldn't meet his eyes, and spoke apathetically. "Could we talk another time, Holt? I'm not—"

"No!" He was adamant. Jerking her inside the small wainscoted apartment, he locked the door.

He was very angry, Emily thought, looking at him at last.

"Emily," he said, "I will not stand for this. You wax hot and cold. For weeks—since I came to Norville House and asked you to marry me—you have been distant, barely noting my existence. Tonight, just now, you melted into my arms. I had hoped that at last we could come to an understanding. But now— *What* has happened?"

Silently, she handed him his mother's letter.

Holt took it with a muttered curse. He read it, his face looking sick. Shaking his head, he threw the missive aside, his lips pressed in a grim line. He drew a ragged breath and blew it out in a rush. Striding up and down before her, he seemed to be struggling with himself. He glanced at her once or twice, but maintained an unyielding silence. At last he spoke.

"I love you, Emily," he said abruptly. "I wanted to marry you, but— I never know where I am with you. At times you look at me as if you want me to eat you. Then you turn to ice. Now, it's obvious that you don't trust me."

He took a hasty step away and stood with his back to her, hands on his hips. When he turned, his face was tormented.

"Why did you not *know* these scurrilous accusations were false? Confronted by such a letter defaming you, I would have repudiated it instantly—no matter *who* had written it. Do you think I'm going to reply to that?" He flicked Annora's letter with the back of his fingers.

Emily shook her head. No words came, but she couldn't help wanting an explanation. She knew Holt thought his honor impugned, but she longed to hear him *say* there was nothing to this rumor about the Ridley woman and her little boy. Why did he not defend himself? A thought came slithering across Emily's brain like a small black viper. Even liars like Annora occasionally told the truth. On the other hand, look how she had misconstrued Emily's dining with her own father at Fenton's.

Holt moved closer to her. "These past few days—ever since I kissed you at the Norville ball—have been hell. You—you are killing me, Emily."

It was a cry. Holt was hurting, but so was she. Why had he driven with an attractive young woman each day? And *was* the little boy his? Emily looked away, out the window, across Mayfair, toward the park. It wasn't his fault. If she hadn't thrown his proposal back into his face, if she hadn't given him his congé in Cousin Mavis's little sewing room at Norville House, she would have been the one riding in his carriage, and she had no doubt that by now they'd have been formally engaged, with the announcement printed in the *Times*.

A dull sense of loss was steadily growing inside her. A jagged edge of pain sliced through her, making her catch her breath. He *had* wanted to marry her, Holt had said. Past

THE MUCH MALIGNED LORD 185

tense. He would go to her father and withdraw his permission to seek her hand. It was over. Emily swallowed a sob as he continued speaking.

"Look at me, Emily. Few people understand that a man is vulnerable to two women in his life—his mother and his wife. Either one can destroy him. I am convinced that men are born incomplete. When we are small we need our mothers. When we are men, we need a woman to love—deeply, unconditionally. For some of us, only one woman will do. But love alone is not enough; there must be trust."

He paused, seeming to brace himself for what he was going to say. "Learn to trust me, Emily, or forget me."

She stared at him almost blindly. It was an ultimatum.

After a long moment in which his burning black eyes held hers, Holt turned and walked out of the room.

Like a ghost haunting its halls, Emily roamed Lester House that night. Fool, *fool!* she kept calling herself. Holt Ingram was thirty-six years old. Of course he'd had mistresses. No woman liked to face that fact about the man she married. A smart woman ignored what she couldn't help and hoped for the best. If she really loved her husband, she tried to make him love her so that he'd never think of straying. If it was a marriage of convenience, the couple all too often bred up an heir or two to the peer's title and went their separate ways, content to have one of these *modern* marriages, engaging in numerous affairs, but scrupulous enough to cause no scandal. The beau monde did not care what its members did, so long as they were discreet. Create a scandal and one was no longer good *ton*.

Emily sat in the dark study on the third floor, huddled in the large window seat, the hard light of the moon streaming over her. Why hadn't she trusted Holt? Why hadn't she seen that he was offering her his heart before it was too late?

The clock boomed four times. Four o'clock, thought Emily, feeling more wide awake than ever. And Holt—was he still up, striding about that great mansion of his in Albermarle Street? Thinking, perhaps, of her? Or had his thoughts already turned to the woman in Panton Square?

Twenty-one

HOLT LEANED against his library table and stared at the chessboard he'd set up. Only two figures stood on it, a white queen and a black knight.

He had been drinking steadily since he left Emily, at Brook's, at White's, at Boodle's. Now home at four A.M., he was still sober and cursing himself for the way he had handled Emily. He couldn't get her face, pale and vulnerable, out of his mind. When he said that she must trust him, her eyes had filled with tears that her pride wouldn't let her shed. Ah, God! If only he could capture Emily as easily as the knight on this board could take the queen.

An arrested expression crossed Holt's face. Then he laughed, running his hand through his tousled hair. Lady Lester's masquerade. Perfect! Isobel had mentioned that Emily would be wearing white. His sweet Emily—his beautiful queen.

A grin kept crossing his mobile features. This must be a total surprise if it was going to work, he thought. Surprise was the first necessity. He scribbled messages to Val Lindsay and Cecil Jennings, giving them the bare details and warning them to tell no one. He would visit Amos Wilton on his way out of town. Holt leaned back in his leather chair. He needed Rupurt's sword from the Armorial Hall at Ravencroft, and his shield. Yes, and a helmet and spurs.

He would go himself, he decided. Ten hours there, another ten to return. By this time tomorrow, he could be back in London. Plenty of time. Val and Cecil would take care of matters here.

Holt watched the first streaks of light transform the eastern sky. There were many things to do. If his trip to Ravencroft was successful, he would still need to go to Greenwich and see about some silver knight's mail. Silver and black: those were Rupurt's and Ravencroft's colors since the crusades. He needed a hauberk and—

Holt laughed, boyishly excited. A queen was waiting; could he win her for Ravencroft?

Amos Wilton received Holt Ingram in his rooms at six A.M.

"Sorry to call so early, sir," Holt apologized. "I'm leaving for Ravencroft and wanted to explain something first. I'm glad to see you're up."

Amos offered his hand. "Doctors learn to sleep lightly. Most of us rise with the dawn. What brings you?" This was a young man after Amos's own heart, admirable in every sense of the word. He would make Emily a fine husband and be a wonderful father to any children they might have. Ingram stood in his riding coat, big, powerful, every inch a man. Amos smiled. "Come in," he urged. "Nothing wrong, I hope?"

Holt felt a little hesitant about what he had to say, but plunged in. "You were aware of certain . . . stories my mother told Lady Hume when she, Emily, and Demetria were staying at Ravencroft?"

"Er—yes." Amos felt that any comment he could make would be superfluous. "You must tell me everything. I was just about to order some breakfast. Would you like some?"

"Yes, sir, if you don't mind. I forgot to eat," said Holt.

"My pleasure, dear boy. After all, you're practically in the family."

"I hope so, sir. But you must know that Emily and I had a disagreement last night at Heathcote House. At first, she was very glad to see me, having recovered from her miff when I hurt her feelings at Allegra's ball. She refused me all that next day. Then she thought my letter, written after I asked you for her, sounded too businesslike. She told Demetria it was 'unromantic.' "

At Amos's raised brows, Holt grinned ruefully and rubbed his chin. "Yes. Well, I'm about to show her romantic, but more about that later. The thing is, my mother managed to smuggle one of her poison-pen letters to Emily via Mrs. Hetty Humfry. Your daughter received it at exactly the wrong time, Dr. Wilton. I'd just managed to kiss her, and she was quite ... er ... quite cooperative. She went to the powder room to wash Caroline Lamb's blood off her—that's another story, sir. Anyway, old Hetty gave her the damned letter. Emily and I had agreed to rendezvous and when she came down the hall, I saw that something had altered her drastically. From the warm, radiant girl on the stair landing, here was this pale, stricken little person who wouldn't look at me. I'd had enough of *that*, sir. After the Norville fiasco, she wouldn't look at me for days. I wasn't going through that again. Something snapped inside me. I was all prepared to propose and get everything between us settled, and then she wanted to beg off.

"I think I reacted like a madman, Dr. Wilton. I felt out of control—furious. I grabbed Emily, and locked us inside that little parlor I'd discovered earlier, demanding an explanation. She handed me a letter. Yes, it was from my mother, and you'll never believe what she had written. Some virulent tripe about Mrs. Ridley, of all people, being my mistress. I had fathered her son, if you please, and was marrying Emily only to get a legitimate heir for Ravencroft."

Amos was shaking his head. "And did you tell my daughter who the Ridleys were?"

"No. I was angry. Something possessed me—a rage at my mother, and perhaps at Emily, too. I flung her some home truths. I said she should *know* such allegations were false. I was desolate to think my mother could cause her to mistrust me. I could see my marriage with Emily going the way my first marriage did. My mother constantly served up lies, and poor Muriel, who had fallen into her clutches from the first, believed every false tale, every insinuation. She died hating me. I knew I couldn't survive that again, Dr. Wilton. My mother is alive in this world, even if I've sent her far away. I cannot live in constant dread that she will write Emily, that Emily might believe her, and this turmoil would become a deadly circle that repeats itself over and over."

"No," Amos agreed. "That mustn't happen. But what can you do?"

Holt had been eating rapidly. Now he swallowed the last of his toast and drained his teacup. He tossed down his napkin, stood up, and reached for his coat. "Emily loves me; I know it—I feel it. I will do anything in the world to protect that love; I'm even prepared to make her suffer these next few hours. You may not agree, sir, but I think that if Emily is convinced that all is over between us, she will learn she must never believe the lies my mother may engender."

Holt shrugged into his riding coat. "Here's what I plan to do, Dr. Wilton. I hope you agree to help me."

"Anything," Amos said. "I'll do anything."

The grin that lit Holt's face transformed it. "I propose to turn Lady Lester's ballroom into nothing less than a living chessboard. At the precise moment, Demetria will engage to clue in all the members of the party. On the stroke of midnight, Emily will find herself alone on the floor. Then behold! the white queen, you see, *en prise*—in position to be captured. And there I shall appear, as the black knight, carrying my ancestor Rupurt's sword and shield. Don't you see, sir? It's the last move. The black knight will take the white queen; simply capture her and carry her away." Holt smiled again, a wicked little gleam in his eyes. "That should be romantic enough even for Emily, don't you think?"

"Very good," said Amos. "In the meantime, why don't I take her to Panton Square? She would have her reassurance about Mrs. Ridley, but more importantly, it will make her think. I expect Emily's shock at the injustice done you by your mother and which she herself compounded when she began to doubt you, will point exactly to the lesson you want her to learn: which is never, no matter what the circumstance, to believe your mother."

"Yes," Holt said. "Take her to Panton Square with my

goodwill. Then later, the night of the masquerade, quite late, I think, will be the time to give her this." He dragged a small package from his pocket and handed it to Amos. "It's my folded glove, sir. Emily will know what it means. I've also written her a short message. When she receives these, her suspense will be over."

Emily screamed and started awake, shaking. She looked bleary-eyed about her bedchamber. Bright daylight flooded the room. Her dreams had been a muddle of horror and joy. In one scene, she thought Holt was dead. She'd awakened crying. That had been about daybreak. She slept again and dreamed he was kissing her, holding her high in the tower, his mouth, his eyes, his hands adoring her. Then he took her completely. But as he did, he turned into a great squawking bird, and Emily screamed again and again.

Demetria ran into the room and gathered Emily into her arms. "What is it, Em?" she crooned, holding her small cousin and rocking her back and forth on the bed.

"Bad dream," said Emily, pushing back her hair and sitting up.

Seriously alarmed, Demetria said, "I know you're upset, Em. You didn't sleep all night, and here it is, almost the middle of the day, and you are screaming. I know Holt left Heathcote House in a black mood, and you didn't say two words all the way home. Won't you let me help you?"

Demetria was fully dressed. She'd already ridden in the park, but Cecil was nowhere to be seen and neither was Val Lindsay. She hadn't expected to encounter Holt Ingram, but if she had, she'd been prepared to tell him exactly what she thought. It scared her to see Emily in such a state.

Emily swallowed water from the glass Demetria held for her, and rubbed her swollen eyes. Her brain refused to function. She wanted to lie back and sink so deeply into sleep that she would never awaken.

The weight of what had happened sat heavily on her as she tried to explain that she and Ingram had a quarrel and he'd withdrawn his suit. "Oh, Deme, I can't talk about it just now. Thank you, but please—may I be alone?"

THE MUCH MALIGNED LORD 191

Demetria kissed her cousin's cheek. "Of course," she said gently, and added, "This came for you a few minutes ago."

At Emily's hopeful look, Demetria shook her head. "No, it's not from Ingram. Your father sent it."

Demetria left and the note was soon opened.

Amos Wilton had returned from Lambeth. *Come take luncheon with me, Emily,* he had written. *I'd like you to go with me to see a young patient of Dr. Scanlon's. The boy is just turned nine and consequent to a fever last year, his leg has withered. Remember little Amy Bonham at home? This boy has the same symptoms. I thought at once of the treatment you devised for Amy—that series of warm baths and compresses, and the regimen of massage and exercises you prescribed for her.*

Gerald's mother and grandmother are taking him home today to their farm in Kent. I believe you can teach the mother what she needs to know in a few minutes. Please come to Fenton's at one o'clock, and we shall dine, then drive to see Gerald. Lambeth trip successful; details later.

The sight of her father's familiar handwriting calmed Emily somewhat, and she was able to bathe and dress. She had decided that she would get this visit with her father over with, doing whatever she could to help the child he'd asked her to see. Then she would come home and write Ingram a letter that she prayed would bring him to her side.

Lady Lester, all solicitation, ordered her carriage to take Emily to St. James. Demetria and Nicole—who seemed sincerely sorry that something had come between her niece and Ingram—waved her off.

Emily walked into the hotel dining room escorted by Jane Lester's second footman. Her father was waiting for her.

Emily was able to inquire about her father's health, to ask for details of his visit across the river, and was trying to listen to his description of his friend's hospital, when Amos stopped and said, "Something is wrong. Emily, are you unwell?"

"No, no. It's Ingram. He and I have—parted."

Amos looked suitably grave. "Tell me."

Emily handed him Annora Ingram's letter. Her hands

shook in her lap, but she did not cry. One did not cry in a public place.

Amos calmly perused the letter, his expression noncommittal. He handed it back to Emily, saying, "The woman is an unnatural mother. Certainly she cannot be considered normal; in fact, she may be insane. It's just as well that Ingram is putting her away. Those lies she told concerning him at Ravencroft, and now this, can hardly be the work of a rational being.

"But what surprises me, Emily, is that you could have allowed her madness to infect you. I'm nearer to scolding you than ever before in your life. Poor Ingram. My heart goes out to him. He had just gotten rid of Annora and she still managed to strike at him through you. How must he feel? He has never known a mother's love. And just when he thought he was going to be happy, he has lost you. It's sad that you permitted yourself to be used as Annora Ingram's instrument."

"But Papa, Holt never said one word in his own defense."

"No. Can't you see that a real man will not countenance aspersions cast on his honor? To answer such allegations would only lend them credibility, more especially if they were untrue, which I can witness that these are."

"How, Papa? How do you know?"

"That's not to the point, Emily. Men know these things. You have lost Ingram because you were willing to believe the worst about him. No man wants a wife who will believe vile rumors against him. To be accused is bad enough; to be accused when one is innocent—that's infinitely worse. Well, well, I'd hoped to have Ingram as a son-by-marriage. He's just the sort of man I'd always hoped you would marry."

Amos cut his eyes sharply at his daughter. Just as Ingram had predicted, Emily was in pain. It hurt him to see the anguish in her eyes, but he must seem to accept the breakup with casual—even callous—regret and a seeming disregard for Emily's suffering.

Emily suddenly raised her eyes and gave Amos such a pitiful look that he almost abandoned the role Ingram had asked him to play. But he couldn't; no, he couldn't do that. He must be strong for Emily's sake.

THE MUCH MALIGNED LORD

However, he could relieve her feelings in one respect. He would take her to see Gerald Ridley and his mother.

Amos allowed the waiter to serve the cheesecakes and said, "When we've eaten these, we shall go."

"Please, Papa. Then may we start home? I don't believe I can face a large masquerade ball. All I want to do is cry. I must write Holt a letter of apology, then I want to leave London forever."

"Certainly not," said Amos. "That would be quite rag-mannered, and something your dear mother would never have approved. Lady Lester has been a wonderful hostess. We must not repay her kindness with discourtesy. But we will leave London soon, I promise."

Emily pressed her napkin to her lips and Amos hurried on when he observed how her fingers trembled.

"I want to get home to my Dora," he said. "And you ... Since you are not to marry Ingram, you will need something to distract you. Work is the best medicine. Also, there is this: Dora and I have discussed a wedding trip, and I've asked Dr. Ellis if he will come to Herefordshire for six months and run my clinic. You will be able to help him. That will keep you busy and make your recovery go faster. Emily, you've had a terrible blow, but"— Amos forced a hearty cheerfulness into his words—"you will recover. I know you don't believe it now, but you'll get over Ingram. Perhaps you shall marry someone else in time. If you don't, there's always a place for you at the clinic."

Riding in the hack her father had hired, Emily thought she'd never felt such pain. Her father seemed very ready to accept what she could not: that all was over between her and Ingram.

Emily bit her lip and looked out the window. No matter what Papa thought, she would never love again.

They were pulling into one of the residential squares that were so numerous in London. The jarvy drove them past the street sign and Emily was jolted out of her reverie. "Is this—?" she faltered.

"Yes," said Amos, helping her down. "This is Panton Square, my dear. Not a good address, but certainly respectable. Come along. Mrs. Ridley is expecting us." His face was bland as he laid down this bombshell.

Rockets were exploding in Emily's head as the door was answered by a woman about thirty years of age, quite pretty and dressed neatly in a serviceable gown of blue kersey.

Amos introduced his daughter, and Mrs. Ridley proclaimed her pleasure. "So happy, Miss Wilton. How nice of you to come. We've heard so much about you, both from your father and from Lord Ingram."

"Thank you." Emily shook her hand and waited as Mrs. Ridley brought her mother, a Mrs. Emmett, forward.

Emily had noticed a little boy sitting in the inglenook beside the fireplace. Now the woman turned to the child. "This is my son, Miss Wilton. Gerald, come say hello to the beautiful young lady."

Leaning on a small crutch, the boy came across the room. He was thin, with black hair and dark eyes, and Emily thought his hesitant smile hid shadows of pain.

Her heart went out to Gerald Ridley. So this was the child Holt had brought to see the doctors. How like him. Now if only the massage and warm baths would help restore Gerald to health. She laid her hand gently on his dark hair and smoothed it from his brow. "Gerald, I'm so glad to meet you. Here is my father. I believe you are already friends."

Gerald smiled and went limping to take Amos's hand.

Children always trusted her father, Emily thought. She closed her eyes. Here then was the explanation of the Ridley woman, and the child as well. Once again, Annora's lies had injured Holt. Her heart faltered inside her all the while her father was examining Gerald.

Amos had seated himself at the table and opened his bag. "Gerald, this will be the last time I see you for a while," Amos said. "I'm returning to Herefordshire, you see. However, Lord Ingram tells me that he has arranged for you to come up to London to see Dr. Scanlon in six months or so. Be quiet now, while I listen to your heart."

Placing an ear trumpet against the boy's chest, he listened intently. He laid aside the trumpet and extended two fingers, firmly touching the boy's back, and tapping with the fingers

THE MUCH MALIGNED LORD 195

of his other hand. He closed his eyes in concentration, listening by touch to the vibrations received through this procedure.

Briskly, he restored his trumpet to the bag. "Very good, young man. Fit as a fiddle. You're going to grow up strong and healthy. Perhaps you'll be a soldier like your father."

In an aside to Emily, Amos said, "You don't know it, my dear, but Private Neal Ridley was Ingram's batman in Wellington's army. They went all over the Peninsula together, I understand."

"Papa," Emily said, "I seem to be learning a lot today." But, she asked herself, was it a lesson learned too late?

As she was rubbing Gerald's legs, and telling his mother and grandmother how to bathe him and use hot compresses, her mind was on Holt and what she'd done to him. Once again, Annora had seriously mistaken her facts. And Emily had believed them. She'd have plenty of time later—an eternity—for regrets. Now she must see to this child.

"Mrs. Ridley, please watch the way I'm wringing these towels in the hot water and applying them to your son's legs. Once you've applied the warm compresses, Gerald's muscles will relax. That is when the massage will do the most good. In the wintertime, when it's too cold to bathe him like this, make canvas bags of salt. Heat these salt bags in a dry iron kettle and apply them just as you would the wet cloths. The warmth and the massage have worked on little Amy Bonham. And the stretching exercises ... Gerald, you should see Amy run and play hopscotch with her friends. It will be difficult; you'll have to exercise very hard. I believe you can do it."

Gerald's grin was wonderful. "Miss, I can if you and his lordship think I can. Ingram says if I do what Mama and Grandma say—if I try to get well—he'll buy me a pony with a little red saddle. Then I can go anywhere!"

Gerald sat up, as if he'd had a sudden thought. "Will you visit us at Grandfather Emmett's farm? That's where Lord Ingram is sending us today in his great traveling coach, all the way to Kent. Ingram was coming with us, but he had to go to his castle. But if you'd come, miss, that would be almost as nice. Can you?"

Emily hugged him and said, "Oh, Gerald, I'd love to, but I'm afraid that's not possible." She looked at her father. "I didn't know Ingram was going to Ravencroft."

Amos shrugged. "Neither did I." He busied himself with checking his bag. It was true. It was only this morning that Ingram had come to his rooms at the Fenton Hotel. He could see that Emily was stunned by the news that Ingram had left town. Amos hardened his heart. He must not fail in his resolve to help Ingram and Emily come together again.

Emily left the Ridleys' in a state of shock. So long as Ingram had remained in London, there was a chance that they could be reconciled. But with him gone . . . As she bade the Ridleys good-bye, a refrain kept running through her head: *He's gone, Holt is gone forever.*

She did not see her father's worried face as he drove her to Mayfair, and barely remembered responding when he said he'd see her tomorrow night at the ball.

If Emily could have seen anything beyond her own suffering that day, she might have noticed that everyone seemed to be leaving her alone. It did not occur to her until much later that a conspiracy of silence had reigned at Lester House during the interminable two days that she waited for Lady Jane's masquerade to be over so she could quit London forever.

Demetria was blessedly absent from their chambers, and Emily, quite numb, sat down to sort out her emotions. Never in her life had she made a mistake of such proportions. It shook her confidence badly. She, who'd always prided herself on *thinking*. So careless, she thought. She'd been so careless.

Slowly, she dragged herself to the bed and lay on the counterpane, her arm thrown over her eyes. How could she have hurt Holt, of all people? He had been her life—her destiny. But that vile letter had taken her by surprise. She should have destroyed it, gone to him, thrown herself into his arms. It was her duty to keep such things from him, to protect him, and, above all, to trust him. Holt was right. Without trust, there could be no love, and no happiness at all.

Even when she had repudiated Holt's first proposal, something—*something!*—had been stuck in the back of her head. As long as he was close by, she had known their estrangement could be mended. At any moment she could walk into his arms and he'd kiss her and their rift would be healed.

She curled into a little knot and wrapped her arms around herself. Where was he? Wherever he was, Emily knew he was hurting. For that, she would never forgive herself. Had he reached his sanctuary? Was he walking the rim of his tall tower, watching the westering sun and thinking of her?

Emily slept, awoke to darkness, and did not move. Someone, Demetria perhaps, had covered her with a down comforter. She was alone now, she thought. As she sank into the haven of sleep, she looked with dread toward the years ahead—years without Holt. Her father was wrong. She would never let another man hold her. And Ravencroft! It would always be the home of her heart.

Emily struggled, swimming up, up from the murky waters of sleep. She forced her feet to the floor and stumbled to the window. The dull morning light that crept inside as she pulled the draperies set the tone for the day. The sky was leaden and gray. A strange lethargy gripped her, but she forced herself to call Grace Garvey, her aunt's dresser, and ask her to send a maid with some tea.

Grace, who had known Emily all her life and was worried about her sleeping so much, said tartly, "About time, missy. I'll come up later and dress you myself. No more of this lying about, now."

When Grace had marched away, Emily told herself that life—no matter what its quality—must be lived. Therefore, she would force herself to move, to function.

Emily drank her tea as she bathed. Then she let Grace dress her in her smartest walking gown. There was a shop in Chelsea she wanted to visit.

She descended the stairs, and only she knew the effort it took to walk into the breakfast room and calmly greet her hostess and her aunt.

Jane Lester bounced out of her chair like a fat little ball and embraced her. "Emily! All rested, I see. How we have worried about you. But now everything will be all right. You look . . . rested."

Jane fanned herself rapidly, and Emily looked at her in surprise. Never before had she seen Lady Jane in such a fluster. Her aunt, on the other hand—Emily turned to her Aunt Hume and assessed her expression. Blank, she thought. *Carefully* blank. Certainly restrained. Emily almost smiled. Her aunt had been coached; that was very apparent. So—no one was to ask questions, make comments, or offer advice. She could well imagine Lady Jane's instructions. *Don't mention Holt Ingram to Emily,* she would have said. *Don't say that he has left town, and left Emily without hope.* It was just as well that there were to be no questions, thought Emily. After all, what could be said?

She greeted them pleasantly and, going to the sideboard, served herself some curried eggs. "Where is Demetria?" she asked. "Has she moved to another room?"

Lady Jane shot her sister a warning glance and said, "Demetria is riding with Meredith Longley. As for her moving out of your room, we thought you needed your rest."

"Yes, I did. I thank her for her consideration. I believe that I was exhausted. Too many routs, parties, and balls. From early morning until late at night—all crowded back to back. I swear I have changed my clothes at least five times a day since we got to town. You have been a most gracious hostess, Lady Jane. And you, Aunt, have done your utmost to see that I was properly thrown upon the Marriage Mart."

Emily passed her fork between her plate and her mouth; she buttered her bread and sipped her tea, going through the motions of eating. As for tasting anything, she might as well have been eating sand.

She spoke, she tried to smile, and eventually she said, "Please tell Demetria I want to go to that old curiosity shop in Chelsea this afternoon, Aunt. I saw a chess set there the other day, and have decided I must have it as a memento of my trip to London. It is very old, of Persian provenance, pure ivory for the white pieces and ebony for the black. It is banded in gold, and very beautiful. I hope it's still there."

Very carefully, she rolled her napkin, sliding it into the silver napkin ring by her plate. Rising, she said, "If you will excuse me, I shall retire to my room. I must write a letter."

Emily made it up two staircases, locked her door, and leaned against it, shaking so badly that her teeth chattered. Her effort had cost her dearly, but she knew she would be glad of it later, when she had grown accustomed to dealing with the agony that gripped her and dissimulation came more easily.

She was thankful she'd been able to demonstrate that her composure wasn't completely overset, but her exertions in the dining room had drained her. She shed her gown and burrowed into her cocoon of blankets like a small, harried animal going to ground. In a few minutes, she was asleep.

Much later, Demetria had to shake her awake. "Emily, if you still want to go to that shop in Chelsea, hurry and dress. Val Lindsay is taking us," she said.

Emily jumped up and quickly made her toilet. Aware that Demetria was watching her closely, she calmly discussed the costumes they would be wearing that evening.

Once, she caught her cousin looking at her with narrowed eyes, but Emily pretended that she was unaware of Demetria's scrutiny. Gathering up her fur wrap, Emily said, "I'm very sorry to be so much trouble, but I do think it's just as well that we get out of Lady Jane's way. Last-minute preparations for a large affair such as this can be quite demanding; one always finds that some detail or other has been overlooked, and must be taken care of."

She was chattering, she thought as they passed through the long front hall. Workmen clad in aprons were rolling out a red carpet. Others hurried about carrying large pots of tall ferns. One stood on a tall ladder, hanging satin streamers for decorations.

Val Lindsay waited for them in the outer foyer, and Emily greeted him and thanked him for escorting her on her errand.

"My pleasure, Emily. I'm glad to see you." Like Demetria, Val gazed at her keenly, then pretended to look away. How she appeared, Emily did not know, but she had been unable to banish the sadness that loomed in her eyes when she had given her bonnet a final twitch in the mirror.

She wore the new creation that Madame Fanchon had ordered for her from Paris, a hat with a curling feather and a deep-poked brim. It matched her latest walking dress, a beautiful blue lustring silk with severe lines that gave her needed height. Even her half-boots were the same cerulean blue, creating an ensemble that turned her gray eyes a luminous azure.

As she sat back in the seat of Val's smart town carriage, she smoothed her kid gloves. No one must know what she was enduring, Emily thought. She still had a modicum of pride, even if her heart was bleeding inside her. She refused to be one of those die-away misses who wore their hearts on their sleeves, indulging themselves in mawkish behavior. She drew a determined little breath. The smart outfit did much to restore her self-confidence, and she took great comfort in knowing that her appearance, at least, did not betray her.

Twenty-two

By the time they returned from Chelsea, and Emily had set up her antique chessboard, she was reconciled to the notion of getting through the evening.

She sent an obviously worried Demetria away, briskly assuring her that she was all right. "I'm fine now, Deme. Go get some rest. You must be beautiful for Cecil. You seem perfect together. I'm so happy for you."

Emily had been composing a letter to Ingram in her head all the time she was buying the old chess set. Now she sat on a cushioned bench before the satinwood lady's desk, and took up her pen.

After a brief, formal salutation, she wrote, *Ingram, you said that I must learn to trust you or forget you. In the past forty hours, I have learned to give you my trust, and not because Papa took me to see the Ridleys. I am fully sensible of my culpability. I am deserving of all blame. I sincerely hope that, given time, you may forgive me, for I believe that I shall never forgive myself. As to forgetting you, I cannot promise to do the impossible.*

If you still harbor some small feeling for me, please grant me one last wish. I have determined to ask Papa if he will bring me to Ravencroft on the way home. If you do not slam the castle doors in my face, I hope that we may calmly dis-

cuss what has passed between us and part not in anger but with the good wishes of sincere friendship.

Ingram was handed this letter by the footman when he strode into his front hall in Albermarle Street. He had just ridden in from Ravencroft. Standing in his tracks, he ripped open the envelope and scanned the lines quickly. A tiny smile tugged at the corners of his mouth as he carried the missive to his study. He stood before the fire, still dressed in his caped greatcoat, and read it again.

Emily wanted to be friends, did she? Never! He would show her *friendship*. He hadn't ridden over two hundred miles in the rain to gain a friend! He rubbed his chin and grinned. The thought of the kisses she would give him when he captured her tonight, and later, when he held her in his tower—the thought of her kisses was what had sustained him during those long hours in the saddle, his newly healed wound aching in the cold. He *would* have her. A great glow of joy spread through him, warming him still further. She would receive his pledge—his folded glove—in an hour or so, and the message he'd written with it. As for Ravencroft, he would take her there himself.

Dinner at Lester House that night was a simple buffet, and Emily was thankful she was spared the necessity of sitting at the long dining table with the others and making small talk. She was free to stay in her room and have a tray sent up. She planned to wait until the last possible moment before going down. A brief appearance was all that was required in order to fulfill her duties as a guest. The dancing was scheduled to start at eleven, and the unmasking would take place at midnight.

She had felt at peace since she'd written Holt's letter. She felt that the quickest way to get it to him was via his steward at Ingram House. She knew Holt was in constant communication with this man, who would forward her message in his earliest dispatch.

It was quite dark now, and Emily went to stand in the huge lunette, the crescent-shaped window that characterized this charming bedchamber. Her room was dark, and she stared down at the hurry and bustle of the street scene before her. Linkboys carrying torches ran back and forth. Guests were beginning to arrive, their coaches lining up to discharge them. Even three stories up, she could hear the sound of shouted words and laughter.

Emily knew that she would laugh again, but she did not know when. Certainly she did not know with whom. A great wave of lassitude rolled over her, and she crossed to the bed. Her refuge had been sleep during these hours of personal disaster. She pulled the corner of the spread across her and closed her eyes. It was all mental, of course, this unnatural languor. It would pass as she recovered from her grief. No one, Emily had learned when her mother died, was capable of sustaining a high state of grief forever. Time, she thought, drowsily. Time was what she needed, and she would have plenty of that when she returned home to Herefordshire.

When she awakened, she felt it was quite late. She lit a candle, and found that it was after ten P.M. Turning from the clock, she noticed a small package lying by her pillow.

With a great flash of presentiment, she knew it was from Holt. Quickly, she tore it open and found his folded glove. She stared blankly at it for several seconds, then read the accompanying message. It was brief, three short sentences: *With this gage, I wage my law. On guard, my love. It's time for the final move.* Ingram had signed his name and all of his titles.

Emily gave a glad cry and cradled the glove to her breast. She read the note again and kissed the words, laughing and crying. Pressing Holt's folded glove to her lips, she knew that this was his pledge, his proposal. With this glove Holt had "waged his law." At midnight, she would return it as required by that old rule of baronial court procedure she had quoted to Holt at Ravencroft: *He shall wage his law with his folded glove and shall deliver it unto the hand of the other, and then take his glove back and find pledges for his law.*

A low knock at the door sent her flying to answer it.

Demetria stood there, wearing a cautious expression. She

relaxed a little when she saw the glow on Emily's face. "Did you find your package, Em?" she asked.

Emily laughed. Grabbing Demetria, she hauled her inside. "You!" she exclaimed. "You brought this! You've known all along that he was coming. Confess!"

Nodding sheepishly, Demetria asked, "Are you angry with me?"

Emily hugged her. "No, I'm too happy right now, but I may kill you tomorrow. Oh, Deme! Holt—*my* Holt! He's coming, isn't he?"

Demetria nodded and smiled broadly.

But Emily's eyes had lit on the clock again. "My God!" she cried. "I've got to get ready. Why did you let me sleep so long? You must dress, too. What time must I come down?"

"Uncle Amos thinks you should be in the ballroom at a quarter of twelve."

"My father! He knew, didn't he?" Emily shook her head. "Well, I shall have something to say to *him!* No, I know he did it for the best. And I've deserved it all, for what I've put poor Holt through. Quickly, Deme. Call Marie. I must bathe and dress."

Shooing her cousin out, Emily went to the armoire and took down the white dress Madame Fanchon had fashioned for her costume.

It was a medieval queen's gown, very simple, patterned after an artist's conception of Eleanor of Acquitaine, Henry II's queen, famed for her Courts of Love. She would wear her hair flowing and twined with pearls. Her white satin mask was outlined with pearls, her girdle low-slung and silver, argent being the predominant color in Ravencroft's shield.

Emily had never felt such anticipation. How sweet is that which once was lost, she thought rapturously. She had been resurrected, brought back, given her life again!

Twenty-three

DEMETRIA CAME dressed for the ball and twirled about, showing Emily the Marie Antoinette costume she had donned; a thin red ribbon *à la guillotine* was tied round her bare throat.

Her hair was two feet tall, arranged on a wire cone and powdered and curled. A tiny live bird in a miniature cage crowned this edifice and chirped nervously.

"Oh, Deme—" Emily said. "Aren't you afraid that bird will—" She bit her lip. "I don't think I'd like a live bird roosting in my hair, no matter how small it was."

"But *non,* my dear Emily!" lisped Deme in an atrocious French accent. "I have told zis bird zere is a hungry cat in the stables, and if he doesn't want to become—mmm—how you say—*denrees*—food?—for Monsieur Matou—oh, drat!—if this little birdie doesn't watch it, he'll find himself in that tomcat's mouth. And I've warned him to sit very still in the *center* of his cage!"

Demetria whirled away, saying the last of the guests were arriving and she wanted to spy out Cecil Jennings and see what he was wearing. He seemed to have disappeared these past two days. "If I can't find him, I'll take any man his approximate size to the Grotto Room and kiss him silly. No, no, Emily, I'm only joking, but if Cecil is late, I'll *say* that's what

I've been doing, and won't he turn green? I can't wait to see him."

Deme left the room in a whirl of skirts.

What would happen, Emily thought, when she saw Holt Ingram? Would he take her hand, and would she have his pledge fulfilled? Her father was right; she must delay her entrance until the last possible moment.

Emily had the curious feeling that tonight would be the last time she was Emily Wilton. If all went as she prayed it would, in a few hours she would be the future Baroness Ingram. A sense of fate flowed over her. Ravencroft truly was her destiny.

Holt Ingram and Ravencroft. That fortress had waited for her for centuries; Holt had chosen her to love and to carry on his line. She seemed to have been caught up in a romance written by some old English bard ...

Emily asked Marie to prepare her bathwater, then sent the girl away. Alone, she stepped into her hip bath.

Settling into the hot water, Emily took a sponge and scented soap and laved her skin, her throat and breasts, until they were gleaming.

The chatelaines of old had bathed their lords, and even their guests. If Holt took her to Ravencroft, would she bathe him when he came to her at the end of the day? And would he bathe her, soap her? Would he lift her from the water, carry her to their bed, and love her, wet and dripping?

Emily suddenly rose from the bath, splashing water everywhere. She wrapped herself in the bath sheet. She couldn't wait to see him. She wanted to be dried and scented and arrayed for Holt Ingram's pleasure.

She called Marie, but Grace Garvey came instead, claiming she had nothing to do, that she'd already dressed her lady and Miss Demetria.

"Grace," Emily said, hugging her, "how nice to have you help me."

"I always dress you when you come to Mursey Castle," Grace said gruffly. "Now stop talking and hold up your arms."

Meekly, she did as she was told. Grace settled the dress over her head, and Emily fastened the silver girdle herself.

Brushing Emily's hair, complaining that it was too long, Grace worked her magic, dressing it simply, pulling the top tresses back from Emily's brow and twisting them in a long rope of pearls. The rest she allowed to flow over Emily's back and curl down to her waist.

Then, trying to frown, Grace stood back and told Emily to look at herself in the long mirror, adding that she had to go see about Lady Nicole.

Emily laughed and kissed the old woman's cheek. "Thank you, dear Grace," she said. "Wish me happy."

Sniffling and contorting her face, Grace growled, "Yes, missy, that I do. And how I wish your mother could see you tonight."

Grace left, and Emily assessed her appearance in the looking glass. Virgins were adorned this way in the old romances, in a plain gown with simple sleeves and a modest neck, and with the long girdle swaddling their hips. They had worn their hair loosely, of course, the way hers was tonight.

How was it she looked more womanly in this stark robe than she had in that modern blaze of a gown she'd worn to tempt Ingram at Allegra's ball?

She prayed Holt would think she was beautiful. Never in her life had she wanted to be more truly beautiful.

What were his thoughts, right at this moment? Was he dressing, as she was? She couldn't begin to imagine what he would wear. She was certain of nothing except that he would come.

It was almost midnight. Taking up Holt's glove, Emily fitted her mask over her eyes and walked slowly down the stairs.

As she reached the bottom, she was snatched onto the dance floor by unseen hands.

The noise was a mad, swirling roar. Emily was surrounded by jostling strangers, all taller than she, a forest of bodies. She could see, could hear nothing. Where was Holt? Shrill laughter, manic laughter, made her clamp her hands to her ears. Panic caught her and Emily desperately pushed it back.

She was engulfed in a Rabelaisian scene and couldn't escape. The dancers—the harlequins and harem girls, the sultans, admirals, the Punches, Judys, Falstaffs—they all crowded round her, and Emily was lost, lost to view.

Holt would never find her. Time was running out. Where was Lady Lester? Her father?

Emily tried to look for Demetria and her bird cage. A scarlet domino begged her to dance, but Emily refused, thankful her mask hid her face from his leering eyes. She felt hot; the room was stifling; she was smothering.

Another pair of arms—a blond reveler dressed as a knight—tried to capture her. Then a king—Henry VIII? A page clasped her and she fought free, striving to claw her way to the edge of the dancers, but she was caught, held in the crush.

The music stopped abruptly. Shrill screams pierced the air, followed by a shocking silence.

All movement ceased as everyone turned to look at three fantastic figures looming out of time in Lady Lester's ballroom.

A wide path opened before Emily. She found herself standing alone and free, facing she knew not what. She pressed her hand to her throat.

A black-mailed knight—Holt!—stood tall and menacing, his gleaming *heaume* riding his coif, the nasal hiding his features, his shield silver and black and blazoned with three ravens.

A thrill coursed up Emily and she smiled triumphantly. He had come! Holt had come to capture her.

Two squires stood beside him. Surely, Emily thought, Val Lindsay and Cecil Jennings were the knight's squires, dressed in his colors and each armed and holding small round shields. These squires crouched slightly behind the knight, one to each side, their swords held *en garde*.

The knight stood absolutely still, magnificent and invincible, sword lowered but ready. Legs spread, he was prepared to do battle.

Everyone, as if on cue, faded back, leaving Emily in the middle of the room—alone and vulnerable.

Holt saw clearly that Emily smiled; he knew she waited for him alone.

The crowd was silent, utterly still.

He handed his sword, Rupurt's sword, to Val Lindsay, his shield to Cecil Jennings. Then Holt removed the helmet—the *heaume*—from his head.

He pushed back his coif as he turned, and Emily saw his face for the first time. His expression was intent, his mouth hard and unsmiling.

Emily could hear his spurs, golden spurs, as he walked toward her. They made small clinking sounds as he crossed the floor, steadily, unhurriedly.

He came from the corner of the room, up and then across. He had made two moves, in effect a diagonal, exactly as it should be, Emily thought.

She looked up as Holt stopped in front of her. She could smell his clean male scent. His black hair lay in damp ringlets across his dark forehead.

Holt reached up and slowly removed her mask, and Emily stood revealed to his eyes and to everyone.

Silently, Holt looked at her. Hands at his sides, he leaned forward and kissed her mouth. It was their only point of contact. They stood, *en tableau vivant,* a stalwart black knight kissing the white queen's lips.

Emily swayed. Nothing, *nothing* had prepared her for this feeling. Holt, possessed of her lips, was ready to take her completely if only she would yield. She tried to resist, clenching her fists, arms rigidly down. She tried to play the role of the white queen who wouldn't yield, but she couldn't maintain the pose.

She moaned. His mouth—his kiss—wasn't enough. She wanted Holt to hold her. Tears slid from under her tightly closed lashes and she sobbed deep in her throat as she fought her losing battle.

Suddenly, it was too much. Emily threw her arms about Holt's neck and capitulated. Her surrender was victory for them both. The crowd broke into loud hurrays, exclaiming in joy and approval, clapping their hands.

Holt gathered Emily to him with a force that threatened to

wound, his mailed arms lifting her clear of the floor, squeezing the breath from her petite frame.

At last he had her, he thought, her mouth under his again. Holt had wanted this—wanted her—for his entire lifetime. Long and long did he hold that kiss, until, after a small eternity, he lifted his head.

Emily, hanging in his arms, seemed disoriented as she slowly opened her eyes and realized where they were.

Holt held her and looked quickly around. He had to get them away from the crowd. Standing her on the floor, pulling her from their laughing well-wishers, he took Emily down the long hall to the candlelit Grotto Room.

Emily's eyes were shining like all the stars Holt had ever seen as she handed him his glove.

"I love you," he said, holding her, smoothing back her hair. "Tell me what you want."

"I—I want to belong to you," Emily gasped. "I want you to know that I will trust you no matter what, forever and ever. And I—I want you to love me, and marry me, and take me home to Ravencroft."

Quickly, with Emily's help, Holt struggled out of his hauberk. He stuffed his glove inside his white linen shirt and took her in his arms once more.

"And do you love me?" he demanded. "Say it." More than anything he needed to hear Emily say she loved him.

"I do," she cried. "I love you, Holt—love you."

"Will you stay with me forever?"

"Yes—yes, and . . ."

"What, Emily?" His heart was bursting, he was so happy. "What are you trying to say?"

"Will you send all the servants away and lock us in at Ravencroft, and—and love me in the tower room where you took me in the storm? I—I wanted you there, Holt." She hid her face against his chest.

Holt laughed. He cradled Emily in his arms and laid his cheek against her hair. He laughed again for the sheer, exuberant joy of it.

"And I wanted you, my darling. I make you my promise: that small room must be our special place. And each year on our anniversary, for the next sixty years or so, I shall banish everyone, lower the portcullis, and love you as you can only imagine. For you and I, Emily—we are bringing love home to Ravencroft, at last."

Avon Regency Romance

Kasey Michaels

THE CHAOTIC MISS CRISPINO
76300-1/$3.99 US/$4.99 Can

THE DUBIOUS MISS DALRYMPLE
89908-6/$2.95 US/$3.50 Can

THE HAUNTED MISS HAMPSHIRE
76301-X/$3.99 US/$4.99 Can

THE WAGERED MISS WINSLOW
76302-8/$3.99 US/$4.99 Can

Loretta Chase

THE ENGLISH WITCH
70660-1/$2.95 US/$3.50 Can

ISABELLA
70597-4/$2.95 US/$3.95 Can

KNAVES' WAGER
71363-2/$3.95 US/$4.95 Can

THE SANDALWOOD PRINCESS
71455-8/$3.99 US/$4.99 Can

THE VISCOUNT VAGABOND
70836-1/$2.95 US/$3.50 Can

Jo Beverley

EMILY AND THE DARK ANGEL
71555-4/$3.99 US/$4.99 Can

THE STANFORTH SECRETS
71438-8/$3.99 US/$4.99 Can

Buy these books at your local bookstore or use this coupon for ordering:

Mail to: Avon Books, Dept BP, Box 767, Rte 2, Dresden, TN 38225

Please send me the book(s) I have checked above.
❑ My check or money order— no cash or CODs please— for $_____ is enclosed (please add $1.50 to cover postage and handling for each book ordered— Canadian residents add 7% GST).
❑ Charge my VISA/MC Acct#_____ Exp Date_____
Minimum credit card order is two books or $6.00 (please add postage and handling charge of $1.50 per book — Canadian residents add 7% GST). For faster service, call 1-800-762-0779. Residents of Tennessee, please call 1-800-633-1607. Prices and numbers are subject to change without notice. Please allow six to eight weeks for delivery.

Name_____
Address_____
City_____ State/Zip_____
Telephone No._____

REG 0193

Avon Romantic Treasures

Unforgettable, enthralling love stories, sparkling with passion and adventure from Romance's bestselling authors

AWAKEN MY FIRE by *Jennifer Horsman*
76701-5/$4.50 US/$5.50 Can

ONLY BY YOUR TOUCH by *Stella Cameron*
76606-X/$4.50 US/$5.50 Can

FIRE AT MIDNIGHT by *Barbara Dawson Smith*
76275-7/$4.50 US/$5.50 Can

ONLY WITH YOUR LOVE by *Lisa Kleypas*
76151-3/$4.50 US/$5.50 Can

MY WILD ROSE by *Deborah Camp*
76738-4/$4.50 US/$5.50 Can

MIDNIGHT AND MAGNOLIAS by *Rebecca Paisley*
76566-7/$4.50 US/$5.50 Can

THE MASTER'S BRIDE by *Suzannah Davis*
76821-6/$4.50 US/$5.50 Can

A ROSE AT MIDNIGHT by *Anne Stuart*
76740-6/$4.50 US/$5.50 Can

Buy these books at your local bookstore or use this coupon for ordering:

Mail to: Avon Books, Dept BP, Box 767, Rte 2, Dresden, TN 38225   C
Please send me the book(s) I have checked above.
❑ My check or money order— no cash or CODs please— for $_____ is enclosed (please add $1.50 to cover postage and handling for each book ordered— Canadian residents add 7% GST).
❑ Charge my VISA/MC Acct#_____ Exp Date_____
Minimum credit card order is two books or $6.00 (please add postage and handling charge of $1.50 per book — Canadian residents add 7% GST). For faster service, call 1-800-762-0779. Residents of Tennessee, please call 1-800-633-1607. Prices and numbers are subject to change without notice. Please allow six to eight weeks for delivery.

Name_____
Address_____
City_____ State/Zip_____
Telephone No._____

RT 0193

Avon Romances—
the best in exceptional authors and unforgettable novels!

THE LION'S DAUGHTER   Loretta Chase
76647-7/$4.50 US/$5.50 Can

CAPTAIN OF MY HEART   Danelle Harmon
76676-0/$4.50 US/$5.50 Can

BELOVED INTRUDER   Joan Van Nuys
76476-8/$4.50 US/$5.50 Can

SURRENDER TO THE FURY   Cara Miles
76452-0/$4.50 US/$5.50 Can

SCARLET KISSES   Patricia Camden
76825-9/$4.50 US/$5.50 Can

WILDSTAR   Nicole Jordan
76622-1/$4.50 US/$5.50 Can

HEART OF THE WILD   Donna Stephens
77014-8/$4.50 US/$5.50 Can

TRAITOR'S KISS   Joy Tucker
76446-6/$4.50 US/$5.50 Can

SILVER AND SAPPHIRES   Shelly Thacker
77034-2/$4.50 US/$5.50 Can

SCOUNDREL'S DESIRE   Joann DeLazzari
76421-0/$4.50 US/$5.50 Can

Buy these books at your local bookstore or use this coupon for ordering:

Mail to: Avon Books, Dept BP, Box 767, Rte 2, Dresden, TN 38225   C
Please send me the book(s) I have checked above.
❏ My check or money order— no cash or CODs please— for $_____is enclosed
(please add $1.50 to cover postage and handling for each book ordered— Canadian residents add 7% GST).
❏ Charge my VISA/MC Acct#_____Exp Date_____
Minimum credit card order is two books or $6.00 (please add postage and handling charge of $1.50 per book — Canadian residents add 7% GST).   For faster service, call 1-800-762-0779. Residents of Tennessee, please call 1-800-633-1607. Prices and numbers are subject to change without notice. Please allow six to eight weeks for delivery.

Name_____
Address_____
City_____State/Zip_____
Telephone No._____

ROM 0193

If you enjoyed this book, take advantage of this special offer. Subscribe now and get a

FREE
Historical
Romance

No Obligation (a $4.50 value)

Each month the editors of True Value select the four *very best* novels from America's leading publishers of romantic fiction. Preview them in your home *Free* for 10 days. With the first four books you receive, **we'll send you a FREE book as our introductory gift. No Obligation!**

If for any reason you decide not to keep them, just return them and owe nothing. If you like them as much as we think you will, you'll pay just $4.00 each and save at *least* $.50 each off the cover price. (Your savings are *guaranteed* to be at least $2.00 each month.) There is NO postage and handling – or other hidden charges. There are no minimum number of books to buy and you may cancel at any time.

Send in the Coupon Below   To get your FREE historical romance fill out the coupon below and mail it today. As soon as we receive it we'll send you your FREE Book along with your first month's selections.

Mail To: **True Value Home Subscription Services, Inc., P.O. Box 5235
120 Brighton Road, Clifton, New Jersey 07015-5235**

YES! I want to start previewing the very best historical romances being published today. Send me my FREE book along with the first month's selections. I understand that I may look them over FREE for 10 days. If I'm not absolutely delighted I may return them and owe nothing. Otherwise I will pay the low price of just $4.00 each: a total $16.00 (at least an $18.00 value) and save at least $2.00. Then each month I will receive four brand new novels to preview as soon as they are published for the same low price. I can always return a shipment and I may cancel this subscription at any time with no obligation to buy even a single book. In any event the FREE book is mine to keep regardless.

Name

Street Address   Apt. No.

City   State   Zip

Telephone

Signature
(if under 18 parent or guardian must sign)

Terms and prices subject to change. Orders subject to acceptance by True Value Home Subscription Services, Inc.

77332-5